MW01670962

PURE SLUSH BOOKS

# MARRIAGE

LIFESPAN VOL. 6

First published as a collection August 2022

Edited by Matt Potter

ISBN: 978-1-922427-30-4

BP#00114



Pure Slush Books
32 Meredith Street
Sefton Park SA 5083
Australia

Email: edpureslush@live.com.au
Website: pureslush.com
Store: pureslush.com/store



Also available as an ePub eBook
ISBN: 978-1-922427-31-1
Also available as a Kindle eBook
ISBN: 978-1-922427-74-8

A note on differences in punctuation and spelling
*Pure Slush Books* proudly feature writers from across the English-speaking world. Some speak and write English as their first language, while for others, it's their second or third or even fourth language. Naturally, across all versions of English, there are differences in punctuation and spelling, and even in meaning. These differences are reflected in the work *Pure Slush Books* publishes, and they account for any differences in punctuation, spelling and meaning found within these pages.

Pure Slush Books is a member of the
Bequem Publishing collective
bequempublishing.com

DEDICATED TO

**EVA**
**MAGDA**
**JOLIE**

AND

**ZSA ZSA**

… poetry and prose by …

Alex Reece ABBOTT • Sara ABEND-SIMS
Amanda ADDISON • Tobi ALFIER • Hedva ANBAR
Kristine Rae ANDERSON • Sandra ARNOLD
Richard BAND • Linda BARRETT
James BATES • Paul BECKMAN
Dev BERGER • Annie BIEN • Joyce BINGHAM
Natalie BLAKE • Mark BLICKLEY
Michele BOMBARDIER • Howard BROWN
William BUTLER • Susan Maxwell CAMPBELL
Hillary CAMPOS • Rachel CANWELL
Robin CANTWELL • John CARNEGIE
William CASS • Con CHAPMAN
Chuka Susan CHESNEY • Jan CHRONISTER
Susy CHURCHILL • Dave CLARK • Peter CLARKE
Christine COLLINSON • Lisa COSTA
Linda M. CRATE • Brenda CULLEN
Steve CUSHMAN • Tony DALY • Tony DAWSON
Dawn DeBRAAL • Albert DeGENOVA
Winston DERDEN • Daniel DIOGUARDI
Michael DURACK • Steve EVANS
Kate FALVEY • Juliet FOSSEY • Wendy FREBORG
Natalie FRY • Leone GABRIELLE
Jeremy GADD • Arthur GARDINER
Delphine GAUTHIER-GEORGAKOPOULOS
Declan GERAGHTY • Nod GHOSH
Alejo Rovira GOLDNER • Rab GREEN
John GREY • Ben GRONER III • Jan HAAG

... and ...

Tom HAZUKA • Ronald T. HARDWICK
Mark HEATHCOTE • Jenna HELLER • Jack HENRY
Matthew HISBENT • Keith HOERNER
Ryn HOLMES • Mark HUDSON
Barbara Schilling HURWITZ • GP HYDE
Abha IYENGAR • Kendra JACKSON
Joanne JAGODA • Caroline JENNER
Kenneth M. KAPP • Alan KENNEDY
Steven Dee KISH • Pam KNAPP • Jacqueline KUDLER
Len KUNTZ • John LAUE • Neil LAURENSON
Christine LAW • Tim LAW • Larry LEFKOWITZ
Joan LEOTTA • Cynthia LESLIE-BOLE
Louella LESTER • Raquel LEVITT
Mike LEWIS-BECK • Ann LISKA
LindaAnn LoSCHIAVO • Lance MANION
Andrea MARCUSA • Jayne MAREK
Jackie Davis MARTIN • Fabiana Elisa MARTÍNEZ
John MASKEY • Sarah MASTERS • Glyn MATTHEWS
Joy MAWBY • Linda MAXWELL • Joan MAZZA
Jan McCARTHY • Pat Murphy McCLELLAND
Trisha Ridinger McKEE • Rob McKINNON
Mandy Toczek McPEAKE • Deborah MELTVEDT
Todd MERCER • Karla Linn MERRIFIELD
Marianne MERSEREAU • Corey MESLER
Marda MESSICK • Neila MEZYNSKI • T.C. MILL
Kathy MILLER • Karuna MISTRY • Marsha MITTMAN
Jennifer MOON • Ray MORRISON • Bruce MORTON

… as well as …

Colleen MOYNE • Remngton MURPHY
AR NEAL • James B. NICOLA • Edward O'DWYER
Louise L. PACE • Carl 'Papa' PALMER • Gary PERCESEPE
Debbie PETERS • Jonathan PETT • Sylvia PETTER
Emma PHILLIPS • Ben PITTS • Margaret PLAGANIS
Diana RAAB • Christina M. RAU • Ivan REHOREK
Lisa REYNOLDS • Lisa RHODES-RYABCHICH
John RILEY • Sharon ROCKMAN • JA ROSE
Biman ROY • Merryn RUTLEDGE • Ed RUZICKA
Angeline SCHELLENBERG • Arlene SCHINDLER
Claire SCHÖN • Robert SCOTELLARO
Phyliss Merion SHANKEN • Judith SHAPIRO
Pegi Deitz SHEA • Josh SHERMAN • Shoshauna SHY
Joan Seliger SIDNEY • Beate SIGRIDDAUGHTER
Cheryl SNELL • Amy SORICELLI
Emily STANFORD • Elizabeth STANLEY
Adrienne STEVENSON • Evelyn Fletcher SYMES
Lynn TAIT • Eileen TRAUTH • Lydia TRETHEWEY
Peggy TROJAN • Lucy TYRRELL • Dianalee VELIE
Pri VICTOR • Lois Perch VILLEMAIRE
Kenneth WAGNER • Tony WARNER
Kresha Richman WARNOCK • Michael WEBB
Rachel WELD • Brian WESTON
Nan WIGINGTON • Allan J. WILLS • Rita WILSON
Riley WINCHESTER • Julianne WOODSIDE
Anne Harding WOODWORTH • Larry WRIGHT
YUAN Changming • Gary ZENKER

# WELCOME TO MARRIAGE

In 2015, as part of my then day job, I delivered training courses on LGBTIQ rights and issues to staff of residential aged care services … so, to people working in nursing homes and hostels.

(LGBTIQ was the acronym we used then. I know that acronym changes almost daily now, but this was seven years ago after all, a whole rainbow life away. Then, and now, along with a lot of other letters on other spectrums, I identify as G, which – rather obviously – was why I was working in the job.)

Whatever the acronym, the training sessions were always interesting, took place across the state (so in country and city locations), and many questions were asked and answered about a whole range of inter-related topics.

Now, at that time, one of the bigger social debates raging in Australia was same sex marriage, or marriage equality as many called it. (I'm on the 'marriage equality' side, myself.)

And the inevitable would be asked of me and my L colleague (who has since moved on to another letter in the rainbow spectrum, or so I've heard): "Do *you* want to get married?"

And we would both answer … "No."

To be followed by … "But everyone should have the right to marry the consenting adult they want, if they choose to. That's the whole point of any kind of *equality*. You can do what everyone else can do."

Yet what I really wanted to say was, "I don't need the heteronormative approval."

And I usually kept that to myself.

Usually …

What you will find in these pages is many different interpretations of what it means to be married, or in a long-term relationship.

Or to be getting married, or having just been married (so weddings, really) which is an entirely different context.

For me, the age and gender breakdown of writers' approaches to 'marriage' has been the most interesting.

But that, dear reader, is a whole other book.

Matt Potter, editor and publisher

August 2022
Adelaide, Australia

# Poetry

# When all this is over

## Juliet Fossey

(After Kathleen Jamie)

we will go prospecting for gold and sieve nuggets
from the riverbed, near a rush town in Alaska.
You will forget your frugal nature and I will give up
darning socks. We will lavish each other with gifts.

Our dogs will stop barking at the fence. Packages
will arrive that are easy to open, containing items
that match their pictures. The annoying little ticks
we've noticed in each other will disappear.

I won't find myself yearning for time alone.
We will re-start our anniversaries and you'll buy
me a hair slide, flowers, a ring that fits. Of course
we'll travel. You will overcome your fear of flying.

I will renew my passport. We'll go prospecting
for gold in Alaska and lavish each other with gifts.

# Bridal Waltz

## Steve Evans

I am up late
        marking students' papers
when you enter the room
        in your wedding gown.
It is beautiful on you still,
        a bit snug now
but you are under sail
        all style and cleavage.

Maybe enchanted
        or maybe under the
humour of its elegant
        and regal presence,
you decide to wear it
        all the next day—
on the train to work
        and interviewing clients,
on your lunchtime walk,
        and shopping for lunch.
You carve a path of calm
        in the frenzy of the city.

By the time you get home
        I am feeling foolish
in my suit with flowers
        and waiting on bended knee.
The choir of neighbourhood kids
        seems a bit redundant
and my little speech silly,
        especially when you say
you've received three
        proposals that day.

Finally, in the house alone,
        we hang up the suit and gown
like ghostly chaperones
        and begin the dance
of the newlyweds,
naked, blessed.

# No man's land

## Mark Heathcote

Between them, separating us, this white piece of paper
all hopes of a future now sadly-annulled.
Their marriage over divorce settlement-finalised
one parent's hand grasped instead of another.
This-is-how-our innocents get taken and destroyed
lying on our beds as if it were an air-raid bomb shelter
like military veterans, clutching-damp wet teary pillows.
But we're only conscripted kids amidst the ongoing war
Crying for what is fundamentally a God-given right.
The rights of two parents that-don't-want to kill each other
allied sister and brother against each other entrenched.
Between them, separating us, the long-awaited ruling,
Nothing's-been-won, but all was irreparably lost.
And it's us weeping kids who paid that significant high cost.

# My Marriage

## Neila Mezynski

Murky as an alligator swamp and plenty scaly. Brooding. Silence. Disappoint plenty. No more hopping up and down chasing round the bed with water balloons in birthday suit. Silence. Vodka bottles heaped high hoping no one will notice in the middle of the room next to the pink elephant. Said I wouldn't go. Stay put too soon. World War 3. That dastardly line was palpable, sticky wicket after I crossed: "It was a mistake." He said. Quiet like. 45 years.

# The Night of the Day

## Larry Lefkowitz

The night of the day
We threw away the red sweater
My wife wore the day I met her
Twenty-two years before
I dreamed she did a wild dance
Not at all in keeping with her non-dream persona
Wearing a red dress festooned in scarves of red
And I thought in the dream:
I didn't know you could dance like that
And when she finished
I whispered in her ear:
"I love you," and was filled with desire.

Upon wakening I felt a pang
Because I was sixty
And I and my wife
Had been young in the dream

And yet, seeing my wife's
Still pretty face,
The still alluring curve of her lips
I felt a pang of desire
As if the dream
Emerging into the waking
Had left me something of a gift

In which
The she\now
And she\then
Merge
Into she/always

# We Are Both

## Jeremy Gadd

We are both the wrong side of forty now
and the fire of our youth burns less vigorously,
lacking the fierce intensity with which it once blazed:
even the prospect life's embers will,
inevitably, flicker, falter and go out
is not the improbability it once was
when viewed through the telescope of time.
Nowadays, my beard before I shave is grey
and I'm careful about the way I behave,
heedful I don't offend others but,
I don't see our faces as worn or lined.
Your beauty remains untarnished to me,
your cheek as smooth, your eyes as clear
as they were when we were twenty-three.

# Dream Wedding

## Marda Messick

If I married my old man and he married me
under the oak tree and a honeymoon,
I'd wear a spring green gown
with periwinkle boots and a jasmine crown,
he in a white smock and new blue jeans.

I'd hire a magician to pluck silver dollars
from the grandchildren's ears,
and a fiddler to play for the ancestors' dance
while our mamas rest on thrones, tapping their toes,
and we all promenade till the stars fall down.

We'd drink champagne to the dear turning world,
our vows made of haikus and the names of birds,
and we'd live ever happily for not long,
if I married my old man and he married me.

# Don’t Change Your Name

## Joan Mazza

I would tell any woman getting married,
don’t surrender your birth name. Your last name
should be yours, yours from birth to death. Don’t
become Mrs. Smith, or worse, Mrs. John
Smith, your identity submerged into

a man’s until you drown. Men don’t change.
They hyphenate with reluctance, revert
to theirs at work, in fame, on bank accounts.
Keep your name and keep your credit cards.
You think this marriage is the exception,

the rarity to last sixty years, bequeath
children a family name to carry—
the man’s name—the woman’s ancestry
forgotten, immaterial. Divorced women
wind up with the debts of big spender

deadbeats, yet often keep that married name
to match their children's name, rather than
restore their own. When they remarry,
their names change again. Keep your name or take
a name you will want to keep. When you change

your name to his, you'll have a permanent
tattoo you can't easily undo. Be who
you are, that one you were born to be, write
and create under your original name,
not maiden name. No explanation needed.

# Without Her, We Could by No Means Be

## Alejo Rovira Goldner

All night she gave birth to her husband
who came out shivering like a mule.
Just by being, he proved the worst of his kind
and yet, at first, she heaped on him her everything
as wings fell from wind chimes that guarded the wind.
His body's mind seemed the color of her body.
His head's eyes told tales of the Great War
packed with poor hygiene and lack of sleep.
"Stop overthinking things, hon," he told her.
"Stop throwing your defunct feet at me," she told him.
He claimed his vintage helmet held her right apostles
but the thumb-sized holy men waved hot iron rods
too close to her nipples and she cried.
Lightning unleashed sea-flies into the decrepit room.
"I'll name you Ephraim," she said
"because you've destroyed all hope."
All night she strangled her husband.

Over a rainbow, a phalanx of storks carried off his remains
but they froze into marble and slammed to earth.
Doctors and congressmen tended to the fallen slabs
and tossed them back skyward.
Some as marble and some as storks and some as human parts
they flocked to the woman and pecked at her face
until she birthed a husband.
She knew to melt his extremities but not in time.
He slew her with a diamond brooch.

# Holy Matrimony

## Declan Geraghty

We looked back on those first days
with happiness
like we were invigorated just with the thought of them
the thought of those first days
and then regret
about the days in the middle
then relief
relief when we think about the last days
days that went by like prison chalk ticks on a wall
walls built on our own errors
trapped in our own stubbornness
sentenced to a lifetime
of Holy Matrimony
even though we were free
free on those first days.

# Mating Ritual

## Marianne Mersereau

They come every spring –
a male and female mallard
to our backyard pool.
We awake to the splash of their landing
often before dawn.
The first five years, we thought it charming.
Now, after thirty years of cleaning up
droppings, we shoo them away
with little interest in their courtship rituals.
After reading that mallards mate for life
we wonder if this is the same pair
from last year, what anniversary
do they celebrate, and
why they choose our pool
when they have a large lake
only blocks away?
How do they find our place each year?
Is it memory or word of beak
that brings them back?

# conversation at a park

## Pri Victor

He asked if I thought the fallen leaves
looked like crabs moving along the shore
I said the leaves looked like an ochre hand
conducting the trees to music so violent
it had been muted for the non-green world
or like a pack of muddied dogs
swarming on a common enemy in decisive hum
I said the breeze sounded like the machine moment
before the MRI begins its rifle fire
head clamped and eyes wide open
or like his breathing when he is finally done with me
I said the bare concrete path looked like our floor
after I gather the children's Lego at the end of the day
or like my face when he comes in and just stumbles to sleep
I asked him if he thought the leaves minded
their fling of curled spines across another's ground
if it was their choice to remain rootless in this dance
He said they were just dead leaves
and I was getting carried away

# Hitched

## Allan J. Wills

Live in the present moment
said my present moment wife.
She sits on the sofa
flicking a touchscreen.
Hitched to a passing thought.

Married to memories, I'm alone.
Sometimes,
in the ephemeral world
a gesture, a skin tone,
long dark hair, whiplash
as sensual phantoms
of a former life.
The thought escapes –
We, both of us,
don't want to be old.

Yet time's arrow skewers all.
What will we have
when we all move on?
All of us bubbles adrift.
Then, pop! Gone.

# Appleseed

## Ben Groner III

*It's the size of an appleseed*
my wife said of the embryo this morning.
More tadpole than human, curled up
like a class 4 plosive "C"
in the soft wall of her uterus, like the
class 4 rapid of parenthood churning
by the headwall ahead. I hope it lives.

*I hope it lives?* What a banal thing
to say. Of course I do, of course
anyone would.

I hope it comes to term, but I also
hope to come to terms with the fact
I may fail to be a good father,
at least on occasion. I have no original
document to scan a copy of, no prophet
of which to ask: *Why do so many
suffer if the world is so good?*

I hope the embryo keeps copying,
fertilizing, swelling, morphing,
that it will be grafted into the
galaxy of humanity, that when
its lonely branch blossoms,
it will relish its earthy fruit
and not be ashamed.

# Semi-colon

## Jan Haag

You can get through your whole life
without one, I told my students.
Really. Periods and commas
will do you fine, if you use them
correctly, if you resist the urge
to polka dot a page or sprinkle
them through a field of letters
like so many chocolate chips.

If a period puts a button
on the end of a sentence,
halts a declaration, and
a comma serves as a mere pause,
when you combine them—
that simple dot over a curvy
wink—you arrive at the spot
dividing two complete thoughts.

It creates parallels;
it speaks of relationship—
your road running next to mine,
each of us equals
holding our own weight
in this lovely dance
of a sentence together.

# *La Piscine* at St. Martin D'Uriage

Joan Seliger Sidney

Why didn't I refuse? Stu meant well, but dammit,
the consequences foiled my husband's intentions
and one honest mistake led to tribulations,
all those years regretting what we can't
undo despite muscle medications,
physical therapy, daily half-mile swims,
or weekly therapeutic horseback sessions.
If only we could travel back to that dim
June morning. Exhausted from friends' visit,
I needed to slip back in bed and sleep.
"But you'll feel fine after diving in deep
water. You always do." Why didn't I resist?
The *maître-nageur* pulled me up the pool stairs.
My left leg spasmed to my breast, my bane to bear.

# Cedar

## Shoshauna Shy

*You don't marry the man;*
*you marry the family*

sounded as clammy as the weight of wet
bedsheets, cumbersome, confining,
chilling as sleet. Yet before the wedding,

I came to learn that holidays happened
with all generations, homemade rhubarb
cobbler and lemonade; any whiff of a sister's
budding romance earned teasing and sly
interrogations; that publications, promotions
and other achievements met a groundswell
of applause.

There were the old stories from childhood –
the peaches in crates under bunkbeds
at the cottage; sisters in fisticuffs over
"borrowed" dresses; that their mother
strained Coke through a handkerchief
when the glass thermos broke at the movies.
Stories recapped so many times till it seemed

I had been there and lived them myself,
like I, too, had grown up in their Wisconsin
farm town, not my suburb on Lake Michigan.
Or that I swung on two playgrounds that day
Kennedy got shot and died on camera; Trick
or Treated both Union and Wesley streets;
played Spud under double the streetlights.
And in decade #4 knotted tight as his wife

I'm well-versed in the dip of the gossip
bucket, feel pride in the skills of athletic
grand-nieces, confide freely in brothers-in-law.
For what sounded like a Doomsday warning
turned out not to be treacherous at all, those

bedsheets woven with merino and silk,
sun-washed on clotheslines,
scented with cedar.

# Praise For the Double Bed

## Peggy Trojan

The double bed we slept in
for over fifty years
contributed to our marriage
in its quiet reliable way.
One hundred twenty-five years old
when we bought it in the sixties,
already had a history of dependability.

Mahogany with five-foot posters,
it provided a visual picture of boundary,
even in soft moonlight.
Allowed easy cuddle, intimate conversations.
If David went to bed before I did,
he often warmed my side with intention.
If we went to sleep with unresolved anger,
an accidental touch during the night
could easily be accepted as an apology.

I would gently poke him to stop snoring.
Would answer when he talked while dreaming,
or check on his breathing when he was ill.
He often touched my shoulder in the night,
making sure I was still there.

Once, he called out quietly,
from a dark king-sized motel expanse,
"Peggy, where are you?"

# Aren't They a Pair?

## Amy Soricelli

The funny little ways people get along with
their blinking eyes and nervous moves of
the elbow. That couple over there are leaning
tight against each other's hands, their fingers
a woven string game.

She probably moves the blanket over the end
of the bed the same way each night, or the long
car trip to visit her sister and the backwards turn
to check the stove. He has learned to live with the
steady hum of her daytime soaps as he cleans

the coffee filter with his insurance salesman hands.
She never asks out loud why he retired so early
to live in a house with no den. They both fill up the
charity bags with clothes the other remembers
from their first date, and still the crumbs in his top

pocket for the squirrels. She bends her head to the
side always when he asks her this, or this, and before
a serious answer she will close her eyes. He has a funny
way of falling in love with her from back when she was
younger and laughed with her mouth wide open.

# Marriage, the Con Artist

## Debbie Peters

Before I knew how you would paint me
in your gallery of portraits
          Renoir-romantic? Klimt-kissed?
          Cassatt-maternal? Picasso-fragmented?
I feared your brushstrokes on my Modigliani-like neck

Yet I posed for your vows, modeled for our *I do*'s
until the day you
          no longer prized me as a masterpiece
          saw only the flaws your sleight-of-hand could not mask
          grew tired of mowing the lawn in front of the house
          sketched the future in pencil

Until the day you
          eliminated fidelity from your palette

# A Pandemic Afternoon

## Joanne Jagoda

Two seniors on a cool December day
sitting on a purple leather sofa
cozy under a puffy red quilt
a lazy pandemic afternoon
days and weeks flow together like a river rushing to nowhere
watching a mindless Netflix movie I think I've seen
time ebbs in boredom and inertia
he takes my hand
and kisses my fingers
we cling to each other these days
out of resignation and desperation
every sigh and breath accountable
knowing we are fighting an unseen enemy
casts a shadow of uncertainty between us
the daily grim statistics hang heavy in the air
grieving loved ones left behind
their lives will never be the same
now with the vaccine so close at hand
we want to build a wall around us
would that our love could keep us from harm
our fifty years together a safe harbor,
but there are no guarantees
a light beckons
at the end of that almost endless tunnel
we are praying to reach it in time

# Marriage – 2017

## Rob McKinnon

Voters asked to judge
who should be allowed to marry the person they love,
a choice between an antiquated narrow view
or an inclusive embrace.

In response, streets filled with rainbows
in seas of "Yes" on placards,
thousands in cities marched
to end the injustice,
while on steps of parliaments and in parks
speakers passionately urged acceptance,
but traditional restrictors
counselled continued exclusion.

A postal plebiscite
because legislators were bound
by narrow conservative views
and internal party politics.

Citizens choosing compassion in a majority,
the voices in the streets heard
and the law changed,
love equalling love advanced.

# Cold Cuts

## Glyn Matthews

The mirror doesn't lie,
only what we see.

The wrinkles round my eyes
are not laughter lines.

I realise now,
the crow that walked across

my face was you. But
I never saw the signs until too late.

Rather than peck out my eyes,
you kept your hate

simmering for years on
a slow heat and ladled poison,

by measured spoonful from
an ocean of regrets,

reheated through a lens
of sleepless nights,

intensified by turning hours
on a spit that sealed the juices in.

A small portion
of your loathing was served

each morning with the toast,
while later, cold cuts were thrust,

designed to slice me with
a bitter garnish of your hate,

though for years my hunger
for your love disguised the taste.

# Games We Play

## Adrienne Stevenson

the match between us was not scripted
no duration was established
no point system assigned, no rules set

nobody was picked for a team
although teamwork is required
we struggle to maintain our own space

frequently clashing over minutiae
from time to time we meld
into near-unity, so briefly

we remember ancient grievances
fail to celebrate joy for long
but welcome its recurrence

our gazes sometimes wander
yet revert like migrant birds
shuttlecocks on a return of service

we are collaborators and opponents
the ball passes back and forth between us
what is the state of play?

# The Milliner's Last Night

LindaAnn LoSchiavo

Her millinery shop had windows bright
With fascinators for madame whose face
Needs artificial lace to help erase
Ten years and homburgs for suburbanites
Disguised as understated socialites.
She scanned the sawdust-trampled street in case
Her customer was late or had misplaced
The payment for this bretonne veiled in white.

Winds cold as fingers of an old cashier
Blew scraps through the boutique as beggars took
Their place. The organ grinder's monkey held
His fez when coins appeared as sunset neared.
A lady, cloaked, knocked with a frantic look
As, in the distance, wedding steeples belled.

# The Bed He Made

## Colleen Moyne

He never meant for it to happen

It had been six months since they traded glances
across that dimly-lit nightclub

One too many drinks led them back to his house
and there she stayed

He never meant for it to last

But too many drinks led to poor judgement
and a positive test result

and his momma raised him to do right –
to lay in the bed he made

He never meant to commit

But now he waits in his ill-fitting suit
for her to walk down the aisle

A lump in his throat – not borne of love
but of regret

He never meant for it to come to this

But the kid needs a dad –
something he never had.

# Marriage Poem

## Corey Mesler

*for Cheryl*

When you sleep beside me
I know the things stars
know, the secrets of
the rill, the instinct of the
ocean itself. It's a large thing,
then, your sleeping beside me,
a thing not to take lightly,
as accountable as dreams.
When you lie there your breath
is the exhalation of the
tired world, the sweet sad song
of the forest. And I am
small beside the enormity of
your sleeping beside me,
but, simply, wifemine, I am.

# Song of an Octogenarian

Jacqueline Kudler

If you want scrambled eggs, you don't
turn up the heat, no, you beat them to
a froth—no milk, for heaven's sake—
then set the flame low and slow, stir
steady till they pull together how you
like them. Hard, soft, up to you.

And if you want your Impatiens to
hold their own all summer long,
you don't over-water please, no,
just one gush each or you drown
your darlings.

Pay attention through the years
and you get to see how things play out:
the one great gift that age delivers.

So marriage, for instance—oh,
never easy and often stops working
right. Well then, maybe the software's
jammed, you know, and you just
need to press Restart. A walk in
the woods, maybe, or a week in
Belize just might do it for you.

But sometimes, sometimes, it's
the hardware that's off and there's
nothing for it but to pull the plug
and junk it.                    Nothing.

Because love needs all of you, really.
You don't just measure it out in small
breaths, no. You give it all the breath
you've got each day—like blowing out
the candles on your birthday cake,
because then and only then, your
wish just might come true.

# Just Off the Driveway

## Ed Ruzicka

A few months before Katrina hit
you thinned lilies at your
rent house on America Street.
Passed a grocery bag of bulbs, stalks, blooms
from the crook of your arm into mine.

That allowed them to escape any singe
when an electrical fire sparked down
to your sedan in the driveway two months later
and your car suddenly erupted into flame
outside your window while you were
snapping toast in your teeth.

By then I had dug a bed next to my own driveway
where the lily blades could rattle and swill.
Instead they languished under an oak's shade.

Less than one year later your gray Mazda
started to crawl past the lilies, park in the carport
off North Parkview as this house became ours
and one more thing to share.

The lilies toughed out a dozen winters.
Grew scraggly inside their skirt of shade.
This spring after the great oak above had to be felled –
        five tons of hardened trunk hauled off,
        after the massive canopy toppled –
we had the emptiness of sun, cloud, moon, star
where leaves, squirrel, branches had been.

This March after their long dormancy
those lilies finally found enough sun
to burst up jasmine-bright
in rills and arcs for our glad eyes,
in the midst of everything
else that blooms for us.

# Speakers

## Merryn Rutledge

He slumped on the couch across from me,
staring, it seemed, at nothing.

*You made me get rid of my Carlson speakers.*

Inside me shrilled an alarm
this stranger who resembled
my husband likely didn't hear.

*You wanted newer ones, remember?*
We had been happy.

*You made me,* he said.

His head, neck, and hands stained yellow from bile.
We were waiting for it to clear his body
so he could start chemo.

No chemo.

Instead, a technician in ER glided
her ultrasound wand over his belly.

Splotches on the monitor behind his head–
red, yellow, orange. Flames.

I asked her what the colors meant.
*I'm not supposed to say,*
she told the monitor.

Martin grunted when the wand kneaded the flesh
on one spot.
*Oh, that kind of infection,* he muttered
to the ceiling.

In my head, I scrolled down
the list of warnings in the notebook
his oncologist had given us.

The patient didn't speak again.

# Blood Money

Winston Derden

The EMTs crowding the bath would not
permit the estranged wife to view the body.
Too much blood, they said.

Whether he fell against the tub
and bled out from head trauma, or
a stroke pitched him forward was

immaterial to the coroner.
He died alone, no foul play in evidence.
Autopsy a waste of time and money.

From the funeral home to home,
to steel against guilt, remorse,
the weight of final arrangements,

the press of bills, the questioning
of settlements, tied-up disbursements,
the crush for cash unrelieved by

a retirement center that
would not return the deposit
with blood dried on the bathroom floor.

Hands and knees, sponge and pail and rubber gloves,
scrubbing, rinsing, ringing out
to liquidate indebtedness.

# Homeland

## Biman Roy

Sometimes a river defines the night.

I met you at the ghat of the Ganges,

you left me at the edge of the Hudson.

We chose a home in between,
an homage to life.

I lived to breathe, you lived to dream.

When it rained in your dream,

you rented a night out.

I just played possum

to the incessant wind.

I took you for granted,
but somewhere a branch broke

with the weight of wet snow,

as you repatriated for a new homeland.

# She Sets the Table

## Mike Lewis-Beck

neglecting napkin holders
and how the knives should turn.
The fire won't take and the wine
glass's for white not red.

I hurt my foot and can't do it.
Over the pasta with our garden sauce
we talk about our niece and my son
and whether they will find love.

She explains to me my new computer
and describes the wine tastes.
Her ideas for our new photo-poetry
installation on Guatemala enthrall.

I pass her a savored Sicilian salt
and the Parmesan chunk to grate.
I worry the bucatini's too *al dente*
hoping to do better next pot.

# Enjoying a Moment

## Tony Daly

We sit in a parking lot full
of dance moms and dads.
All with running engines,
face masks dangling from our ears,
ever ready for the mad dash
to the door to collect
our little girls and boys
before they can be too exposed
to the outside air.

We sit in a parking lot,
silently, side-by-side.
My wife in the passenger seat,
earphones in, watching videos
that make her snort
when the laugh surprises her.
Myself, typing poems in a tablet,
looking around for inspiration
in the simplest of things.

We sit in a parking lot,
just the two of us,
decompressing from a day
of work from home desks
and loaned computers,
from reaffirming the words of teachers,
correcting inattentiveness,
listening to constant chatter
of grade schoolers
as we try to take notes
from teleconferences
we may have to report on.

We sit in a parking lot full
of dance moms and dads,
silently, side-by-side,
just the two of us,
enjoying a moment.

# For Worse

## John Grey

I plan to be generous with just about everything
Love is just the beginning.
There are also my books to be considered,
my collection of old vinyl,
my habits of course,
my taste in food and television
and, let's not forget,
my infatuation with ancient
Fred Astaire and Ginger Rogers movies.

When I said "I do"
under the nose of the priest,
in front of that conglomeration
of friends and family,
I made a commitment to not hold back
one New England Patriots cap,
any Playboy magazines,
an addiction to Coca Cola
and an appreciation for all things Disney.

The honeymoon is over
and up from the cellar,
like the Beast from 20,000 Fathoms,
comes my collection of souvenirs
from my trip to Paris,
while down from the attic,
like heavy smelly snowflakes,
float the sneakers I will never wear again
but haven't the heart to throw away.

I'm sorry sweetheart.
This is your reward
for agreeing to marry me.
Yes, you love me.
But love is just how these things start.

# Wedding Couplets

## Natalie Fry

I kept my arms covered all that week and washed
my skin so that it smelled of flowers

but the feel of the fabric didn't make me
regal as I'd imagined and needed to be stitched

with dust on the stairs. I waited in the square
for the 50-metre drive to the Town Hall.

No, it wasn't a religious one, and I swore
as I got out of the car, I would never do this

again, hearing the blur of quartet that I couldn't
for the life of me string together.

A snatch of angry words, rose petals,
sweat running down the back of my neck

a lack of chairs for guests, legs heavy in the heat
and the soon-to-be Mayor droning on

the way Italians do about the responsibilities
of bringing children into the world.

And in the pictures, later, all I saw
was my inability to hold the bouquet the right way.

# Community Property

Wendy Freborg

I saw this book upon our shelf.
Although the flyleaf bore your name,
I was sure I'd bought it for myself—
I am sure I had one just the same.
I used to know what all was mine:
I had my own games, my thoughts and books
And always knew just where to find
The things I owned, all on their hooks.
Now I am not sure what's part of me
And what I've gained or lost to you.
Things that are ours are all I see,
Yours and mine mixed without a clue.

# Things Change

## Ryn Holmes

Hearing an old song today
memories come flooding back
in where you have no business,
and I got to wondering how you are,
where you are these days
as you go about your life without me in it?
Do you keep the same old routine
or mix it up in new ways with new women –
perhaps less troublesome sorts eager to please,
happy to take the place of one sworn to forever,
still tethered by bonds thin as spidery silk?
You were packed away as part of an old story
but here you are still.

A smiling man once came to me,
sexy little guy with big things to offer,
open hand holding a forever proposition.
Me oh my could he ever run rings around
words too gorgeous to resist,
so being foolish I jumped into romance,
chose poetic rhymes over reason
all smart-alecky certain any big problems could work out if –
big if – we put our hearts into it,
after all we were both named for saints.

There is a saying that women grieve and men replace –
not so sure about that myself.
I'm only certain about the empty space
                                                            over there
on your side of the bed.

# where had the years gone

## William Butler

swept away in a tidal bore of passion and discovery
which lasted over a year, the first months were easy
ensuing years added up as kids (2),
and car payments (2), mortgages (1), vacations came and went
where had the years gone he would ask himself repeatedly
sitting in his backyard chair, his life wafting into the summer sky
wispily, wistfully as he watched the grill pop and smoke
I'm waiting for something he excused himself smugly
glancing about, nervous someone would call him on it
waiting for what, someone would ask,
a promotion, junior partnership, more territory, what
what, he questioned, but clinging to his excuse
for another set of years, graying hair, kids gone
separate bedrooms, cruise vacations, golf buddies,
no expectations, and restlessness
the grill rusting, the pool empty, cars eleven years old,
bad back, and little to say when he looked at her now,
she was another person whom he didn't know
where had the years gone, he asked, received no response
anniversary cards, birthday cards, fixed smiles,
bad hearing, and a stroke

he saw her slip away, pass into the plastic stick-on stars
of the room, swept cob-webs from the closet
late one night, standing in his driveway,
staring sightless into the dark sky,
he wept but could not remember for whom or why

# Rest Your Head

## Jan Chronister

Cousins born four days apart
rest their blond curls
on forearms,
gaze at cut glass bowls
of mixed nuts, pillow mints
set out for the wedding.
Dressed in their best,
they inhale the aroma
of almonds, cashews.
Noses tingle at the scent
of sugary pink,
yellow, green puffs.

Their aunt stands at the altar
lost in a dream,
innocent of the weariness
that comes with being a wife—
the dairy farm,
four children,
holding too many ends
while her airline pilot husband
flew from city to city,
gone for days,
nights not spent alone.

# Marriage: a Comparative Definition

## Yuan Changming

In the West:
It is like a fortress besieged; those who are outside
Want to get in, and those who are inside want to get out

In the East:
It is like a chicken rib, unappetizing and yet
Not bad enough to be discarded as sheer waste

Though it's actually an open bottle, where bees
Get bruises one after another as they charge toward
Light, but flies can thrive as they settle in darkness

Or a cage with the little gate always open
But only for the untamed bird

# To Have and to Hold

## Richard Band

He comes home to only his stuff
and the bed unmade on one side,
and she is not there,
bestowed with conversation,
picking up where they left off that morning.

About the house:
a solitary coffee cup,
the books are his alone,
the wildlife calendar marks
none of her appointments,
no photos of a couple
in a clutch, in falling snow.
There is no two of them.

He is not to blame.
Something failed to happen.

I know that could have been my lot
had she not chanced through a doorway that day,
at that time, amazing.

Yesterday,
we laughed at a man in a silly hat.

# Caprice

## James B. Nicola

On weekends he wears the baseball cap
from the team he was on in his teens.
He forgets how she used to sit on his lap.
She reads singles' magazines.

It was not their initial dream
to sign on as husband and wife.
His was to play on a pro ball team.
Hers was an à-la-mode life.

She keeps in a drawer her old photo book.
In his workshop, he slips on his cleats,
then places them back on the rusted hook.
Each season the sequence repeats.

And each season neither one finds
that their marriage is taking a toll
like the gradual losing of minds
or the possible loss of a soul.

# Partner

## Peter Clarke

We have lain side by side
for nearly fifty years,
the wonder of her stays with me:
Black depths, golden heights,
burned in the fires of anguish,
shocked in the ice of death.

Her breasts have changed
from pert to round,
her bottom,
large and milky white.
Grey flecks temper her
blonde pubes,
her sex lips rubbered.
Thighs stumped, legs veined,
movement stunted to
pre-arthritic mooches.

Her black and white thinking has been
repainted into a myriad of colours,
layered from flat to almost sculpted.
A whole rich companion unfolds.

But the girl flares through
her bright green eyes,
playfulness leaks out her tongue,
captured by her infectious laughter.

# How I Met My Second Husband

## Lois Perch Villemaire

On an unmarked, unexplored path,
a detour, an escape route, a byway,
stinging from injuries and bruises,
no dreams or expectations,
still freshly alone, relieved,
mature but unaware,
unappreciated,
hiking along, eyes soft,
we collided at an intersection,
fell down together, and
on best behavior,
initiated conversation.

Two very different types,
we had lots to learn, to teach,
It made for careful listening,
patient explanations.
Moving slowly,
discovering common ground,
developing communication.

What makes you smile?
What makes me laugh?
Long bike rides, movies, books
for discussion.

In time, love arrived and settled in
like a carefree day on a lounge chair
at the beach,
Sand, seashells, wailing gulls
sailing just above the ocean currents.
Making plans to construct our lives
in a new formation,
Figuring it out together,
reinventing that unmarked,
unexplored path
where we started.

# I'll Take My Chances

## Mandy Toczek McPeake

*But why?* I asked, and luckily he laughed.
*I've seen the worst of you,* he said,
*Now will you marry me, or not?*
I love the man; he knows his mind.

*I need to know we'll talk,* he said.
*One unfaithful wife is enough.*
*Can we be honest even when it hurts?*
The only way to make this work, we agreed.

*I'll never turn away from touch,* he said
*Can you promise me the same?*
*We talk, we touch; this marriage will survive.*
Touch becomes the salve for bitter words.

Hard times, harsh words, they happen.
I learn to temper my temper,
To consider how it feels
To bear the brunt.

In time we know each other well
Have children, watch them grow.
We know, point out, accept
The worst of our flaws.

Again and again, I see that I come first.
So, I feel free, as does he, to give and take.
To know when to concede,
no loss of face, no shame in that.

Thirty years later, our eyes still watch the ball.
*You've got to keep working at it*, he says.
Appreciate each other's good intent
Celebrate the best of times, share the worst.

My own family, we fought to win,
Which isn't winning, so we lost each other.
This life he and I made is worth fighting for,
together.
That's how we win.

# The Gambler

## Steven Dee Kish

Mama was a gambler; she never betted money,
only other people's lives.
She took a gamble and moved out at eighteen …
it didn't pay off.
Mama flunked out of college in her second year
and struggled to make ends meet.
She found herself with an important life decision to make.
Her choices were limited; she could move back home
or find someone to shoulder the load.
The betting odds were against her,
but she got lucky and found someone.
It was a quick engagement, and after walking down the aisle,
Mama found some stability.
Married life didn't suit her; she couldn't get rid
of her thoughts about the nightlife.
So, Mama gambled … After a quick divorce and lines of coke
up her nose, Mama was busted.
Her new home was her roach-filled apartment by the river;
she had to get out.
So, Mama rolled the dice again and looked for another mark
to get her out of the gutter.

Bingo! She found one, but he decided to raise the stakes;
he asked her for a kid.
Faced with eating another mayonnaise sandwich
on stale bread, she fulfilled his wish.
Mama doubled down, she had to give a little to get the jackpot.
Husband number two didn't read the fine print.
Mama hated kids.
She got a new Buick in the driveway and a manager's job.
With a steady amount of cash flow, Mama's life was flourishing.
Job promotions, motorhome, three weeks' vacation,
and a second car.
Mama was living her best life with a cig in one hand
and a cocktail in the other.
Life was good, she was rubbing elbows with the elite,
but that made her jealous.
Mama didn't want to be in the working middle class.
She wanted to host parties and have a house on the lake.
So, Mama upped the ante and left it all behind
to bask in the warm sun of Las Vegas.
Fights started to happen more frequently,
and another divorce was on the horizon.
Mama got her next man lined up;
he offered her the life she wanted.
She thought her horse had finally come in
and was ready for her big payday.
Mama didn't see the Vegas con-man milking her
for all her money.

Her gamble didn't pay off; she was feeding her kid
mustard sandwiches and was bankrupt.
The extended family offered a helping hand,
but Mama refused to swallow her pride.
She was all in on this new life she desired
and sacrificed her kid to get it.
Mama left the kid alone at night while
she looked for another winning horse.
While Mama was getting wined and dined,
some Joker started to abuse the kid.
No amount of cries or failing grades from the kid
could sway Mama's decision.
After five years of playing the game,
Mama's ticket finally came in, and she won.
She didn't win the jackpot like she hoped, but she broke even.
Husband number three bought Mama a house,
cars, boat, and a motorhome.
Finally, Mama was satisfied with her winnings;
now, all she had to do was get rid of the kid.
The kid was broken and held no more value to her.
She pawned off the kid and got what she could for it.
Mama got the life she wanted because she was a gambler.

# the very definition of

## Jack Henry

we walk
together down a well-trodden path
made of dirt and stone,
hike through old hills
Southern California,
pause a moment
to take it all in.

he kisses me, soft,
and smiles.
we keep moving until
we stop at the edge of night,
a long path still before us.

we make fire,
eat a simple meal.
there is no need
to share many words.

fire out, cold creeping in,
we coil together in double sleeping bag
deep in our tent, settle into sleep,
wait on the coming of another day.

# Passing a Dead Squirrel on the Way to the Marriage Counselor

Kenneth Wagner

You say *you know squirrels mate for life*
*her mate is going to be sad she's gone*
*I bet they loved each other*

and I wonder out loud
do squirrels know they mate for life
and how do you know it's a she
did this dead squirrel have a ring
was there an engagement party
was there a ceremony a bouquet a cake
did uncle squirrel get drunk and crash through
the sliding glass door did it rain on the honeymoon
how many years married how many kids
do they carry a mortgage on a pine branch
close to her parents' tree

and on this dark day how does he mourn her
is there a parish   a congregation   a parson
squirrel who delivers the sad news
and stays with the family all night
is there a support group in an old oak
a greenish room 12 limbs up
is there a little bark table with a plate
of acorns and an urn of bitter nectar
do they sit on folding chairs made of twigs
are there tissues made from sapling leaves

and what of the squirrel's children who have
to cope with death   are there long nights
of staring into space   when their tails twitch
does the ache of loss twist their hearts
do they stay home from school for a week
is a week enough time for a young squirrel to grieve

and what of the in-laws in the next tree
do they come and help out or are they
still angry their daughter married the wrong
squirrel and secretly blame him for her death

and I wonder are you truly sad for the dead squirrel
for the mate of the dear departed or just your squirrelly self

because when I say   *I know for a fact squirrels don't mate for life*
*but I think black vultures do*

your eyes narrow and squeeze out a thin line of tears

# Nuptial Rites

## Pat Murphy McClelland

For bride and groom
and members of their party
for cousins, friends
and college roommates
weddings implicate
beholden deliverance
from siblings, parents, cast-off lovers,
bars, meet-ups, hook-ups, dates,
from frowned-upon,
suspect single states.

For bride and groom
bartered deliverance
gowned in tulle, veiled in white
conservative in tie and tux
revives abandoned orthodox
one more time. Bearing something
old, wearing something blue
she aims her flowers, he tosses
garters to the optimistic
next in line.

For mothers of the bride
in sheer chiffon
for fathers prevailed upon to pass
their daughters on to dubious
substitutes with feigned benevolence
weddings re-incarnate
once young and daring leaps
of faith, bygone dreams made
sacred by the prospect of increase.

For tender-hearted aunts in hats
and suited uncle cynics
for withered elders of the clan
weddings instigate
stirrings of elapsed pasts
of promises exchanged
of memories cast in sepia tones
of bittersweet eroticisms
demanding that we turn.

Dearly beloved
generations stand
gathered in this ritual place
attending different ceremonies.

# Wed Lock

## Anne Harding Woodworth

1

Imagine yourself a non-traditional bride,
in love with the man waiting down there
at the altar. Your arms are linked
with your father's and mother's,
and the organist strikes up the processional.
Your mom wanted 'Here Comes the Bride',
but you read in *Cosmo* that 'Here Comes the Sun'
suits the non-traditional wedding just fine.

What's so non-traditional about this one?
The groom to start with. No chance
you were marrying your father.
Young unadventurous women
marry their fathers. You aren't that.
Your groom's a joker. A shredder.
Your groom's rich. He doesn't have to work,
but for fun he loads skiers onto a chairlift.
He says, "Have a good one"
with a flirtatious twinkle in his eye.
His father's best friend owns the mountain.

Imagine yourself without a trust.
The reception your mom and dad
are paying for is at a hall in Denver.
Dad is spending an unfamiliar bundle
on this wedding, proud that he's paid every bill
so far. Just one more. The band.

2

The band wants cash. Dad has seven C-notes
in his tux pocket to give to the band
when the reception is over.
But right now, you and the groom
have the first dance, bearhug-style.
That's all he knows how to do on a dance floor.
Dad's a good dancer, likes to dance and cuts in
after leaving his tux jacket on a chair.
The groom should go ask Mom to dance,
but he doesn't. Imagine your mom relieved.

3

Imagine how you feel when the party's over
and the cash is missing and Dad
has to drive to a few ATMs
to get as much cash as he can for the band.

Imagine yourself going off for a honeymoon
in the Caribbean. You're crying
when you say goodbye to Mom and Dad
(because of the missing cash)
but you tell them you love them
and you thank them for this special day.

The groom is antsy to get going
and tells you anybody can afford losing
a buck here, a buck there.
Imagine yourself feeling better.

4

The early weeks of marriage go pretty much
like the late weeks of living together.
You have your job at Starbucks
and the groom helps people onto lifts
when he isn't shredding. You look
at your heirloom diamond rings
every five minutes. Imagine yourself
feeling just married. You can't wait
to see the wedding photos. And the video.

Imagine how you feel when Dad calls
about the video. You're dancing with Dad—
clearly that's the focus of the frames—
but in the background the groom
sits in a chair, and there he is, *flagrante delicto,*
sliding his hand furtively into Dad's jacket.

# Distance

## Ben Pitts

You were wearing the just-right amount
of everything.
The air licked with rosemary
and lilacs.
Laying on cool pavement while planes
like needles
dwindled in the clouds above our heads.

We said even back then
*Let's turn this desert*
*Into a memory.*

Light split—
prisms around your ridge
made it
        difficult to tell which direction to move to.

Your hometown?
My hometown?

*Our hometown.*

A romance like ours
is pocket-sized, it slides
perfectly in place
no matter the place.

# Husband Poem

## Michele Bombardier

*After Yehoshua November*

Whatever grief comes for us,
knocks its slow knock on the kitchen door,
we will stand together to meet it.

Those years of doctors, prognostic indicators,
first-line-second-line treatments, our learning
a whole new lexicon, what held me together

were your small kindnesses: the glass of water
on the nightstand, the morning tea,
the phone calls you took when I kept the phone

in the garage, under a blanket. *I'll give her*
*your message,* you'd say and your lack of promise
that I'd call back a deeper kindness yet. I remember

once the white of your shirt a sail
in the backyard: you were mowing the lawn
in the dark, it was late, I was at the window,

you'd come towards me, turn, clatter
into the dark and I could hardly bear it,
your visage and transience, a little rehearsal

of what we know is to come.

# From the Unfolding

## Christina M. Rau

The me was you
close to the skull
where the real life is.
Your body abroad
untouchable in the miles.
Your vacancy an ice pick
pointed end stuck in the freeze.
In the residue of dreams
a lucid wakeaday world
rises,
        dreams the ash
tamped down into fresh grave.
It wasn't ever really living—
that rack of moments between us
replacement for the void.
A habitual rhythm is not a choice
but we deem it something.
The not being alone but being alone together.

Still every sensory detail
floats as if alive and awake and full of its own
volition. A life of its own but not ours,
mine, yours.
Your hold a harpoon. My grasp a shiv.
The you is me no longer who the me was before.
Your mind stateside
border over border
ethereal realness of clouds
the kind that are pretty at first
and then turn gray
and then all sky
turns to cloud
roiling in an angry tundra
overwhelming earth
no me no you no us
just this not-life
unraveling quick.

# Owed to Oskar's Park Hotel

## Bruce Morton

*for Bärbel*

As the fiftieth anniversary approaches
I do not want to answer the question
For the umpteenth time, "How did you
Two meet?" So here it is once and for all,
The short and sweet of it: "I won her
In a poker game." Badaboom! True story.

I had all of her brother's money and he
Wanted to play out his hand—a straight.
What to do? And as if on cue in walk
His two sisters. So he says to me,
"Will you let me bet a date with one
Of my sisters, you choose, if I lose?"

Well, I drew a full house, "Sure,"
I say. I am thinking to myself, what
Do I have to lose? Innocence? I don't
Think so. So I raked in my chips,
Stacked them neatly and played on
All these years, still pot committed.

# The Wood We Left Outside

## Con Chapman

We have a tradition here; once a year
  on our anniversary,
  we build a fire. I guess we aspire
  to togetherness, to slough off
  the indifference that builds up
  day after day, the way a snake
  sheds its skin, to begin again.

Whoever thinks of it first opens
  the flue and then the second, in an
  excess of attentiveness, does it too,
  which means it's closed now, not opened,
  so when the smoke begins to rise
  from the paper and the kindling, it fills the room.
Amidst the panic the fire department is called

  and they come with hoses and a giant fan
  to blow the smoke outside. We've done it
  at least three times, you'd think we'd have
  learned by now to listen to each other, and not
  save the solicitude for special occasions.

We bought a half cord of wood
today, stacked half in the garage, and the rest outside.
"Don't you think you should put a tarp over it—to keep
it dry?" she said. Naw, I said, it'll be fine, I said.

"That kind of defeats the purpose, doesn't it?"
she said skeptically as she walked away. I explained
that we'd use the wood in the garage first, and
when that ran out, we'd bring the rest inside to dry.

"Okay," she said over her shoulder.
I went inside to take a nap but before I fell asleep,
I thought about the anniversary coming up, got up
and threw a plastic sheet over the wood we left outside.

# We're the Same About Different Things

## Dave Clark

Some look at shoes
Like others stare at cars and figures.
Drawn in, fascinated,
Studying sleek lines and rousing curves,
Yearning to get their hands on them.

'Nothing happens during a day of cricket,'
Some say, while nattering over cuppas
For hours
About inconsequentials of daily life.

Some love the journey,
Others the destination.
Both love going somewhere.

You hate being embarrassingly early.
I hate being embarrassingly late.
I'm tidy but dirty.
You're sprawling and clean.

Some are tight with budgets, some with calories,
Some with time. All are crunching numbers.

One watches Disney, the other, Bruce Willis.
Both want happy endings and snuggles on the couch.

Finding pockets of peace through bricklaying, prayer,
Cooking, darts, deep breathing, cigarettes,
Snorkelling, yoga, demolition derbies.

In so many differing ways
We're the same.

# The Anniversary

## Remngton Murphy

—Was it all worth it?
—Hah?

—You know, our thirty years together.
—Of course, it was worth it.

Why would you even ask such a thing?
—Thirty years is a long time.

And you know, in a lot of ways
I'm really not the same woman.

—What do you mean?
Haven't you always liked cinnamon buns

And creamed asparagus on toast?
The evidence convicts you. Case closed.

—Well, I suppose you have a point.
My tastes haven't changed.

—Look, this here's our anniversary.
In so many words, a cause for celebration.

And here we are, sitting in a midtown hotel
With a decent view of Rockefeller Center.

There's an ice bucket on the table,
And rammed inside, hey,

Courtesy of yours truly,
A gen-u-ine five hundred dollar bottle

Of Chateau Chevy Blanche.
What's so funny?

—It's *Chateau Cheval Blanc.*
And please, don't get me wrong.

I appreciate all you've done for me.
Working hard.

Building a business up from scratch.
The expensive car. The vacation home.

Making life easy for me.
—But?

—It just seems like something's missing.
—Missing?

—I can't put my finger on it,
But something doesn't seem right.

—Did you find somebody else?
—No.

—What is it then?
You're not happy with me?

—No, it's nothing like that.
I'm happy with you, and I'm pretty sure

That you enjoy being with me.
Aren't you happy?

—Say look, do we need to get ourselves
All bent out of shape

Obsessing over upsetting topics?
Tonight of all nights

We ought to be thanking our lucky stars,
We ought to be dwelling on what we got.

Due to my shrewd financial planning
An early retirement, I'm happy to say,

Certainly looks feasible,
And our kids, at long last out of college

And schlepping for their daily bread,
Oh happy day,

Are finally weaned off the money-tit,
And it's sure to be a beautiful evening,

Because—drumroll, please—
I've managed to wangle two theater tickets,

And what I mean is, premium seating,
Fifth row center.

As for me, and you've heard me say this
Till I was blue in the face,

When it comes to Broadway musicals
I can take 'em or leave 'em.

Speaking personally, I think I'd have a much better time
At Yankee Stadium.

But I know what it means to you,
Saying goodbye to the dreary same old

And hello to a captivating night on the town.
—In that case, we better shake a leg.

We wouldn't want to miss the beginning.
Especially since you paid so much.

—Believe me, honey, it wasn't just the cost.
You have to know somebody too.

—You're still the kind, considerate man I married,
Always going above and beyond.

# I'll Do Anything, For You, Dear, Anything

Keith Hoerner

She holds two swords
of societal success.
Her career of achievement,
her marriage of love realized.

Nice
house,
nicer
car.

The look that
men look at –
even her
husband.

Meditative dreams
on summer days
under a comforter
of cool breezes.

Still, one regret
reflects
the swords'
sharp edges.

Cut her
caesarean style –
deep
as you like;

take out the child
she cannot
carry …
his son.

The single
thing
she cannot
give him.

Justice, she feels,
is not
in the cards
for her.
She seeks
to be satiated
through
gluttonous eyes.

Where are her
maternity clothes,
the infant boy
she must steal?

# Who's Going to Heckle Us If We Get Married?

## Josh Sherman

One of the first things you told me
was about how you were in
Guildwood Park one time
with some friends
You told me about it
when we went there
on our second date
on January 12, 2019

I want to set the scene right away:
Wikipedia describes the park as
a "beautiful sculptural garden
located along the Scarborough Bluffs"
These kinds of places exist everywhere
in some form,
so I'll leave it at that
I'm more interested in what happened
that one time
you went to Guildwood Park

Some people were getting married there
They were getting married
in a public space
Was the Distillery District
already booked?
These things happen, you know
You have your dream wedding planned
at a popular tourist destination
And then you end up
in a suburban
Scarborough Park

You mimicked the bride's vows
in your most bridely voice,
and, man, you made connubial vows
sound so dumb
But sound carries,
the sky is big out there
by the lake
So she heard, and a friend had to tell you
to stop

You hadn't realized
that you might be overheard
(Really, I don't think
you considered the possibility)

Suddenly they were all looking at you,
the wedding people:
the bride's maids, the ring bearer, the groom
—especially the groom

And that's when you made your exit
You walked away as they stared
Then you stepped into a Smart car

That's the best part

# Villanelle for a Suburban Marriage

Kristine Rae Anderson

Words and signals intersect—or miss:
two figures hurtling through the day.
Though when we part, we always kiss.

Your Ford turns north; my Honda, west:
the split of lives, facts of our age.
Words and signals intersect—or miss.

At work you call my empty desk.
"At the tone … " the message says.
But parting—yes—we shared a kiss.

Your inbox full, you scan the list.
My name blurs in a numbered haze.
Our words don't intersect again—they miss.

Your office lit against the dusk;
I'm first back home, to empty space.
So long ago, that parting kiss.

At night in bed we acquiesce to rest;
new dawn will thrust us separate ways.
Words and signals intersect—or miss;
though when we part, we always kiss.

# What You Make Me

## Larry Wright

I am glass
You've known me forever,
familiar as the streets of our home town.
But when you look at me, I am glass.
I can tell by your eyes that I am glass.
Your eyes keep tracking through and past me.
You leave and the volume of my thoughts expand
within the vacuum of your absence.

I am stone.
I've known you just as long, but never wondered
about the different roads we've each traveled.
Had my highs and had my lows,
I suppose you've had yours too.
When you speak
I am stone before your words
and so the sticks of them cannot hurt me.

I am air.
Light and empty
You walk around all day with summer for a smile
and every laugh is low and soft as the rains of spring.
But I only feel the cold wind of autumn
blowing through my heart
when I see you failing to see me,
and again I find the winter in your eyes.

# The Tides

## Albert DeGenova

How many Christmases do we truly
    remember? Tide rises unseen
    like mist before our eyes.
Rocks and footprints
    drown like paper boats.
    So much decoration,
    so little buoyancy –
    this journey begun
    with feet in the sea.
Once upon a time
    you wore fishnet stockings
    for me – that Saturday night
    backseat battle of the bra
    ended in surrender.
    I lived in the shadow
    of your skirt – pleasure-bent,
    you were my cowgirl in black pumps.

How many days was it
in Naples, waiting
for Vesuvius to erupt –
the fury of it all, no freedom
for those who love, never,
as long as your mouth tastes
of my skin.
How many anniversaries do we clearly
remember? Time to unravel
the navel of years, the ingested
sun and breakfast silences,
that soupçon of regret.
This afternoon you wake
in the recovery room –
a careful new scar to mark
this year. *Volare mia cora!*
Let's just leave the car at the red light
and walk away hand
in hand.
Let's crawl into the bass clef
and sing.

# Anniversary Gift

## Jayne Marek

The front door clicks. You're back
from a blind afternoon shopping
for a gift for me, whom you do not
understand in terms of gifts.

You open the door and step into
our anniversary as if the heat
of decades ago still cloaks your
shoulders with the unshakable

partners: joy and uncertainty.
*So Main Street is closed*
*again*, you call to me from around
the corner, a crackle of bag

verifying that you won't let me
see you yet. *Well, I'm feeding the cat,*
I call, offering a little grace for animal
and spouse alike, *can't talk right now.*

But I don't say *Do you recall the field*
*rough under our shoulders and the dry*
*grass that clung to the blanket*
*where we lay flat underneath*

*that Fourth of July night?* I will be
the one to shake out the blanket
while you discuss how French philosophers
argued over the American Revolution.

Then the guillotines, of course,
in France, of course, although I shudder
for a moment thinking that Salem's
witch murders weren't so different.

*I bet there were guillotines*, I mutter,
and you hear just enough to say *What?*
I clack the cat's bowls, a celebration
of sorts. What we've come to, or left.

# Love in the Age of Dementia

## Karla Linn Merrifield

Farewell, fellatio.
Farewell, cunnilingus.
Farewell, dildos.
Farewell, vibrators.
I'm into a new brand of intimacy
with bed scenes and shower scenarios
involving nether parts.
My intimate secret is not clothed
in Victoria's, rather XXX-size t-shirts
washable, replaceable, multipurpose—
sleepwear and bathroom floor cover
when you— gasp— run out of towels;
only takes a couple days to need another load.

I have become intimate with
piss and shit
shit and piss
piss piss shit
piss shit shit
urine stink shit stink
sodden Depends, trousers,
sometimes socks and sneakers,
regularly bathroom tiles and bed sheets,
despite GoodNites disposable pads.
I have become ever more intimate with
all manner of incontinence products
to share intimacy with my beloved husband.

# Aesthetics Behind the Sofa

## Karuna Mistry

Should be angled, not straight behind that sofa
Never mind, no one to catch an ugly sight
        Except for the one who knows – of course

Soap drama, kitchen spill, morning palaver
A tad melodramatic or so you might think
        Mop up, leave baby, and throw out bad water

Steamy episode with bare-naked clothes
Ironed out to a hot temperament
        Every top, trouser, t-shirt – and underwear

Stampede madness, checklist chores
Against the hanging circular countdown
        Before a rush for the ride in raging hour

Time to come home says the boss
Better judgement than the employer
        A superior is she – home life manager

# in a long marriage

## Susan Maxwell Campbell

sleeping with someone
the gentle snore or sigh or mumble
his cold foot on her calf
the tug of midnight blankets
and the cycle of waking
the bathroom and a drink of water
the child crying in the next room
the dog needing out
and sometimes the intimate touch
patting his warm hip
stroking her smooth back
sweeping away the tickly hair
and the blessing of biological need
the off-center kiss goodnight
the clicking off of the reading lamp
settling pillows and smoothing sheets
the secret inner flight
through prayer
past the day's cares
toward the dreamless
dark

# A Mate of My Own, 1774

## Pegi Deitz Shea

(Based on the life of Jeanne Baret,
the first woman to circumnavigate the world.)

Sabbath and, after church, I'm boiling water
in the tavern's back room. Out front, a clamor!
A French soldier stumbles in, slumps over a table.

"Rum, beer, wine, whatever you have."
He wears the sour, stale vapor of sea vessels,
the bruises and joint swells of scurvy.

But has straight white teeth, bulging muscle—
he's not beyond saving. I bring him wine
steeped in citrus fruit, then salad, cheese.

As I tend his sores, I learn his story. A second son,
he'd grown up in a village, apprenticed as a blacksmith
(Tata would approve), left to seek excitement, adventure.

Found beauty, found death, took pleasure, took lives.
Now a sergeant, he seems as broken as I, and heartsore
how powers claim ownership of others' blood.

His sable eyes lift into mine. "And your story?"
I tell him truths, about Tata and healing, about Docteur,
disguises, discoveries. (No pits, no violations—not yet.)

Wide-eyed, he touches my hand, says, "I'm Jean Dubernat."
*Jean.* He learns *Jeanne Baret* when the mayor barges in
and charges me for serving on Sabbath. Jean pays the fine.

Months of healing walks later, he pays our marriage license fee.
We leave Île de France on the next ship,
hug the Cape of Good Hope,
and head for real French soil where we will sow love.

# Mr / Ms Partner

## Sara Abend-Sims

These words of yours
a prophet's speech
filled with zeal
imbued with certainty
overflowing with conviction

I try on your wisdom
like a perfect garment
an absolute note
in the latest vogue

I shorten a sleeve
tuck in an inch of width
stand by the mirror
and turn around

I bend
stretch
and look again
before storing this garment
of words-not-mine

what I favour most
when opening my wardrobe
are the familiar ones
the tattered garments
of well-worn-words

the ones I've made myself
to inhabit my rooms
of home-grown knowing

trying hard, still trying
I add a patch of yours
mix and match some bits
wanting to make it fit

when this doesn't work
I give the garment back to you
with thanks and gratitude
for the attempts you've made
to share your knowing
to show me that you care.

# weddings are meant to be happy

## Linda M. Crate

my friend made me a member
of her wedding party,

and i remember that whilst it was a
fun and good time there was
also this awkwardness

heavy and thick in the unspoken
corridors of the wedding hall;

beautiful october wedding
full of joy
and yet also melancholy—

the ex who cheated on me and had
married the woman he cheated on me
with was a part of her wedding,
and i had to clench my jaw and keep
every anger and every wrath i felt inside
to keep the peace;

and there was a part of me still that
loved him and that scared me because
i knew he was no good—

and so when i think of her wedding
i think of the fun i had with our fellow friends,
and i write him out of the narrative because
weddings are meant to be happy
not funerals for our ugliest emotions.

# Marlboro Man Versus the Man I Thought I Married

## Lisa Rhodes-Ryabchich

It's late in our relationship,
still the evening sits with us,
as the large television screen jumps
reflecting bright, beautiful colors
through a large, antique mirror—
the one given by Leo, who survived
Hitler's wrath as a child, bless his soul—
he always wanted kids, but his wife
wouldn't give him any— not that she
couldn't have any, but she refused
to show any human warmth.

This is something I'm always questioning
in my husband— is he cold when he ignores me
when I ask him when he is going
to quit smoking? Or does he lack common sense
or not understand human concern?

Maybe he never felt loved & doesn't know
how to love himself, let alone anyone else.
What remedy can I find to help me endure
this relationship, where cold creeps through
my veins at night, numbing my body, erasing
my savior faire, dragging me down into despair?

But why do I still care? This question continues
as I rest my ear against my pillow, gently wishing
Marlboro & my husband were not having an affair.
He saves box tops from his leftover cartons of cigarettes
& boasts about his Marlboro man clothes
& paraphernalia redeemed from prized box tops,

saved from many months of vigorous smoking.
He risks his presumed good health by sneaking
off to smoke outside during the wee winter hours,
even if it means waking my sleeping parents
living a floor above him, as he opens
& closes the old barn door to excuse himself.
What spirit will save him from the Cancer ward?
Will his best friend, the Russian doctor have mercy on him?

# We'll Always Have Vegas: You and I Traveling Together by Greyhound Bus to Get Married There

Linda Barrett

We'll always have Vegas
  It was a memorable journey
  In the aftermath of 9/11/01
  as a test of our love
We'll always have Vegas:
  You the kite
  Me the string
  That kept you down to reality
We'll always have Vegas:
  Me the Patriots fan
  You the Philadelphia Eagles'
  Liberty Bell Cheerleader

We'll always have Vegas:
You the one
Who introduced me
To The Prince of Peace
and the Lord of Love
We'll always have Vegas:
Even without you,
I still know the Fun City
Brings back happy memories
of our marriage years.

# 4MyC

## Brian Weston

I tried
I promise you.
I tried.

She did love me.
A distant memory now.
Early spring afternoons
Warm sun.
Hot hands touching.
Talking about our dreams.
Our dreams.
The world happened around us.
But she was my world.
Excited about what the future would bring.

A few years passed
Of happy marriage
You joined our bubble.
My overwhelming love now shared.
Was this the moment?

I wish I knew when it changed.
Did I do something wrong?
Smother her too much.
Rely on her too much
Love her too much.
I would go back in time just to know what I did wrong.
The time for talking has stopped between us.

The world is a different place.
But my love for all of you is the same.
She may not love me anymore.
My love for all of you.
Is what keeps my heart beating.

# Her Candle

## Carl 'Papa' Palmer

So many candles I've never burned.
A marriage candle,
two first communion candles from my kids,
a bicentennial candle,
millennium candle.
So many candles I've never burned.

Her candle I've burned for over twenty years,
not every day, but most every day.
A memory of what once was,
of what we had
me and her,
her candle.
Originally voluptuously large,
beautifully ornate,
burning bright hot and fast.
We were young then.

Gradually her candle grew old,
became hollow.
Most of the outside still holding fast,
dusty with age,
the wick long lost,

in darkness temporarily filled
with a tea light candle.
Certain songs, movies or moods
rekindle the freshness,
remind me of when her candle was new.

In the light of day reality blazes,
her candle actually an empty shell.
So hard to visualize as it once was,
as in last night's memory.

Beginning to wonder,
continuing to wonder,
if, after all this time,
I shouldn't just throw it out.
This foolish vigil,
this senseless old man,
end this memorial,
this ritual and move on.

But, as the room grows dark,
the many candles I've never burned
remain so.
A new tea light candle
and she is back.
We, me and her,
her candle
and my thoughts
of twenty years ago.

# After the Wedding

## Michael Durack

Between Slieve Bernagh and Lough Derg
we shared our first kiss. October,
the wee small hours, back seat,
motoring from Ballyvally towards Tuamgraney,
stragglers from a country wedding.
The driver, I remember him well
but not the make and model of the car.
It was blue, automatic shift. It broke down.
But that is of no importance.

What matters is that somewhere in the dark,
in Ballycuggeran or Ballylaghnan,
in Raheena More, Raheena Beg or Caher,
in Ballyhurley, Ballyheefy or Bealkelly
your lips touched mine for the first time.
The townlands undistinguished and untraced,
we might have been voyagers lost in Space.

But now those ancient tracts of land I bless
because somewhere on the road between
the tribal Ballys and Raheens
our mouths connected in a loving kiss.

# pomegranates

## Lydia Trethewey

among the things I cannot take, the pomegranate tree we planted in the backyard. It's flowering again, fleshy red droplets like words from lips in undecipherable language, the symbol of Aphrodite's romantic love (ironic) or like Eve's knowledge when she swallowed the seeds and had to leave, she'd always been told she was made from (for) him. I could never speak the way I needed to. I was an aphid who dreamt of being a moth, I'm so very sorry, I never meant to promise what I didn't know. pomegranates, shaped like lanterns we never hung from our trip to Vietnam, we never painted the walls that brighter colour or went to Iceland or met each other in the deepest recess of our glacier dreams. when we hug our goodbye, I can't remember what was real and what was caused by the flight of a bumblebee around a pomegranate a second before awakening. I hope you'll look after yourself when I'm gone. maybe I'll be a visitor in our house, I'll bring the dog, when I grow back my skin hard like calyx. I hope you'll water the tree in my absence, keep it alive. I hope you'll eat vegetables sometimes and not just fish and chips. I hope you'll rest at least a little bit. among the things I cannot take, the knowledge that you'll be ok.

# On Loving

## Lisa Reynolds

Once in a while I think back to the beginning,
how we hushed thoughts to spare feelings
Do you remember those days Darling,
when loving should have been easy but wasn't

We were two halves eager to be whole,
harbouring wounds neither could see

What did we know about love
other than what we wanted it to be –

A safe haven when life became too much
A gentle touch when words weren't nearly enough

Everything we have now, and more

# Asparagus and Salmon

## Eileen Trauth

I used to cook alone
answering only to myself.
You lived inside your silence
accepting, so it seemed, the plate

I set before you
never offering up warm words
or tastes that made you smile. Instead,
negotiating the TV channels
like world peace,
we ate our détente, until the day

your inner decay grew like rancid meat,
turning grey within its wrap,
and you poured fear like sour milk,
and consolation slid from my grasp
like slimy vegetables.
Then your words rose up
like baking bread.

Now, beyond our kitchen window
I watch you watching
firm flesh grill to pink perfection
while verdant stalks beckon
from the stove.

# Old Wives' Tales

## Kate Falvey

Most of them mosey along,
more in step than off-track,
fearful after the kids are gone
that shared purpose will unbraid,
fraying the rope they counted on
for safe passage through the more
treacherous winter peaks.

One says, what will I do when he
retires? I can't imagine him home
all day. We'd have nothing to say
to each other, nothing to do besides
grocery shop or mend bits and bobs
around the house. Stuff he never got
around to doing. Stuff I end up
ignoring or hiring someone for
or trying to do myself. Of course,
I love him, after all these years.
We were kids together. We raised
a child. I just don't know what
we'd talk about all day.
What we'd do.

One says, he is a gem and I'm aware
of how good he is. He is light years
away from his savage brutal childhood.
He cracks jokes, washes windows, oils
creaky hinges, tends damsel, clown,
and rusty angelfish, bubble coral, snails
in his glowing reef aquarium; plays
softball with his slightly beery buddies;
cherishes me.
He's hard on the boys, though, rather
relentless, surely the ghost of his father
reasserting dominion. I try to get through
and he hears me, but it's sad and wearying
to be perpetually eyeing the keyholes, and
shuttering that dead bag of brutal wind
out of our airy, comfortable home.

One says, without her and her penchant
for pragmatic organizing, the buzz of
chemo, specialists, side effects, imminent
demise, and existential terror would be
unbearable, fatalistic and religious though I am.
There's no comfort in second-guessing a
divinity I stoke with prayer but never really
warmed to. It's praying with my wife that
lights the spark of faith, her body next to mine
in the grave regions of the trackless dark
a warm certainty, a pronouncement
of an edgy, companionable, trustable god.

One says, I want to swat him out of his
hypochondriacal distortions, his on-the-boil
olio of self-limiting qualms and alarms.
I make him eat the gluten-free, mashing
cauliflower with garlic, portioning out
the penne with pesto, made from the basil
we grow when he gets sick of the skinless
imposition of spineless chicken breasts.

I listen from my armchair, recalling
marriages of yore, my own included,
hearing grandma and papa, sixty years
together, bickering over the cantaloupe,
a vivacious aunt gone mute in the reverberant
rumble of her husband's bungled chances
and misgivings, hisses of pent outrage leaked
through flat-lined lips pressed tight in front
of the children or the guests. There is this
white noise of chafing, the perpetual rub
of irksome impositions, the intricate
crosshatchings of one personality
upbraiding another in a closed,
but still mutual space.

Alone, I twitch toward the phantom touches
which arc from the ghosts in the room
though my long-widowed mother,
who clearly loved my challenging father,
assures me that it's sweeter to be free.

# Hand in Marriage

## Deborah Meltvedt

What seemed a million kitchen evenings,
I watched my mother's ring play hide and seek
a glimpse of gold as her fingers dredge pink flesh
of thighs and breasts through muds of margarine and flour,
then, with a thud, plop poultry and routine into
a dented pan that never seemed clean.
Her knuckles so large
she sometimes joked
*I couldn't take it off even if I wanted to.*

But I liked to picture her hands naked
dribbling basketballs in high school
cupping coffee in a book store
or waving to my father home from war
before he proposed
before my mother knew to say *yes*
before she turned ovens to four hundred degrees
sweated out dreams
and fed our demanding open mouths.

# Mrs. Rosenberg

## Dianalee Velie

They called me a traitor, a spy,
I owned none of those labels.
My sin, loving the wrong man,
typing up his stolen secrets.
Even my brother lied about
my involvement with their
unlawful, snooping escapade.
I told the rabbi this as they
strapped me into the electric
chair but no one believed me,
no one cared for the truth
and now my name is soiled
in history books forever linked
with espionage and the death penalty.
I, Ethel Rosenberg, was an innocent
typist and loving wife who trusted
her husband with her short life.

# Don't Watch Rocky Alone On A Friday Night After Your Wife Leaves You

## Steve Cushman

Or like me you might find yourself
running around the neighborhood

after midnight in your white Jockeys
and her pink flip flops. Your legs will

hurt, probably your head and chest too.
Your heart like a muscle about to explode.

The next morning, asleep in your front yard,
curled up next to the pansies you'll wish

you had your keys and hadn't locked the door.
But you're damn sure not calling her because

this is just another example she'd point to as
why it was time for her to move on and what could

you say, really, standing there in your underwear,
dirty-kneed and bloody-toed as the sun scorched

your eyes, welcoming another beautiful summer day.

# Love in Rooms During the Pandemic

## Lynn Tait

We live together in rooms,
we occupy rooms apart.
My favorite room is one I don't have.
It's under construction in my head.
It's a three season room.

We spend time in our backyard,
visit neighbours and friends on porches and patios.
My husband packs snacks, plastic wine glasses
because we're all breakable.
It's hard to tell these days who's brittle
who wants to break things.

We wear masks, disposables, fifty in a box.
We have a friend who stitched care into cloth.
My mask is not as colourful as my man's,
because I chose to be quiet.
It seems to be working.

But when masks fog up my glasses,
and our world—a haze of good intentions—
we're not sure goodness and mercy follows,
but for now we're safe in our rooms together.
We listen to wine, drink music,
we dance and there is love.

# In the Shadows

## Marsha Mittman

i leave the new york school at the
end of the day when classes are
over and see her veiled and alone
this anxious tiny slip of a figure
always waiting in an alcove just
inside the double doors that open to
a busy street and the world outside

one particularly beautiful day when
i see her in the alcove's shadows
as i pass by i ask *why not wait*
*outside it's so lovely today* and
she replies *i'm not allowed out*
*alone i have to wait for my chaperone*

these few words eventually lead to
repeated brief conversations one day
i ask as she waits alone in the dark
alcove *are you going to college*
tears well in her eyes as she explains
*i can't it's too much trouble for my*
*father or brother to accompany me*
*back and forth and they would never*
*allow me to live on campus they also*
*want me home to help with siblings*

towards the end of the term after
many discussions over the year i stop
for an impromptu chat and she surprises
me by asking eyes lowered blushing
*what does it feel like to love* laughing
i answer *you're young you'll find out*
*soon enough* shaking her head she answers
*no my marriage has already been arranged*
and then glancing around to check we're
alone she asks in an anguished whisper
*i mean i want to know how it actually*
*feels to love please you're the only person*
*i can ask* and not catching her implied
meaning i repeat my previous comment
*you're young you'll find out soon enough*

in a strained hushed voice the restricted
veiled sad young girl waiting in the
shadows awaiting her arranged marriage
whispers     *no*     *i won't*     *i've been cut*

# When I Was Married I Gained Many Pounds

## Julianne Woodside

You brought:
    Your grandmother's spaghetti recipe
    Your aunt's chutney recipe
    A cousin's pumpkin pie.

I brought:
    Canned tuna with Campbell's mushroom soup
    and canned peas over rice.
    Frozen fish sticks
    Oreos.

With only one car, you got the first job so
    I learned my way through a thrift-store cookbook,
    with a strong preference for
    anything complicated enough to take all day.

I remember especially:
    Chicken Kiev
    A 'crown roast' with all the little paper caps
    Nine-layer lasagna

Homemade butter whipped with honey slathered on thrice-risen, freshly baked bread

Threading bacon into a hunter-friend-gifted, giant venison roast for our first Thanksgiving, with all the trimmings and traditional dishes as outlined in the cookbook, including a huge turkey to go with the roast. (We had five people to eat it all. There were still leftovers in the freezer when we moved to
a new apartment the next year.)

Finding out your aunt's chutney went well with beef.
With pork. With chicken. Eggs. Tomato soup.
On sandwiches. With soft cheeses. On toast.
On potatoes. (Together we learned how to
'can' that chutney in those discount store Mason jars,
so we could have it nearly always.)

We traded cooking days, you making your favorites.
(You didn't care for your family,
but we loved their recipes!)

I remember:

Buying larger pants at the thrift store. And then even
larger pants. The weight not exactly from the good food,
but because on the days you cooked, I came to realize:
You would or could not believe I liked the food, or
Appreciated your efforts, or, to be precise, *loved you*
Unless I had taken seconds at least, preferably thirds.

When I got a job, you started cooking more and more often.

My bottomless, youthful, overfull love for you, my chosen one –
It stuffed me, padded me, overtook my bones
Until I was buried inside of making you happy.

I wanted:
    Less spaghetti
    Less pie
    Less weight of fearing your disbelief

You gave me:
    A lifelong love of food and cooking.
    Many days (and nights) of true joy.

But also:
    Unspoken annoyance if my food tasted better than yours
    Anxiety if I didn't eat enough,
    if I read while you watched tv,
    if I laughed while on the phone or didn't get your joke,
    or talked in my sleep
    Disdain for my growing curves,
    also jealousy if anyone else noticed them

    Frozen days of silence if I was too happy when
    you were feeling unhappy (which was far too often
    for our really very lovely circumstances, as I tried to
    show you, in my youthful, overfull, loving optimism)

Eventually I realized:
the pains we caused each other were actually optional.

I had dozens of pounds to lose, but the weight of your censure
and control fell away
as soon as the decision was made.

When I moved out you hid:
Our wedding photos.
Your recipes.

I missed:
You, for a very long time.
(But all these years later, I still dream of that chutney.)

# Ruthless

## Neil Laurenson

To make the wedding more affordable
Dave suggested that they only invite
people they would still be in touch with
five years later.

So there was no room for Steve
who he'd only spoken with a few times at the pub.
Rob was an old colleague
under the impression that Dave cared about cricket
so he couldn't come
nor Andy, who was mad
nor Scott, who still hadn't returned
the DVDs he'd borrowed.

Dave paused when he thought of his nan.
Surely he had to invite her?
But he definitely wouldn't be in touch with her
five years after the wedding
due to her terminal illness
so for the sake of consistency
she was off the list.

More and more names
off the list
till he got to Ruth
his fiancée
and he removed her from the list as well.

# Crumbling

## Linda Maxwell

The two stand together,
Beside the tall, much-talked-about cake
She, in her new shoes, borrowed ivory lace,
her hand on the knife.
Delicately, she tosses the morsel into his waiting mouth
Delaying, he whispers he doesn't know how to do this
She apologizes for his discomfort,
the big wedding she thought he wanted
To him who smears the sugary paste against her cheek,
her shrinking smile, her lipstick,
Berry Blush.

On the honeymoon,
He blames the photographer.
"Sammy thought it would be funny," he explains,
"So don't be mad at me,"
Then wonders aloud
Why his Uncle Junior didn't attend.

For their first anniversary,
She got a job
That paid half of the one she quit
For him.
Months before, he lost his
And said unemployment paid him more to stay home
Than most people earned sweeping floors, scrubbing toilets
Which were her duties—along with taking out the trash,
And scraping stickers from windows and doors.

Sometimes she'd forget to buy his razor blades,
He'd point out,
His dinner fork waving,
His stomach full,
His tone prodding and pricking.

One day (and a baby) later,
He says, "I hate the way you cook, keep house and dress.
Oh and I don't love you anymore."

So she packs up her baby,
Her battered pride,
Her schoolbooks, pots, pans and mixer
And bakes a cake
To celebrate.

# Never Too Late

## Mark Hudson

Today is my dad's birthday.
I think he is eighty-four. My mom
has been deceased for about ten years.
According to my family, my
dad has about three girlfriends in
Florida. But at his age, it's innocent.
He wines and dines them, but it's
really in the spirit of friendship.

We were on a vacation
recently in Fort Lauderdale,
Florida. We were eating dinner
at a place called The Parrot
Lounge and my dad told a story.

"I was in church, and
the pastor said, "Are there
any announcements?" And
a ninety-year-old man
stood up and said, "Yes.
I'm getting married,
and we are spending our
honeymoon in Hawaii!"

It's never too late
to get married. But if
you don't want to
get married, trust me,
don't do it!

# If these walls could talk

## Brenda Cullen

There is silence throughout this house, my home.
Our home.

I listen to YouTube, The Moth,
or Audible books in 'my' room.
The room with my walls of books and
cachets of wool all waiting.
Intentions to create something beautiful.
Not for myself but as gifts.

He watches the American Football, a Grand Prix
or whatever on the backroom computer.
Always, every day, except for the morning dog walk
which he is starting later and later in the day.

He puts on headphones, so I am not there.
Sometimes he will shut the door to my room
if I am 'listening too loud for him'.
Shuts the door on me.

When I like to be alone, I like to be all alone.
Have the run of the house and yard
with no sound except the birds
and the neighbours' kids playing in their swimming pools.
And that's not lonely.

The silence in this house when he is home
is a silence I cannot navigate.
This silence is audible, a noise I cannot converse with.
Shut in, shut out.
Cohabitation.
Once we were lovers, a couple, married, a family.

There are too many walls and doors in this house.
The silence is violent.
Now there are too many walls and doors between us.
Even if I were to open them all,
his ears would be covered, blocked.

We both still sleep in our marriage bed.
He snores. My dreams are always vivid.
Often, I dream I am screaming.
Screaming at someone, at him.
I wake weary and wrung out.
I wish now for no more dreams.

# Sandy and the Turtles

## John Laue

My wife Sandy returns
from the black sand beach
on the island of Hawaii
carrying her snorkel gear,
her bathing suit dripping wet.
She finally got to swim
with the turtles. *They don't mind*
*if you gawk at them*, she says.
*They just go about their business.*
*And do you know some live*
*to be a hundred?*
Her face aglow with pleasure,
her body radiant, pink,
she looks twenty years younger
than when we arrived.
I'm as pleased as she,
glad as if she'd found
the fountain of youth,
or tapped a reservoir of bliss
vast as an ocean
she could swim in happily
like a giant sea turtle
for a hundred years.

# Prose

# Mine

## T.C. Mill

My husband liked to make love in the dark.

As he climbed toward me, I lay back on the pillows—two thin ones stacked on my half of the bed—and switched off the lamp. We were plunged into night. The clock, before his shoulder eclipsed it, showed *11:35*. Dom had warned me he'd be home late. I'd worried anyway. I always did, since my parents' accident.

In between wrestling with worry, I used the hours alone for myself. I made lasagna, which we never ate together because Dom didn't like it. Just as we didn't make love with the lights on.

I stripped off my comfortable sweatshirt and reached out my arms. He settled over me, and as our bodies found each other, I tucked my face against his neck.

What I smelled wasn't his familiar scent. Feminine, not a body's natural musk, and not a perfume I'd ever use. A hint of baked good. Vanilla.

Dom didn't seem to notice my stillness, or maybe he took it for a state of sensual surrender.

He moaned against my ear. "Mine."

*You're mine*, he meant. *My wife. My lover.*

*One of my lovers.*

*All mine.*

It was supposed to be intoxicating, his possessiveness. He did want me. I felt it in his body against mine, how his hands clasped and stroked with the pattern our lovemaking had long ago settled into.

"Mine." Dom kissed my earlobe.

Automatically I kissed him back, my lips catching the corner of his chin. Affection would be hard not to return. I was hungry for it, to be honest.

"*Mine*." He drew out the *i* sound, but still didn't seem to expect a response. Absorbed in his own desire. Unless he said it calculatedly, putting on a show of devotion. At one time I would have been sure he moaned that word purely from wanting me.

Now I couldn't be.

The realization felt like I'd dropped something and it rolled away, under this bed, out of reach.

Dom's knees came between mine, nudged outward. Both of us still wore pants. I hadn't even taken my underwear off before learning he cheated on me. All the same I felt my muscles flexing as if of their own accord to spread my legs wider.

"Hungry for affection" prettifies my feelings. I hadn't just been lonely, but horny. I'd debated masturbating after putting away the leftover lasagna. But I decided to save my passion for him, in case something like this happened. (Hoping he'd come home earlier than expected.) I'd never been able to make myself come with the intensity Dominick could. All my biggest orgasms were from him, were—

"Mine," he moaned, between other words harder to make out. As he turned his head I smelled more of the vanilla, the scent I'd never wear, so sugary it would make me sick.

My legs wrapped around him, so passionately it threatened to roll us to the other side of the bed. To his side, with its single thick ergonomic pillow. He pushed down with his hips, returning my passion, but also pinning me in place.

I'd never felt trapped with him before.

His knuckles brushed my breasts as he unbuttoned his shirt. Should I have been doing that for him? How long had it been since I last did?

I reached for the skin he bared. Approaching his forties, Dom didn't exercise—unless this counted—but kept a flat stomach. Good genes. Flatter than mine, harder, but I did not regret the lasagna. *We both had something for ourselves tonight.*

Of all the thoughts flickering through my mind, it was the only one that seemed petty.

With such good genes, he still wanted the lights out. Not to hide his body. Because of me? Yet I couldn't imagine him keeping the lights on with the vanilla-scented person, either. Maybe just a failure of my imagination.

I kissed him so he wouldn't say *Mine* again.

His lips felt and tasted like they always had, like his own. But another woman knew his texture, flavor, scent. Knew the sound of his voice.

Might have heard it claiming her as *Mine.*

Her perfume and his possessiveness both disgusted me. I'd never felt trapped by Dominick before, but neither had I ever really liked being claimed by him, even when I felt I should. It cloyed. Excessive. Like that stinking vanilla growing stronger as he pressed me down.

You can't really belong to another person, or own them.

Under my distaste, a different frustration swelled.

I felt achingly aroused. At this evidence of someone so different from me, but who was wanted by my husband. Who left her perfume on him while I snatched solitary pleasure—lasagna!—in the empty corners of his life.

At the proof he lied when he called me *Mine*.

I nudged him back to pull my yoga pants and underwear off. In the dark I heard the rustle of him getting naked, too.

Had he used a condom? The question occurred as he came into me. Instead of shoving him away, I pulled him close, nails raking up his spine.

Made him mine, you might say.

But that was a side effect, because as I breathed in her scent again, it felt like I was reaching *through* Dom to touch someone else.

We moved with passion neither of us had shown in this bed for a long time—something I realized only now. You think you know what a thing would feel like, until it happens and you learn you'd had no idea.

Worry because someone's out late doesn't compare to opening the door for a police officer's solemn knock and news of an accident, for example.

Neither of which compares to making love to another woman on your husband's skin. I hissed something as I came; I don't even know what. But I'm sure it wasn't *Mine*.

# Civil Partnership

## Rab Green

There's a scene in *Orlando* in which she, previously he, contemplates the weight and emptiness of her ring finger in the age she's living. I'm doing the same, for one last day, by myself over tea in a Benugo in Westminster.

She was caught off-guard standing at a window, if I remember right, suddenly aware of the expectation on her. I slowly came round to the idea: first discussed after eight years together, on our anniversary night out at a Pizza Express, took another two years, tomorrow exactly, to get us here.

Still difficult to picture tho, even so close at hand:

me in a kilt, him in a suit, leaving the town hall with matching rings. I get a little wobbly and wet-eyed, almost completely feel the significance.

Then he calls and we talk

and he annoys the fuck out of me.

Says he's going to cut across town, to double-check the set-up at the pub for the do tomorrow evening.

Says he'll be quick, no bother, just pop across town, even tho there's a Tube strike on and the buses are rammed and the traffic's hardly moving.

He calls back ten minutes later to say: he's been standing at the bus stop and can see up the road at the bus he's supposed to be getting, watching it stuck in traffic that hasn't moved since he last called.

So he's just going back to the hotel.

I'm only round the corner and I've finished my tea, and I feel vindicated at having won the argument we never had, so I head back to get him.

# Hard Decisions

## Tobi Alfier

Stuck at the crossing of another glass of red and time to go, he weighs his options even while signaling the barmaid for another. Not a tough choice for him, she'll be righteous and pissed-off at home no matter what. Thinks she keeps it to herself, but he can tell.

The barmaid brings him a boilermaker instead of merlot. What the hell, the sound of glass clunking glass is nostalgic, like when he used to run across the gravel lots down by the water, toward or away from someone, the crunch that said you're almost there, keep going.

The crunch like ice in a tall glass of rum and coke, drink of choice for the steal booze from your parents set. They never noticed even as the levels fell down, down, down like Alice down the rabbit hole. How some people survived is something he'll never understand, though he knows he barely made it himself.

Those gravel lots are now stacks of soulless condos and he's a fugitive in a soulless life, one he would never admit to. His nerves strung tight as new fenceline over acres, insomnia full of guilt and smalltime phantoms—but it's all her fault, or so he claims. The words she spoke to him so sweetly now beyond remembering. He thinks of her silence as doing him wrong.

He signals for another, then his time is up. He shuffles toward the door with something less than grace, a country-western song on the jukebox singing him goodbye. Tomorrow he'll play their first dance if he can remember it. If he has to ask, her eyes may look away and never look back.

# Planning to Fix Something

## Todd Mercer

For thirty-several years Jane was more fully alive than I was. Then the fire tore through our canyon. It killed her in a minute, they tell me. I'm having difficulty moving forward. Firemen brought me into the hospital. I was narcoleptic by then. On purpose, at first. I'd fall asleep to conjure-dream a visit with Jane, convince her to meet me at a house we used to live in. I arrive ready to work on the place, planning to fix … something. Jane's not really gone, she's throwing an Open House at a Cape Cod. She's readying the Stickley we sold before the kids were grown. I sleep, then wait to sleep.

# The Simple Little Things

## Abha Iyengar

She would fix a broken button on his shirt immediately, her deft fingers threading the needle, her keen eyes fixing the new button in the right place, making sure it went through the buttonhole with ease, and was the right size and colour.

She would toast the bread to just the right crispness and butter it well while it was still hot. The fried egg, done to perfection, she would place over a slice of toast. The bacon, the cheese, the coffee and the orange juice would be on the table and ready. Her man should have a good breakfast before he left for work.

She prettied herself up to receive him at 6 pm, when he returned home. Showered and perfumed, a light lipstick applied, her hair curling around her shoulders, she made sure she presented a charming picture.

They would have a drink each and then laugh and kiss and grope feverishly for each other's bodies, the heat of passion excluding all else. Then a smoke in bed, a goodnight kiss, and they would sleep with their legs entangled, not wanting to leave the memory of what they had just experienced with each other so soon.

As his wife, she believed in doing these simple little things and they had stood her in good stead. When marriages were breaking all around her, hers had survived.

Now, forty years of married life later, he read the newspaper with his feet up, constantly feeling the back of his balding head as if he could replace the hair there by doing so. She did minimal work in the kitchen with shaking hands and failing eyesight, her body in a nightgown most of the time as she hobbled on painful knees. Dust gathered in corners and the bathroom tiles no longer gleamed. Even the toast was burnt sometimes.

Those simple little things she had done with ease were no longer simple or little. She could not do them anymore. She wanted to sink into bed all day and rest her body, have someone press her feet if possible.

They exchanged a smile now and then during the day. At night, in bed, their backs were turned away from each other as they removed their spectacles, swallowed their blood pressure pills and said goodnight, hoping to have a good night's sleep. An occasional moan escaped her lips if her knee hurt. He bore his aches with silence.

She wondered about all this and reached for his hand in bed. She smiled as his fingers curled around hers. From wildly entangled legs and laughter every night to the quiet holding of hands and gentle smiles, they had indeed travelled together over the years. She believed the journey had been made easy with the help of simple little things.

The warmth of his body next to hers every night was enough to hold on to for the rest of her life.

# You Only Live Once

## Joy Mawby

He's waiting outside the tutorial room. 'Will you come with me and help buy the food for the party?'

Her stomach jumps. 'I'd love to.'

Josie had teased her earlier. 'I'm surprised you and Philip haven't got it together. He's been looking at you all week. I thought he'd make a move in the bar last night.'

She'd laughed but known Josie was right and that she had been *not* looking at Philip on purpose, had slipped away early last evening. After all, she is married – happily, on the whole – and now, on this last afternoon of the course, he is waiting for her.

'I'll fetch my jacket and meet you in the carpark,' she says.

*It's only shopping, hardly big deal.*

In her room, she picks up the photo of her two children smiling at her.

*Just shopping. Love you!* And, going downstairs, *After all, I'm thirty-nine and much married.*

He's waiting by a blue car and holds the door open. She suddenly thinks of the two attractive young women in the tutor group.

'Philip's really handsome,' she'd heard Kirsty say.

'Gorgeous, and what a brilliant sense of humour,' Freya had answered. 'But married.'

'When did that ever stop anybody?'

He starts the car. 'Have you enjoyed the course?'

'Very much. I think it will change how I write.'

'Same here. I heard you tell someone you're a teacher?'

'Yes. Primary school. What about you?'

'Teacher, too. Secondary. English literature. Have you any children?'

'Yes, two, a girl and a boy – eight and six. And you?'

'Two girls, two and five.'

*Four young lives. We can't risk their happiness.*

They've arrived at the supermarket. Now, they talk about what they should buy but underneath their chatter, tension, desire. They choose cheeses, paté, salad, French bread, cake, fruit and wine.

'We've earned a coffee,' he says as they pile the bags in the trolley.

She sits and watches him as he queues for the coffees in the supermarket café. She sees him joke with the cashier.

*He's perfect. But he can't be. No-one is. I really like him. I so much want to be with him.*

He puts the coffees on the table and sits down opposite. He says nothing but reaches across and puts his hand over hers. She feels her face hot, her hand burning under his.

'We've skirted round each other all the week, haven't we?' he says. Grinning, he adds, 'I've been taking cold showers every night. Are we going to miss this chance of happiness? You only live once'.

*

The feast is over and darkness has fallen. They are all outside on the lawn, dancing to snatches of music from an old transistor. Philip holds her close. She has never felt this way before – as if she is joined to someone else – to this man. She's muzzy with wine and with longing.

At last, they sit to rest. He puts his arm round her and they talk about their lives. He's from Yorkshire, she from Cornwall.

*Couldn't be much further apart.*

They talk about poetry, books and love. They find that they each married young – their childhood sweethearts.

'Our marriages fit us like old gloves,' he says, 'Familiar, beloved but what of passion?' They kiss and cling to each other.

*This is passion.*

'Spend the night with me,' he says.

She tries to conjure up the faces of her beautiful children, of her husband but she feels light-headed, disorientated.

'Please don't leave me,' he says. 'If you feel you can't sleep with me, make love, we won't. Just come and sleep in my room. You can have the bed. I'll be ok on the floor. Let's just be close to each other on our last night.'

Afterwards, she can hardly remember going to his room. She remembers him wrapping a blanket round himself, kissing her and saying, 'Are you sure?' She remembers nodding her head and pulling the covers over herself. She remembers not sleeping and remembers him, restless on the hard floor. She remembers crying softly so as not to disturb him.

⋆

Early the next morning, they embrace once more and she creeps to her room, heavy-eyed.

They sit opposite each other at breakfast, making small talk, pretending not to notice the knowing looks of the rest of the group. She feels sick, can only nibble a piece of toast.

'I'll drive you to the station,' he says.

In the car, she puts a hand on his knee, loving him.

*How can I bear to lose him?*

'It's best if we don't stay in contact,' she manages to say, her voice unsteady. 'We've both got commitments and we live too far apart.'

'You're right. If only ...'

'Yes, if only.'

They are at the station. 'Please don't come and wave me off.' They clasp hands once more. She jumps out of the car, grabs her bag and runs into the forecourt, not looking back. She stands still, shuts her eyes tightly, trying to stop her tears.

*I'll never see him again but I'll never forget him.*

On the train, she stares through the window, unseeing, filled with sorrow.

Her husband meets her. He's alone.

'Are the children all right? I thought you'd bring them.'

'They're fine. They're still at your mum's. We need to have a chat before we collect them. Let's go for a coffee.'

*What can it be? He can't know ...*

They sit down with their coffees and she waits for him to speak. He tells her that he has fallen in love with a twenty-one-year-old woman at work. He has already moved most of his things into a flat they are renting.

She's numb, can't take it in.

*Oh, Philip, Philip.*

'I'm sorry to hurt you,' he says, 'but I've been seeing her for a while and now we've had a chance to be together, properly, I know there's no going back. I have to grab this chance of happiness. After all, you only live once.'

# Greta's Marriage Vows

## Margaret Plaganis

"Pass me that ketchup bottle. Hand it to me this time. Don't spin it round on that lazy-susan, you'll tip it off! Why on earth your mother spends money on things like that, I'll never know. I never wasted good money on such-like. Years ago, I didn't have any raising a houseful of kids. But that didn't stop your grandfather. He spent it on himself steppin' out with his cousin, down the road. Me, pinching pennies to put eight kids in church and school, washed and combed in clean clothes. The minute I found out he was cheatin' on me, I took the oldest and three youngest to my mother's house. Your grandfather told the court I broke our marriage vows! Tried to buy me off with a flimsy divorce. But I stopped him in his tracks. No divorce, I told him. I won't sign any papers unless you give me my full share of what I'm entitled. The Law says I got Dower Rights. He wouldn't pay so I wouldn't sign the papers. I held out all these years. No divorce. He still rides high on the hog with his hoity-toity cousin. I know they're still at it. They're the reason my own sons won't invite me over, even for christenings or weddings. Your grandfather thinks he's gonna pull one over on me, but he's got a surprise comin'. He owed me then, he owes me now, he'll owe me when he's dead. I bide my time. I'll get what I'm entitled when he's gone. Grab me one more beer outta the fridge, a cold one."

# Nothing to Prove

## Sylvia Petter

We didn't want it. We wanted to "live in sin". So, we did for twelve years after G. moved in that first night. He had to. I had fallen out of a window – well, not a window but through the back of a bus shelter – it was cold, and I leaned in and there was no glass and I fell and cracked my head. So of course, my blind date had to take me home and stay by me in case something happened. That was in Vienna. He was, still is, Viennese.

When I got a job in Geneva, I said come along. Your turn to be a foreigner.

You're a foreigner, too, he said.

I'm used to it. This'll be your first time.

Twelve years later we decided to have a go at having a child. The clock was ticking, but we weren't desperate.

On a trip back to Sydney, I told my parents about our plans. Dad was a golfer. He took my man down the back and showed him the driver. Hit him in the balls. Didn't mean to. Sorry. Got my man hooked though. On golf.

⋆

We should get married, I said, back in Geneva. The bit of paper thing is our problem. Not the kid's. The kid'll have enough problems in a foreign country with foreign parents from different countries, not even a language to call their own, expressing themselves in a trilingual mish-mash. We called it communicating.

In Geneva you had to announce to the world that you were getting married. The banns or you were banned. No way.

We were going to the US anyway – an unlimited mileage holiday with the best friend who had brought us together. All over. Even Las Vegas. Not a chapel! If it rains, no go. If we fight, no go. We never fight. Always a first time. Why? Why not? Everyone does. No rings. Had to listen to the JP's trip down the Rhine. $25. We caught Kris Kristofferson for double that and toasted our best man with Tequila Sunrise.

The next year I was sent by my employer to a conference in Rio. My man was recovering from a knee operation. I'll get us some rings, I said. I wanted ones that would fit his and hers, and his should look ok with hairs on the fingers. At H. Stern's in the hotel lobby, I saw a guy with his hands, asked him what sort of ring he would wear. A coiled one was cool. I got them.

★

A colleague was going back to Geneva. Please pop this into our letterbox. My husband's wedding ring.

We've always forgotten to celebrate anniversaries. How many is it now? I made a mnemonic. 6781. We don't wear the rings anymore, haven't for years; the kid's now knocking 40. This marriage so far has been one cool ride.

He golfs, cooks, shops. I wash up and write. Maybe that's the recipe? Nothing to prove.

# Future proof

## Sandra Arnold

Barny was enthusing about inviting relevant people to their wedding. Relevant to his career, he emphasised. Future proofing. But Fleur's attention was focused on a young couple sitting in a far corner of the restaurant. She had never seen them before, but she knew the man's name was Thors Bulwoork and that he would go home that night and strangle the woman who was now sitting beside him. This woman, she knew, had stuck pictures of rotting gums on her child's bedroom wall to ensure the girl never forgot to clean her teeth. The child, Fleur understood, was called Willow, and Willow felt safe only after dark. Then she opened her bedroom window and jumped out into the garden. She climbed into a tree every night and sat beside an owl.

"Have you been listening to a single word I've said?" demanded Barny.

"Of course," Fleur smiled. "Wedding invitations. Relevant people."

After Barny's outburst she determined to close the door on all revelations about the lives of others. Not that she had much control over them, coming unbidden as they did. Such insights had unnerved her as a child and unnerved her now. She was marrying Barny, not because she loved him, but because she believed his pragmatism would future proof their life together.

After they were married they moved into the house Barny had bought for them, a large brick villa with extensive lawns in a posh suburb in the city. On their first day there Fleur dreamed of dogs and children charging over the grass on days bright with sunshine. She wandered over to a flower bed and watched a bee wiggle its way inside a foxglove. "I love to watch their fat bottoms wriggle and to listen to the way their drone turns to a high-pitched sound once they're inside," she said, turning to Barny, but he was too busy fretting over the weeds in the lawn to listen. He stabbed out a number on his mobile to summon a contractor.

In the following years Barny trained the dog and the three children to stay off the grass and keep to the concrete paths. He walked along the edges every evening looking for worm casts and calling contractors to deal with any he found. Other than that he admired the perfectly manicured emerald green lawns from a window.

While he was away on a business trip Fleur arranged a birthday party for five-year-old Daisy. She took a video of the twenty invited children dancing on the grass and throwing sticks for Harvey the dog. As she watched them running about Fleur flipped without warning to that place where she knew three-year-old Emma would die in a car accident in fifteen years' time. Daisy, five, would have a disastrous marriage. Fabian, seven, would be bullied all through school and in the workplace. Before she slammed that door shut she knew that Thors Bulwoork would be released from prison on parole.

Barny died of a heart attack at the age of sixty. The lawyer told Fleur he had left the house to their two surviving children who now lived in another country. She didn't mind. She'd moved out of the house the day he'd gone ballistic at the state of the lawns after Daisy's birthday party, which included screaming at Fleur, smacking the children and taking Harvey to the vet to be euthanised. For the past three decades Fleur had lived in a tiny cottage with an untidy garden full of foxgloves and bees and dogs she'd rescued from the pound who chased each other in wild circles on the grass. Barny, with the help of his lawyer friends, had won custody of the children and allowed them to visit her only once a month. After the will was read, Fabian and Emma sold the house to developers after telling their mother by phone that they never wanted to see the place again.

A few weeks after the sale Fleur drove to the city, parked her car and watched as bulldozers smashed the house and left deep muddy tyre tracks in the churned-up garden. She paid one more visit six months later to look at the seven new townhouses with tiled courtyards crammed together on the grounds, and noted that there was not a blade of grass to be seen. She was glad that no children would grow up in these townhouses. As she turned away she saw the notice on the gates: **Thors Bulwoork Builders.** She wasn't surprised. Very little surprised her these days. She reflected briefly that she could have warned Barny about the heart attack. She shrugged and walked away.

# The Man Always Carves

## Arthur Gardiner

The roast chicken on the sideboard was golden, succulent, and nestling in warmed chafing dishes were crispy potatoes, while over there were sweet onions baked to translucence, caramelised parsnips, roasted and perfect. The new bride's hesitant hand spooned parsley carrots and buttered peas, while her groom made a show of sharpening the already razor-edged carving knife.

"When you've carved, will you serve the wine, dear?" said Beatrice.

She had selected a Chenin Blanc to be the perfect pairing. The tears of moisture rolling back into the ice bucket were proof of correct and accurate chilling of the wine. This was their first dinner party, and Herbert's boss and his wife were their first dinner guests.

"How many are we?" Herbert asked.

Dorothy giggled, thinking this was his attempt at humour.

"Oh, come now, there are the four of us. You know that, Herbert."

"Preference?"

"I'm so sorry. What was the question?" asked the lady.

In those far-off days, one used the euphemism 'dark meat' for thigh and 'white meat' for breast, but after over thirty years of bachelorhood, the new groom took etiquette to a new level. He adjusted to more nautical terms.

"Bow or stern?"

The wife of Herbert's boss tinkled a polite chuckle.

"Oh, I'll take from the front end, if I may."

"Like the Duke of Plaza-Toro, I'll take the rear."

A guffaw from Roderick, her spouse, showed how he enjoyed the joke he had made. Poker-faced, but with alacrity, Herbert dismembered the fowl into four equal lumps, two front, two back, and distributed the resulting four indelicate quarters. The breast and wings went to the ladies, thighs and drumsticks to each gentleman. A brown smudge of grease was all the forensic evidence of chicken on the serving platter. Proud of the admirable efficiency with which he had accomplished his mission, the newlywed husband took his seat.

"Plonk, anyone?" he asked.

His bride froze, mouth agape, a crimson flush of embarrassment oozing from cheeks to bosom. Instead of sophisticated slices of delicate white and dark flesh to offset her graceful plating of vegetables, each plate boasted a single chunk of chook: bones, skin and flesh hacked as one. Her bum slumped to her chair: she was mortified.

The man always carves, except, thereafter, in their household.

# Married Bliss

## Christine Law

I met them briefly on the train while travelling to Oxford late one Saturday afternoon. He wore a navy suit with a silk tie. She complemented him dressed in a navy floral tunic over leggings. He slim built; she taller and broader. They were smiling and seemed happy together. "We're going to a wedding," she remarked, holding onto her fiancé's arm. Looking at my watch I noted the time: 3.45pm. Isn't it late? Oh no, he remarked, we have been together some time. She waved her mauve posy as they stepped off the train. No white wedding for them or a wedding breakfast, but did it really matter? If they were happy with a register office wedding and a drink with their friends, who was I to comment? They were happy together having lived together first. I wished them well, thinking how marriage and weddings had changed over the years.

# Second Marriage

## Lucy Tyrrell

After my mother died at age 55, my father, seven years older, was bereft. He tried to find solace in his horticultural workplace until he retired, his pursuits like roaming in a VW camper van, voracious reading, and keeping the homeplace grounds tidy with his gardening skills. From his own unkempt appearance, with food stains on his shirts and unraveled trouser hems, my sister and I could tell—despite our flights or long drives to spend holidays and other visits with him—he wasn't himself.

After thirteen years living alone, my father remarried. Connie came to live with him in Georgia. It was good for him to have someone with whom to share life, a relief to see Dad happy with Connie in the picture. He dressed better, laughed more. They both talked with their mouths full, false uppers a bit loose and fidgeting. He tolerated (or maybe liked) eating the pimento cheese sandwiches she made, the overcooked peas that came from a can.

After they were married, I spent Christmas at my own home, enjoying my own traditions, hanging my own ornaments on my own tree. I was unaware then that I would be accused years later of staying away, of not wanting to spend the holiday with Connie. It simply wasn't true. At least not at first.

When I did visit, I offered to help Connie in the kitchen. She said, "This isn't your kitchen anymore. I don't want your help."

The year after they were married, when I turned 40, Connie bragged to me, "When I was 40, I was already a grandmother." It was clearly a deficit in her mind that I had produced no offspring. My issue instead was my small collection of advanced degrees and my experiences and adventures, which clearly didn't count in her estimation.

When I asked my father where my mother's journals were, journals of our family vacations when my sister and I were growing up—including two trips out West on camping tours of national parks, and a trip to England and France—so I could refer to them when writing memoir essays, it appeared that the journals were no longer around. I don't recall whether my dad admitted that Connie threw them out, but they were gone.

On another visit, on the day they would drive me to Atlanta for my flight back to Alaska, my dad asked me what I wanted to do for lunch.

I said, "Let's have sliced ham and tomato sandwiches on pumpernickel, right here at home."

I loved the view out the sliding doors toward the shiny-leaved magnolias and stately loblolly pines, while blue jays shrieked, calling in words my mother used to interpret as "Snake! Snake!"

He nodded in agreement, disappeared into their bedroom where Connie was readying for the two-hour drive.

He reappeared.

"We'll stop at Hardees on the way. That's what Connie wants to do."

I refrained from saying, "I'll only be here today. You can go to Hardees anytime."

I took my last look out the sliding doors and we drove away. Little did I know, it would be my last look at the property. They moved to Tennessee to be near her daughter.

One Christmas, I received from them a nicely tailored wool L.L. Bean jacket, fancier than I would wear except on special occasions. I traded in the navy one they gave me for a black one. I was content with the gift. She was irritated I swapped the color. The next year I received from them another of these classy jackets.

I carefully asked my father, "I enjoy the one jacket, but I'm puzzled why you gave me a second one."

He had a ready reply. They must have discussed this. "We think you should dress better at your workplace."

I kept calm. This was him channeling Connie's thoughts.

"Have you ever seen me at my workplace and what people wear?" I knew he hadn't. Alaska was too far for my aging father to fly.

"Jeans and t-shirt are the everyday standard, except on most days I wear a National Park Service uniform."

He had no answer. How could he answer without consulting Connie?

When I turned 50, I sewed my father a special blue quilt, using a pattern called "Magic Tiles," in honor of his being my father for a half century. When I visited their new home in Tennessee subsequent to giving him that gift, I found the quilt spread over the back of her fine couch, where the unneutered cat would spray and claw. The quilt protected and spared her couch from his abuse.

After 15 years of marriage to Connie, my father fell when he had the flu and was admitted to the hospital. The reality was that he would never go home again—he was dying of sepsis, pneumonia, and congestive heart failure. He hung on for weeks, first conscious, then unconscious, giving my sister and I time to travel there and spend precious time with him in the hospital.

Apparently, the "for better or worse" they had pledged, did not mean she would come visit him in the hospital when he was dying. She had declared she did not want to see him in his compromised condition. She would only talk to him by phone. My dad acquiesced.

I felt so badly for my dad, who gave and gave and gave in. But I also recognized that he relinquished fulfillment of his own needs to address hers, in a frustrating co-dependency that made things as they were.

Yet, without her intrusive presence at the hospital, it made it easier for my sister and me to stand watch for him, chat with him in his lucid moments about old times, feed him pieces of ice when his throat was dry, and call the nurses if the morphine drip was beeping "out."

His marriage to Connie helped him live a few years longer than he would have without her, I'm sure of it.

# Winter Solstice

## Evelyn Fletcher Symes

The chair complains loudly as he leans back, his hands behind his head, legs extended in a full body stretch.

His secretary stops at his door. "Rough day, huh?"

"Jesus Christ, yes."

"Well, Friday got here just like it always does."

He chuckles and nods agreement. "See you Monday. Let's hope for a less eventful week next week."

She snorts her thoughts on the likelihood of that and leaves.

The office is quiet now. Early darkness shuts the campus down by four. Bitter cold brings a bleak solitude which hurries faculty to home and hearth and students to the steamy warmth and clamor of the dining hall before an evening of conversation and friends.

"Maybe even a few stories will be told," he murmurs. "Life in the mead hall has changed very little, Beowulf, my friend." Through the fogged glass window he watches two young men, mufflers over their noses, trudge resolutely across the hard ground of the square. The wind is bitter. They break into a trot as they round the corner and bob out of sight.

He leans forward and flips open his appointment book. It's a satisfying part of his daily ritual. He scans next week's appointments and notes the fine red line drawn precisely from the 15th through the 17th. It's discreetly placed, a hair's breadth above the bottom line which frames the days of the week. Only one who knows what he is looking for would notice it. But a thoughtful person, noticing it, would recognize its importance immediately. It's drawn with a draftsman's pen and a fine stainless steel straight edge every time he marks the days on the calendar. He's proud of his ability to calculate them correctly, especially since she's so casual about it. She's never had to keep up with where she is. From the beginning of their marriage, she's known she was safe. He's seen to that.

Her passion took him by surprise, her reserve belying her sensual nature. By the third month with her, he knew she was always ready for him; by the fifth, he knew her fertile days from the fervor of their coupling. It was during the fertile days of their fifth month, as he held himself above her and watched her lift her pelvis to meet him, that he knew he would calculate and mark them on the calendar. He's a man who appreciates anticipation, something he has yet to successfully teach her. She holds nothing in reserve, gives everything, takes everything. Yet she has learned to follow the pace he sets, though at times she whimpers. She concedes it is better slower. He wonders if she knows how much he enjoys teasing her. It doesn't matter. He knows her, knows what drives her wild, knows what satisfies her, as she knows the same about him. They're a perfect match.

This last week has been especially delightful. Surreptitiously, he'd slid his hand up the inside of her thigh as he leaned over her desk. She'd gasped and opened her legs to him. He'd patted her knee, straightened her skirt, and hurried to his meeting. He chuckled at the memory. All week he had "bumped," "patted," and "brushed" her, delighting in the way she squirmed. The meetings, though, were legitimate. He would have come to her sooner, if not for the meetings. He's been aching for her. He wonders if he will have his usual control, then chuckles. "To hell with control."

It's almost the winter solstice. The barren winter ground seems to hold no promise of spring. Tonight, he will reaffirm life. She will open her legs to him, and he will plow her furrow and plant his seeds deep in her, like the sacred corn of which the very sowing symbolizes the coming of spring.

In spring he will take her in the fresh plowed ground of their garden, warm and pungent from the sun, her belly swollen with the life he gives her tonight.

He smiles and flips his appointment book shut knowing next month he will not need to calculate the days. He pulls on his heavy overcoat. The light in his office blinks out. In a few moments, the campus is empty. Only Grendle's jealous voice clamoring in the wind howls against the barren night.

# The way I think of you

## Sarah Masters

'And then the young woman came out and sat down, naked,' Don says to his dead wife, Laura. 'Naked.'

'I heard you,' Laura says. She's lying next to Don, her right arm folded behind her head. He can see the freckles on her shoulder, the curve of her breast squashed and half hidden. He wants to stroke it, but he knows she'll dissolve the moment he touches her.

'Stop looking,' she says. 'Tell me what happened.'

He clears his throat. 'It was Marjorie's fault. "You're turning into a hermit," she tells me.'

'Well, you *are*.'

'Alright. "I'll be there," she says. Only at the last minute she can't make it.'

'But you still went?'

'I nearly didn't, believe me. Anyway, I go in and I'm looking round for the table, you know, with the fruit bowl or flowers. The tutor tells us to find a place and he'll introduce us to tonight's model. I'm still thinking, *okay, Don, you can do this*, because she's in jeans and a jumper, perfectly normal. Becky, that's the model's name.'

'Pretty?'

He frowns. 'Nothing special.'

'Don't be coy.'

‘She was our Chris’s age.’ He looks across at Laura’s caesarean scar, and then at her wrinkled hand on the sheet, bare of her wedding ring. He wants to breathe in her scent but there is no scent.

‘Have you finished?’ she asks. ‘So, what did she look like?’

Don squints at the ceiling. ‘Long hair, brown, in a ponytail. Like you had yours.’

‘A long time ago,’ she says. ‘Go on.’

‘So, then we sit down with her in the middle and the tutor tells us we have to sketch her like this.’ He mimes a furious circling of the pen.

‘And she was naked?’

‘Not yet. We had to scribble for two minutes, while she changed poses. I’m thinking, *this is going to be rubbish.*’

‘Alright, what then?’

‘Well, *then*, the tutor says we’ll take five minutes. The next thing, Becky’s walking into the middle of the room and she’s starkers.’

‘And you didn’t have an inkling?’

‘Not a bit.’ He imagines her rolling her eyes, but doesn’t check. ‘She sits down and we’ve got to sketch her. As she is.’

‘How did she sit?’

‘Well, she’s got one arm round the chair back, one arm’s loose along her thigh. And one’s leg pushed out in front of the other, kind of pointing her toes.’

‘Where’s she looking?’

‘Down.’

‘Okay, let me try.’

‘You won’t manage it on the bed. Don’t be daft, Laura. Oh, I’m sorry, love. It’s just too – ’

‘I know.’

‘I miss you.’

‘I know. Tell me about the woman.’

So he casts his mind back to the evening. All around him is the shuffle of pencil on paper, sighs and intakes of breath. The model in the centre, she’s the realest thing in the room, and she should seem like a caged animal, but actually they’re the caged ones, because everything about her radiates control. Don can’t imagine how he’ll capture her on paper, so he sits there pretending to draw. Her ponytail slopes down her shoulders and it’s beautiful. He stares at its slivers of light, and is transported to a studio flat in North London, forty years ago, where he and his new wife Laura are lying together on the bed. A long mirror on the wardrobe doors reflects her leg draped over his. She adjusts herself so she’s half sitting, then she curls her fingers around his penis.

‘I’m still here,’ Laura says, drawing him back to the present. Don catches a flicker on the wall opposite and though there’s no mirror in this bedroom, he sees a ghost reflection as she lifts her leg to drape it over his.

‘She had a rose tattoo, the model,’ he says. ‘On her thigh.’

‘A rose.’ There’s humour in her voice.

‘A ruby rose.’

In that room in Balham all those years ago Laura had leant back against his chest. With one hand she had rolled her fingers over his penis, while with the other hand she stroked herself to wetness. In the mirror her face and neck had bloomed pink. Don had reached his arm around her to cup her breast, loving the fullness in his palm, pinching the nipple, releasing it, pinching it to the rhythm of her hand.

Afterwards, she had asked him to pass her handbag. ‘I’ve never done this before,’ she said as she pulled out a compact mirror. Then she opened her legs and positioned the mirror so they could both see.

'A rose,' he had said. 'A ruby rose.'

She had laughed. 'If you like.' Then he had pulled her hair over her shoulder and kissed the soft nape of her neck.

'You old romantic,' Laura says now. She's sitting up in the ghost mirror and her face and neck are flushed. He can see her breasts, and they're different from forty years ago but also just the same. 'So did you draw her, or just look?'

'Honestly?' he says. He opens the drawer of the bedside table and takes out the sketch. He has to turn away to do this and the next minute, the mirror is gone, and Laura is facing him. He lowers the paper, so she has to dip her head to look at it and he can gaze at her pretty neck and her grey curls.

He can hear himself breathing.

'This is me?' she says.

'You.'

They both contemplate the drawing, of a woman in her sixties. She touches the paper, and he could swear it moves. 'You haven't got the hand right, though,' she says.

'I know.'

'You'll have to go back, get some more practice.'

'Maybe,' he says. 'I'll think about it.'

'Do that.'

And he thinks, maybe I will. Then he closes his eyes and feels the soft pressure of her mouth on his. When he opens his eyes again, she'll be gone.

# Cats and Dogs

## Tony Dawson

Mark lay back in the warm bath, eyes shut, the water soothing his aching limbs. Dozy, still convalescing from a severe bout of flu, mind wandering, and conjuring up all sorts of peculiar thoughts, he wondered, for example, why was his wife, Georgina, so fond of dogs? "She'd have been one of those women who thought that happiness was a warm puppy," he mused.

He, on the other hand, loathed the damned things; he much preferred cats because they kept themselves clean *and* buried their crap. "Happiness is definitely a warm pussy …" he sniggered.

True as it was, he wasn't getting much of it these days. Correction. He wasn't getting any. Georgina had just hit 50 and had become an instant oestrogen-free zone with zero libido.

When he was ill, she had been a wonderful nurse, both tender and caring. He felt cherished and enjoyed the fuss she made when she massaged his aching body and plied him with honey and lemon drinks. Now that he was in recovery mode, she had reverted to what had become her normal arm's length approach to the intimate side of marriage since her menopause: hardly any overt displays of affection, and if he hugged her, he could feel her stiffen. Touching was now tabu. Even though he was a number of years older than her, he still enjoyed kissing and cuddling, and some intimate fondling. He missed it, for Christ's sake!

At that point in his musings, he heard the swish of the shower curtain and saw his wife emerging from the shower, draped in a towel. She picked up the hairdryer and aimed it at her dark hair.

"I heard what you were thinking," she called out above the noise of the dryer.

"What are you talking about? How can you possibly have heard what I was *thinking*?" he shouted above the din.

"We've been married long enough for me to know exactly what goes through your grubby little mind," she bellowed back.

She dropped the towel and stood in front of his face giving him an up-close view of her pubic hair as she played the dryer over it, teasing him with the sight and sound of her pubic hair rustling in the air flow. "How's that for a warm pussy, then? That's the last one you're going to see." And she grinned as she held the hairdryer over the bath and let it go.

# Marriage or a Squirrel

## Claire Schön

'Mummy, the man in this video is singing to another man – about love.'

Maggie is watching music videos while I get ready for work.

'Yes, baby. Some men love men.'

'Do some women love women?'

'Yes. Like Jack's mummies: Sara and Janine.'

'Oh yeah. Do men also marry men and women marry women?'

'Yes. And lots of people don't marry at all; they love each other without that.'

'Or they get a cat, like Mrs Jenners, and they love the cat.'

'That's right.'

'Or they get a dog. Or a squirrel.'

I don't comment on the squirrel. I just hope that won't be Maggie's next pet request.

'But that man is singing that he loves the other man, but he needs to leave him. Why?'

'Sometimes we love someone, but they aren't good for us; they don't make us happy.'

'Is that when they get a cat or a dog or a squirrel?'

'No, not necessarily. They might meet someone else.'

'And marry them?'

'If they want to. Marriage isn't proof of love, baby. Some people choose to marry, some don't, but it doesn't change the feeling.' I taper off a bit, not completely convinced by my own words, reflecting on the way love has changed since I married and wondering if it would have been different had we chosen not to. 'Marriage is a social construct.'

A social construct takes longer to explain to a six-year-old, and I quickly focus on the feeling again. We're clear by the time I drop her at school.

Walking through the door after a long and tedious day at work, I am greeted by socks tucked into pants, nestling in a pair of trousers, lying in the middle of a messy living room floor. They belong to my husband; he walks around them to give me a kiss hello.

'This is why some people don't marry, little girl,' I say, indicating the heap on the floor and immediately regret it when I see her slight frown. She's a daddy's girl; bringing her into our arguments is wrong and childish.

'Marriage is a social construct, Mummy. Focus on the feeling,' she answers brightly, not sensing the tension in the air. 'Or we can get a squirrel.'

# Life, cultivated

## Natalie Blake

Six years ago, I divorced my then-wife, the frumpy thing that she was, and moved back onto campus. Tenure had come with a two-up two-down townhouse she never appreciated due to its postage-stamp of a backyard. But I can buy a bunch of flowers just fine—then have them arranged in a vase by a pretty little thing who is herself as easy to please as those flowers.

I drape my arm over the back of her chair, the pretty thing, who goes by the name of Lucy. She plays with the potted stems adorning the center of the restaurant table, then dares a glance at her parents.

"And how did you two meet?" The mother, Susan, nurses a diminutive glass of white wine and casts her cautious gaze between us.

"I needed a research assistant. Lucy applied," I reply, and the girl nods along in tandem. I haven't revealed, of course, that I've weathered this storm once before and that it didn't go well; or that I fear she'll outgrow me and graduate, our affair destined to become nothing more than a well-pressed bloom between the pages of her college textbook.

"That's right, I beat out fifteen other applicants." Lucy strokes the inside seam of my trouser leg and barely contains her wry little smile when I'm forced to clear my throat.

"Fulfilled the criteria, did she?" Susan purses her lips.

Halfway through his second beer, the father raises his bottle with pride. "Lucy's always been a smart girl. Top of her class and on the honor roll." He sucks foam from his upper lip and gives Lucy an encouraging nod.

Perhaps his approval can be cultivated.

"Daddy, don't be embarrassing," she scolds. The poor thing flushes when she looks at me, but there's nothing to be insecure about. We all went to high school, one decade or another. "Anyway, school was *years* ago," Lucy adds.

"Not that many years ago—" the mother mutters into her wine glass, and promptly shakes the bottle from its cooler for a refill.

"Sue," David sighs, and shoots me an apologetic look.

Despite her age, I top up Lucy's wine to the brim and bask in the sunbeams of her approval. "Are you a hunting man, David?" I make it sound casual, off-the-cuff. Lucy nuzzles my shoulder in thanks because she'd insisted that I ask. Said it would win her Daddy round 'big-time'.

"Oh, I've tried my hand at it," he chuckles, ears pinking. "Nothing big. Got a deer once though," David fumbles his key chain to the table. A flaccid lump of antler hangs from the ring. "*Biiiig* buck it was."

Susan's lips curl. "I detest the killing of innocent creatures in the name of sport."

"I think it's very masculine," Lucy argues, determined to propagate her opinions away from her mother's. "Joseph has a black bear head above the mantel." She pecks my stubbled cheek with pride, then waits and watches for her parents' reaction when she adds, "The pelt is in our back bedroom."

David sputters. *"... our?"*

"Yes," I interject. "Lucy moved in after Spring break." Sometimes, I think if you were to cut my chest open, you'd find the roots of her wrapped around my ribs.

Susan presses her napkin over her mouth, paling. "This is your fault, David; you know that, don't you?" She sounds like my ex-wife. "Always away! If it wasn't a business trip it was a *hunting* trip," Susan continues, David skulking off to the bar for another beer instead of listening.

"*Mom.* Why are you being like this?" Lucy hisses once her father is out of earshot. "I don't see what the big deal is."

Playing my finger under Lucy's bra strap, I lean close to whisper, "Don't start, princess." She flushes and sits back. "We're all adults here, Mrs Birch," I re-assert, so her parents are clear on this fact. "I understand meeting your daughter's first boyfriend can have a somewhat … *aging* effect, but I hope I can rely on you not to judge our relationship at first glance."

"You must admit it's awfully hard not to—"

"Lucy knows what she wants. I think it's time you respected that." My words may be cutting, but Susan's the rotten vine that needs plucking and pulling up before it sucks the life from its surroundings. "In truth, it was not me who did the pursuing."

"That's right," Lucy spouts at her mother, "and it's not like it's against the rules." She restlessly tears faux petals from one of the flowers that had, moments ago, decorated the restaurant table. "He's not *my* lecturer, we're not even based in the same building."

"Indeed. I teach classics. Latin mostly," I offer, before the conversation derails. "And we're really very happy together. So happy, in fact, that—"

"Oh Lucy," her mother starts, "I want to be happy for you, I do, but when you said you were bringing someone to dinner, I just got so *excited.* I didn't expect that someone to be …" Susan's eyes dart to me, then she twists her napkin into ever-tightening tubes before abandoning it with a troubled sniff. "Well, someone who calls you *princess,*" Susan finishes, lowering her voice, as though in the midst of a scandal. "You're a smart and capable young woman who doesn't need taking care of. Life is not some fairytale."

"Maybe I like being taken care of," Lucy bickers back, and the two women immediately have at one another like clucking chickens, caught in fraught debate. Her petite fingers, like tendrils, burrow into my skin and cling ever tighter to me, the harsher her mother's words become.

I start to wonder if love is not unlike a slow growing creeper, flourishing only when it can feed on the detritus of its predecessors. But like all wild things, love has a habit of running away with you.

"—that we're actually getting married in the Fall."

# Round 1

## Jenna Heller

Freya perches on the tree stump, cradles her hand in her lap, rocks silently under the sweltering sun. Feels the heat in her maternity jeans and double-XL Iron Maiden t-shirt.

At the corner of Amber's eye, a bruise blossoms like the silent poison that's been building for weeks. A temporary tattoo. A branding. A prophecy.

Freya rubs her belly and waits for fluttery movement before saying, 'This isn't going to work.' She massages her swelling knuckles, stretches her fingers, clenches her fist again.

In the distance, thunder growls even as the sun dances in the newborn distance between them.

'I'm sorry,' Amber says and feels the sting in the corner of her eye. She looks for a way back in. 'Come on. I'll take you home before it rains.'

Freya stands up. Places Amber's hand on her belly and as the sky rolls, the baby kicks.

Amber can't help but smile. Freya smiles back and looks into Amber's eyes. Sees the blooming shiner. 'Don't make me hit you again.'

# The Things We Do For Love

## Jennifer Moon

FOR SALE BY OWNER: Just married and need to sell much-loved pearlescent white motorcycle. Partner dropped veiled hint they are not enamored by high speeds and open-air travel. Motorcycle is in excellent condition and runs rings around bikes of similar vintage. Bike is not worse for wear with recent decline in time spent on its upkeep, but will be even better with a few years of respectful attention and meticulous care. Some dents and scratches, but perceived imperfections are hardly noticeable once you embrace the lifelong potential of spontaneous adventure and carefree rides. Perfect motorcycle to treasure; price negotiable.

LOOKING TO BUY: Just married and have vowed to find a sensible, inexpensive car. Must be reliable and require little maintenance; suitable for use in richer and poorer times. Mileage is unimportant. But, committed to a clean and comfortable interior, big enough for two passengers. Bonus if winter tires are included, as we trust that future plans will include year-round travel and long road trips conducive to conversation. Looking for a vehicle to love as we begin our shared adventures. Budget is limited to avoid sale of cherished motorcycle.

# Home

## Cheryl Snell

We came together from opposite ends of the world to meet in the middle. As in all romances, there was a chase. Ours revolved around geography: Boston, Cleveland, DC. Every time I'd leave a place, he'd arrive. Was I playing cosmic hard to get? Not possible. I didn't know him in real life. So how did I recognize him when we finally did meet? All the women I've ever been embraced him instantly. He moved into my building, and my cells, and we finally knotted our string made of time and distance. He is my house and I am his.

# Hope is a Dangerous Thing

Emily Stanford

Sunday mornings were always peaceful. Jenny would go down the shops to buy the sausage and bacon to go with our usual breakfast of eggs and bread. I could sit and watch 'Match of the Day' without interruption. No chores to do until she swept back in the door. An absolute treat.

The gate squeaked and her voice drifted in before she bundled herself into my space – early, I might add.

"Darling!" she shouted from the open front door, the waft of the crisp morning air tickling the back of my neck. I barely moved, not wanting my morning calm to be broken just yet, but I could tell this was to be no ordinary regalement of the goings on in this little town. Lord knew what was about to assault me. Front door slamming. Thump-thump of shoes being kicked off. The produce hitting the table, muffled by the cotton shoulder bag she kept them in, the beans rolling across the table and onto the waiting seat of the chair below. Swift, shuffling steps grew louder until she stood in front of me. Eyes wild, breathing fast and clutching an M&S bag. A vast departure from our norm. The only place we bought our bacon was the butchers.

"Darling," she said again, shaking the bag at me. "Did you not hear me call you?"

"I heard you, dear."

"Well, you should have come. I have excellent news!" she said, "I've heard, on the grapevine of course, we are to be grandparents!"

She dipped her hand into the bag with abandon, I could already see the sheen of the vinyl words printed across the front of the tiny piece of fabric. Panic spread across my chest, thickening in my throat as she pushed the baby grow toward me.

*Awesome like my daddy* was emblazoned across the front. Like the daddy we hadn't seen in almost seven years. Who had told us never to contact him or his new husband again.

"Jenny," I said as evenly as I could muster, "you can't send him that."

"No, Mark. We have to try. He's our little boy."

The hope I saw in her eyes hurt me more than she would ever know. He had made it clear to us we weren't welcome in his new life, even if it was lived just a few roads away from the place he grew up. From us.

"Just let me send it? It can't do any harm," she said, pleading for me to be with her on this.

"OK, his address is in the book," I said, defeated by her optimism. Knowing that in a few weeks' time, the parcel she would so lovingly wrap would come back through our door angrily repackaged, another note of warning to **leave us alone** affixed. Breaking her heart all over again.

# Norman Leaving

## Kenneth M. Kapp

Norman looked at his nails. He was standing at the kitchen table, hands pushing down, his knuckles turning white. He didn't want to be late for work again, but Sheila had started up, complaining about something from last week when he either did or didn't do this or that. He swallowed the bile in his throat.

A sigh escaped. "I need to leave now. COVID's over, no more working from home." *I wonder if I blew it and told Sheila that I was glad to be working in the office again?* "Can't we discuss this when I come home. We can open a bottle of wine and sit in the living room. We can talk then if you want."

"We don't have any more wine and the wine you bought the last time was cheap and shitty. Sort of says it all, doesn't it?"

"Look, I'm a beer guy. Sure, I asked for a decent wine that wasn't too expensive, but that bottle set me back $20, not exactly cheap."

"It was still shitty."

"You say. I'll tell you what, I'll stop on the way home and get a $40 bottle, Pinot Grigio, that's what you like, right?"

"Amazing. You remembered. Someone would think we've been living together for years."

"We have. Look, let's do this later, OK?"

"Yeh, what you say. It's always what you say, isn't it?"

"No, hardly." Norman tried his best not to make a face. *I could be wearing a death mask – totally neutral – and she'd still say I was making a face. Hell, wouldn't have made a difference if I graduated tops in the Method Acting studio downtown and smiled at her like Paul Neumann.*

"You're thinking, Norman. I can always tell when you're thinking. Don't – it's not one of your strong points."

"Right. That's why I'm still standing here when I need to leave. Probably be late again."

"Says a lot about our relationship, doesn't it? You always rushing off to work. Rather be anywhere but here. Wouldn't surprise me if you've a girlfriend downtown. Showering and putting on clean underwear. Who do you think you're fooling? I wasn't born yesterday in case you forgot."

"Jeez, Sheila. That's what people do when they go to work. Shower, clean clothes, those kinds of things. COVID hasn't been that long, has it?"

"Depends on what you mean by long. Sometimes living with you even one day is too long."

"You say."

Norman had a warm feeling between his shoulder blades and the black coffee started to gurgle in his stomach. He could barely remember the love and goodwill they once had.

"You know, Sheila, I think it's come down to you and me just cohabiting, sharing a bathroom and stuff – but there's certainly been no "privileges" for a long while."

Norman paused, putting air-quotes about privileges. "I'm going."

"So go already. Staying home isn't going to get you any "privileges." Don't even think about it. I'm meeting Marge for lunch anyhow."

Norman sat down at the kitchen table. "Meeting Marge" seemed the sound of defeat. He missed what they'd once had, thought that possibly they could have it again, get around this corner. He stared at his fingers spread over the round coffee cup stains on the table. The same conversation week after week, ever since he had to return to work downtown.

He stood up abruptly, knocking the chair on its side.

"OK, I'm leaving!"

"OK, so leave already."

# The Wedding Dress

## Riley Winchester

The bride was pregnant but nobody else knew except the groom. It was early, thirteen weeks into the pregnancy, and she was naturally small, so the bump had yet to emerge. Ava thought she could feel the child kicking inside her the nights leading up to the wedding. She never told John about it because she knew it was too early and he would have thought she was crazy. But she had a deep motherly preternatural feeling that the child was metaphysically kicking inside her, that it meant something, that the child was a harbinger of something, that *something* special would come of it all. Perhaps, she thought, it was natural for all soon-to-be mothers. But perhaps not.

Ava walked down the aisle with her father, their arms locked together. She wore a sleek dress made of bone white alençon lace that her mother had hand-sewn. The way the veil hung down the back of her shoulders and rolled along her dress, swathing every angle and contour of her body, it looked as if she had been born in the dress and lived her entire life in it.

Ava's father hugged her at the altar. He wiped tears from the wrinkled ravines under his eyes and then he turned his attention toward John and nodded. John, looking down from the altar, nodded back.

Ava and John stood across from each other. Ava wiggled; she was nervous. John exhaled and scanned the pews. They exchanged vows. They exchanged rings. John said I do. Ava said I do. When they kissed, Ava expected the baby to kick. But she felt nothing from the child.

Years later, moths in the attic gnawed away at the wedding dress until it became nothing but shreds of lace.

# The Wedding

## Beate Sigriddaughter

He found her on the terrace behind a row of fragrant lilacs, mascara staining her cheeks.

"The piglets," he said.

"Yes," she said. She pressed her cheek into his white shirt, mascara and all. "Even salamanders in love would have been better. Don't know if I should laugh or cry."

"Both. And talk to me. If you want."

"I didn't even want to have her there. But you can't very well not invite your own mother to your wedding."

"It's been known to happen."

"When I asked her to read a poem at our wedding, I wanted to honor her. What I had in mind was something like Shakespeare or Barrett Browning, not some doggerel about piglets in love. We deserve Shakespeare. And then those rose quartz piglets."

"Such a valuable wedding present," he said, then, imitating her mother's voice, he raised his to a high breathy story-telling pitch. "*They're considered lucky in many cultures. I want you two to have all the luck in the world.*" Then in his normal voice: "With her in the mix, we need it."

Giggles interrupted her sobs. Her cheek was still pressed into his white shirt. "Dad had this mildly disdainful half-smile on his face as though to signal to the world: *See? This is why I'm no longer with her.*"

"He must have experienced his fair share of her benevolent sabotage. Or unfair share, as the case may be."

"That's it. That's exactly it. Benevolent sabotage. With the flowers, too, earlier today. Kelly agreed to do the flower arrangements at cost. Because she's my friend. They were supposed to be Mom's treat, so I let her do the organizing. I was there when Mom talked to her on the phone and said something about white roses and white lilies. I heard it myself, and I was surprised. Mom never liked lilies. Then when the flowers arrived this morning, Mom was all indignant. 'I told her I hate lilies.' Must have been her mysterious whisper voice. Cause I heard 'white lilies' too, not 'hate lilies.' So, Kelly said there'd be no charge for the flowers."

"I know. And it's taken care of. I have paid Kelly for the flowers. She did accept in the end."

"Oh, wow." She looked up from his chest into his eyes. "Oh, thank you. I already felt terrible for having wedding flowers with bad karma. And I don't mind white lilies in the least. She doesn't mean to hurt anyone, you know. Mom, that is."

He raised his eyebrows.

"No, really. She's just clumsy, despite all her obvious sophistication. I always feel like a country bumpkin next to her elegance."

"A piglet rather than a princess?"

"Something like that."

"You look nothing like a piglet to me. Shall I compare thee … ?"

Her mascara-stained face was about to disappear into his shirt again when she noticed the smudges. "Now I've ruined your shirt on top of everything."

"If we have to explain it, which we don't, we'll chalk it up to wedding emotions. Maybe we shouldn't even go back in. Leave surreptitiously. I'm sure it's the sophisticated custom somewhere in the world for honeymooners to just take off. Let all the guests get drunk and silly on their own. And it appears we have every right to *piggy*back on such traditions."

She laughed out loud, then slowly turned her head from side to side and interlaced her right hand with his left. "What I am really afraid of is that one fine day she'll come after you with her—what did you call it? Benevolent sabotage? And it can really hurt. I don't ever want you hurt."

"I didn't marry her. I married you."

She let go of his hand and picked up the flowing lace of her dress with both hands to make walking easier.

"Let's go cut some cake and then split."

# The First Baseball Game of the Season

## Kresha Richman Warnock

My husband hid his passion for baseball from me before we were married. I don't think it was intentional. We had all-encompassing jobs and were doing the work of falling in love with each other. And it was quick—we started dating on Valentine's Day, were engaged by May, and Jim left in June and July to help the nation celebrate its bi-centennial. Yes, we've been together since 1976. Our wedding was that September.

Eventually though, like all obsessions, his baseball relationship broke through. I wouldn't call it "a mania", and maybe even "passion" is the wrong word for my even-keeled husband. When Jim watches a baseball game, he keeps score. I mean a lot of folks will fill in the boxes at the end of the program at the ball park, documenting the strikes and pitches and errors and runs. (True confession: I can't do this.) But not everyone, in his seventies, has two still-growing plastic bins full of spiral-backed score books that accompanied him, and therefore us, on each of the many physical moves we've made in forty-five years of marriage. Not everyone assiduously researches options for the BEST scorebook available in early February of each year. Not everyone keeps a packet of mechanical pencils in his meticulously organized desk, just the right kind, so he has one available for each game.

When we retired to the Pacific Northwest we had big baseball plans. Of course, Jim would buy the cable baseball package and have the in-home option readily at hand. We'd go to a few Mariners games up in Seattle in person. But we live ten minutes away from Cheney Stadium, home of the Tacoma Rainiers! Minor league ball has charms of its own, and we dreamed of attending multiple games a season, knowing the players, maybe even having some ball park buddies.

The immediate outcome of that dream, like so many, can be summarized in one word: Covid. We moved to Tacoma in January 2020. That first minor league season was cancelled entirely. In 2021, we were still too cautious to enjoy a crowd. But it's 2022, and we make it to Cheney Stadium, for the second game of the season, in early April.

The stands are half full, which is a pretty good crowd for a spring school night. We find our seats and check out the food. Jim is happy with chicken and strips, but I find nothing edible and end up grabbing a five-dollar bag of peanuts and a two-dollar bottle of water. (Note to self: Eat at home next time.) We're medium-sized people, but the seats are a little tight and hard. At least I'm short!

We always get to the park early so Jim can set up. This time, he eats before the game starts, and tidy as ever, he goes from the last fry to the pristine pages of his score book, a mystical graph of squares and angles, avoiding any crumbs or grease stains. Using his mechanical pencil, he writes in the name of each player in its proper order on the page in tiny, geometric letters, each identical in size. An early and fanatical adopter of computers and smartphones, this may be the only time Jim puts pencil to paper these days.

We stand for the national anthem, the announcers play ridiculous games on the jumbotron – one of them involves the man running around the stadium finding someone who has ordered the mac and cheese from the barbecue joint and asking if he wants pepper on it, which is provided by a companion with a three-foot-tall pepper mill. We avoid being in any of the panning shots of the crowd, smiling and waving. Definitely not the one where they catch you kissing.

Our team hits a home run in the bottom of the first, and that is probably the most exciting play of the game for me. It's all one for Jim, who continues to scribe the game, making tiny gray marks in the squares with the mechanical pencil. Jim began this mystical habit in 1963, a twelve-year-old boy faithfully following the San Francisco Giants on the radio. It was the years of the Great Dynasty: Willie Mays, Willie McCovey, Juan Marichal. Maybe even I would be obsessed with baseball if I had grown up in the midst of this mythical era. I can visualize his mother, when she realized Jim's interest in baseball, visiting a dusty sporting goods store in the San Francisco Tenderloin neighborhood where she worked as a bookkeeper and buying Jim that first scorebook. What lessons about order and statistics, about masculinity and grace, even about race in America did this shy teenager learn from the many evenings, sitting with his ear to the radio, his pencil to the scorebook?

Meanwhile, back in Cheney Stadium, I watch the game, check my Twitter account, and engage in another sport nearly lost to Covid – people watching. By the seventh inning stretch, though, I've pulled up the maroon hood of my hoodie and started complaining about the cold. It is April in the Pacific

Northwest, and I should have brought a lap blanket. Jim asks if I want to leave, but I remind him of his inviolable rule: "You can't go home until the game is over." How else can the scorecard be complete?

It's a long game, because the pitchers have a hard time getting anyone out, and the Rainiers lose, nine to five. We walk to the car and half of my brain is fixating on a cup of tea and a warm bed. The other half is jabbering on about how fun this was, and we need to make it a regular part of our summer routine, because, after all, summer is baseball, and now we live ten minutes from the park.

# Challenging Behaviors

## Nan Wigington

I read all the manuals, know what to do. Wedding gown off. Marriage on.

Forget the mother. I am the wife. All pats and belly rubs come from me. Whistles. Praise. Food, too. We go out, I hand him his food, cut his steak, feed him on a silver fork. My husband likes being babied. He wriggles in his chair, grins, sticks his tongue out.

There are still some challenging behaviors. He goes out with his litter mates, gets drunk, howls at the moon, and doesn't come when I call. Some manuals suggest I change his name so it's easier for him to hear. Jonathan just takes too long to say. I start calling him Jack. It's a little better. Some manuals suggest surgical necessity. I shudder at the thought. I want a tame husband, but I need children. I put off calling doctors. I do nothing, pat the spot next to me on the couch. He takes his place, curls up, passes out. Maybe loyalty is enough.

★

We argue. He needs to help with the housework, see his litter mates less often, stop drinking. He says woof or maybe what. I don't know. I quote from a Harvard article about happy marriages and housework. I throw in something about drinking and liver damage. I roll up the paper the article's printed on, hit him with it. On the nose.

He cocks his head and stares at me with his big brown eyes. The kitchen window is open, and he sniffs the breeze as if someone somewhere is burning some meat. He runs to the window, smells something new. Grass? Cat? I take the hint.

"Let's go on a walk," I say. I get my hat, his frisbee, and we go.

On the way home, he says, "I'll moderate, and I'll take over the dishes."

I ruffle his curly blond hair.

"Good boy," I say.

How do you measure happy? I should be happy about Jack. His challenging behaviors seem to be gone. I've taught him how to fetch, heel and claw his way up the corporate ladder. He wears a tie now. I tell him it's sexy. I like the red striped one best. I take it between my two fingers, sometimes my mouth, and lead him to the bedroom. But sex is always the same, fast and from behind.

The litter mates have wives. Now I go out, too. We bowl. We drink beer. Talk about what it is to be happy.

"Shag carpet makes me happy," Sandra says.

"A good go on a green couch," Ellen says.

Lisa frowns and pats her belly. She's 9 months pregnant.

I tell him all I want for my birthday is a new house. He growls a little bit. He likes our place, its familiar smell, the ratty bed, the muddy backyard.

We hire a realtor. Jack scratches his right ear with his right leg. It doesn't faze her. She asks us what we want in a house. "A big backyard," he says.

"Shag carpeting," I say.

The realtor shows us house after house. He runs around with his tongue out opening every door, putting nose and fingerprints on every piece of glass. He lays down in the shag carpet and rolls around in it.

"Uh. Uh. Ah," he says.

We put an offer on a house. He comes to closing, whines, but obeys. I take his hand and stroke the fur on the back of his knuckles.

But this doesn't make me happy. I tell him I want a baby. He's a good boy. We have so much sex, my knees get calluses. His litter mates smell my desperation. They each have a turn. I get what I want.

My husband won't go on walks, won't curl up on the couch next to me. I try to look it up in the manuals. There is a chapter on trust. I close the book.

Six months in. I say, "But it's yours!"

Jack cocks his head, trots to the kitchen. I hear him. He's peeing against the wall.

"Bad boy," I say.

He growls, walks out the door.

Two weeks pass. I put up LOST posters – Curly Blond Hair, Big Brown Eyes, Responds to the Name of Jack. No one calls the number at the bottom.

I dream that he's back, hair matted, hands bloody, smelling mostly of whiskey and women in heat. I give him a bath. I pull out the burrs, bandage the wounds.

"I'm sorry," I say.

We watch TV and he crawls onto the couch, curls up next to me.

★

The night my water breaks and the contractions start, I go to the door, pat my thigh, whistle, call, "Jack. Jonathan. Here boy." He doesn't come. Of course, he doesn't.

# The Clicking Keeps Me Company

Alan Kennedy

## 1

Despite the biting chill of November making her wheezing worse, Catriona insisted on having all the windows wide open. But, even after scouring the freshly sheared fleece five times in lukewarm water, the stink of the Jacob's ewe impregnated the most remote corner of the cottage.

Through a gap in the feather quilt that shrouded her, she threw me one of her ever-rarer smiles.

'I'm icing up over here. Get off your lazy arse, shove a couple more sticks on the stove, then plonk your Sassenach feet on the pedals.'

Every Friday after fixing frozen pipes, putting in second-hand water heaters or whatever moonlighting odd-job I could close my mitts around, I would trudge from house to house picking up leftover scraps the neighbours laid out for us to make the organic dyes Catriona needed to stain the yarn.

Sacks overflowing with onion skins, beetroot tops, and used tea bags lay scattered round the kitchen floor. Strips of banana peel shared hooks with spanners and pipe cutters in my workshop. Jars full of rusted nails, steeped in apple cider vinegar to fix the pigments, piled up in the garage.

We spent every weekend carding the wool with a special contraption she salvaged from her uncle's farm, combing it out meticulously so as not to snap the fibres. In the evenings, Catriona would tease it through her grandmother's spinning wheel.

While I pumped the pedals, she twisted the yarn till a filament of irregular thickness snaked round the teak spindle. For her, it was perfect.

'Every knot in the sweater will remind you of me.'

All the while, she sang Gaelic waulking songs picked up from her mother and studied me with tearful eyes. We both knew she didn't have long.

'I want this to be a special present for you. Only for you.'

Before carrying Catriona upstairs to bed, my last task of the evening was to stretch my hands out for her to wind the roughly spun sheaves. Then I'd leave the balls of wool to steep overnight in one of three tin buckets according to the colour she wanted to dye them.

Crimson, ochre or lavender.

## 2

She presented me with the knitted sweater on Christmas Eve, the last we would ever spend together. When I tried on her marvellous present, a ticklish tingle, a pleasant glow I had never experienced before, coursed through me. A creation of art and of love. I felt my muscles more vigorous, more sculpted. It was as if Catriona was hugging me in the same way she did when she was able to.

Everybody remarked on how grand it was and how handy it would be for the dismal winter we were having.

On the twelfth day of Christmas, the afternoon of her funeral, I put it on instead of the conventional black.

## 3

On the last Friday of April, during a cold snap, I got to know Gloria when I followed up on a call to fix her boiler. We went out the following evening for a drink. On Sunday morning, while we were having breakfast in her living room, she commented on the jumper draped over the sofa. I didn't fancy going into many details and limited myself to stating it was a gift.

When I got out of the shower, Gloria was wearing it and admiring herself in the mirror.

'Hey. What do you reckon?'

Before she could finish the sentence, the bay window gusted open with a savage force. The look on Gloria's face tightened. Her grin evaporated and an expression of horror took over her.

'I can't breathe. Get it off me.'

The jersey was tightening more and more round her neck and wrists with every second, rendering its removal impossible. Gloria's hands turned waxen white, then blue. I tugged and yanked in vain. She nodded towards the back garden, but I didn't understand. Desperately, she made a scissor cutting gesture with her swollen fingers.

The pruning shears snapped into pieces. The hedge cutters went blunt immediately, but I took some half metre pliers from my tool case and, strand by strand, cut her out of the woollen constrictor.

Gloria was discharged from the hospital three days later with four cracked ribs and both wrists sprained. Since the accident, she hasn't returned my phone calls or read my messages. I spotted her two months ago on Johnson Street, but she bolted across to the other pavement and hailed a taxi.

I used to scoff at Catriona's belief in magic, but every time I visit her grave, I wear only cotton, just to be on the safe side. Nowadays, even the aroma of roast lamb gives me the jitters. Her spinning wheel still stands in the living room. I don't have the heart or, I must admit, the courage to dismantle it. Once in a while, I sit on her favourite stool and work the pedals.

The clicking keeps me company.

# Licking the Wound

## Mark Blickley

Laying naked in this bed on my back, I tilt my head and I look down with so much pain in my face. This is the third time today my husband has gone down on me. Shouldn't a girl be happy?

I would be, but this is how he apologizes for the blunt fist to the face he gives when he loses his temper. I tell myself every day I need to leave. Just get my shit and leave. But I don't. I let temptation win every time as soon as his tongue strokes me slowly up and down until the abuse feels distant.

I look down at him in between my legs, my natural fluids moistening his face. I am in such heartbreak and awe over how the man I love can deliver such pain and pleasure. It's insane. I stare at him. He looks up at me and whispers, "I love you, baby."

I search his eyes until I can find the apology for the black eye and the blood from my nose that stained the satin sheets we just purchased. My moans grow louder and drown out thoughts of me leaving until I hear my mother's voice echo inside my head pleading, repeating, "Don't you ever let a man hit you the way Daddy hits me."

I married a man who one day will take my life and I continue to do nothing but look at him as we lay in this bed of lies, the same bed I retreat to after he beats me until I'm numb and then licks me until I can feel again.

Today something is different. Something is very, very off. I can feel his darting tongue actually trace individual letters inside of me that turn into words that form a full sentence that rises up through my body and explodes out my throat, "You are not my suicide note!"

His mouth jerks back and he jumps off the bed. For the first time ever, I can see he is afraid. And I am not. It must be true that the third time is a charm because I am going to save myself and leave this cowardly son of a bitch. I wish my mother were alive so I could thank her.

# Friendly Fire

## Pam Knapp

I considered storming out but felt it was better to stand my ground – push the point home.

The row grew quite fiery, and now we have a standoff. Him out the back, unnecessarily hammering a nail into something in the yard; me in the kitchen unnecessarily scrubbing something in the sink. Gender stereotypes, I know, but you've got to do what works in your own territory.

It feels as if it has been hours, but it's more like ten minutes and I am all tension. I feel the pressure to broker some kind of negotiation but I'm unsure of where the lines have been drawn. There's no sign of a white flag to show hostilities are ended but no, 'And another thing …' sniper fire either. Nothing but the unmistakable atmosphere of something unfinished. I hate it. The hiatus. He's so much better at silence than I am. Inertia: the weapon of choice for the bloody minded.

So, I ask him, 'Do you want something to eat?'

I get the silent treatment – apart from the passive aggressive humming, that is. So infuriating!

In retaliation, I use excessive-force cupboard door shutting. Everything on the worktop that could carry a crash, smack or wallop by being bashed back down in its place, I use to trumpet my indignation. Frying pan: clang on the hob. Cutlery drawer: kerching open and shut – repeatedly. Plate stacking with gusto:

clacking like a ratchet rattle. With the whole armoury of noise, I make sure he hears just how mad I am in case he wants to be first to open any conciliatory advances. But nothing. No reaction at all. So infuriating!

I raise my voice and repeat with unconcealed impatience, 'Do you want something to eat?'

From outside comes the response, 'I'm not fussed.' Just that: 'I'm not fussed.'

Well, he's got the advantage now, hasn't he? My trojan horse sandwich has failed to break his defences and is left looking like a snapped olive branch. I stir a cup of tea like a woman possessed, the frenzied spoon, a reveille. I'm so piqued that I've lost high ground, that I strike back: 'Or would you rather have something so rich that it's hard to swallow?'

'Oh, here we go.'

Bingo! He's broken cover. I prepare for the counterattack and move to face the door. But he doesn't come in. There's no follow up tit for tat. No offensive defence. Nothing. The void unnerves me. So infuriating!

I release a short volley to pre-empt any stray in-coming offensives. 'I'm just saying that life is short,' I say, 'and when you get something wrong you should just own it and get it out there that you realise you have made a mistake,' I say. 'It's not worth a row. Confession is good for the soul,' I say.

We both hear the trigger-happy bickering bug in my words. I bite my lip. Tell myself, don't say another word. Just stop talking.

I wait and gauge the impact.

'I'll make it myself,' he says.

I can't hear anything for definite, but I ask anyway. 'Can you stop that humming please?'

As soon as I say it, I know I've conceded gained ground with a petty shot in the dark remark and the armistice is over. I fall back and momentarily resume the audible kitchen utensil protest.

A guilt induced peace treatise retreats at pace. A change in strategy is required. I leave the cover of the kitchen and move to open ground to utilise face-to-face tactics.

I look him straight in the eye. 'So, are we eating or not?' I say, ostensibly, sensibly moving on.

Not a word is exchanged but eye contact is held between us. I feel the warm glow of victory building with every second that ticks by. I'm confident now that he'll fold, maybe even apologise – well, let's not get ahead of ourselves; perhaps he'll shake his head and sigh his readiness to surrender. The gaze is steady, steady and then he looks up to the sky. Yes! And then back at me. Yess! He takes a deep breath. Yesss! Any second now he's going to crack. Hold his gaze. Keep the silence. Keep it …

Peace in our time.

I *knew* he was being hysterical.

# Two to Tango

## Amanda Addison

She wants to tell her friends, but knows this date is one she should keep to herself. She showers and blow dries her long hair, then carefully considers what to wear in a way she hasn't done for months. Black is always good. Both smart and casual. She lines her eyes with kohl and paints her lips ruby red. By the time she's on the Tube she's feeling rather good about herself – back out there – in the world.

He can see her waiting for him at the top of the steps between two neoclassical columns. She looks out, as if on a balcony. His Juliet. Hair blowing in the light breeze. It's longer now – down past her shoulders and the little black dress hugs her figure nicely.

From her vantage point the square is busy again. What was I thinking, agreeing to meet here for a date? she thinks.

He crosses the road and sprints up the steps. He kisses the woman on both cheeks. It's been months since they've been out – just the two of them.

A sensual Latin beat fills the square. 'Shall we?' he asks.

'I didn't know you danced the tango,' she says.

'Online tutorials,' he grins, taking his wife's hand and leading her down the steps to the square.

# Resurrection

## Cynthia Leslie-Bole

"Anything dead coming back to life hurts."
Toni Morrison

Anything dead coming back to life hurts, especially if it's a part of yourself as vital as your marriage. When your connection with your beloved is severed, when you both retreat into the curled privacy of your shells, you lose your way and float without direction or design, feeling nothing but empty sky above and bottomless ocean below. No land is in sight, no safe harbors or welcoming shores beckon. There is simply unanchored drifting.

Becalmed in the doldrums, you grow so far apart you can barely see each other, even if you squint and shade your eyes against the glare. You become tiny specks with indiscriminate features to one another.

You begin to forget the beginning, how you looked at each other and felt flooded with an effervescent joy. How a touch could send you into hot flashes of the most delicious sort. How your eyes, when locked, fed directly into the heart, and from the heart into the soul.

You drift into somnambulance, neither awake nor asleep to each other, and any effort to reach out seems too hard, too strange and stilted. Gradually the revelatory eye contact you used to feast on becomes glances from the blurred edges of vision, just enough of a look to verify that the other is still there, but not enough to risk exposure. Those little affectionate touches that used to populate your days fade into paler and paler versions of their former selves until they disappear completely. And passion expires with only the tiniest curl of smoke, a guttering flame snuffed out by lack of fuel and fresh air.

Then you coast along, without a breath of wind in your sails, too dull to respond, too desiccated to save yourself. Neither of you wants to initiate turning on the engine so you can power your way out of troubled waters. You both stubbornly wait, insisting that you will only make progress if, and when, the other person fills your sails again. So you wait. And you wait. And you despair. You grieve the loss of spontaneous laughter, stimulating discussions, easy companionship, and physical nurturing that used to be the essence of your marriage.

And then suddenly you can wait no longer, and you resolve to break through the inertia. You are both told that you must independently turn the love-light on again rather than waiting for the other to begin, so you start small. You bring each other tea, and it is accepted with thanks. You apply a tentative pat to the hand, the shoulder, and it is not rebuffed. You dare direct eye contact and risk a guarded smile. When the smile is returned with delighted surprise, you open up a millimeter and the smile feels right and real, if only for that second. You make an effort to bring more of yourself back to each other, confess a few fears and concerns, and report the small stuff of daily life as a good-faith offering. Then you try a full-bodied hug—not too bad. In fact, it suddenly feels so desperately needed that you hang on for longer than strictly necessary and revel in the familiarity of the body you once knew better than your own.

And those calcified shells begin to crack open, often achingly at first, and the skin exposed is raw, but somehow this seems right and real. That flesh has been too tightly bound for too long, and the fresh air feels fine.

Soon signs of resurrection are coursing through your bond. It is awakening, stretching its arms sleepily, and yawning to greet the sunrise. It feels newly hatched, yet it drags history in its wake. It's time to sort through the narratives, to bring onboard the treasure of your shared memories and growth while tossing overboard the what ifs, the should haves, the blame and bitterness.

It's time to revivify and recommit, to be born into a new marriage with eyes and heart wide open, risking both redemption and annihilation, knowing that anything coming back to life hurts, but the reward is well worth whatever discomfort it entails.

# Bat

## William Cass

It was Saturday, a crisp late-fall afternoon full of white light. Pam rearranged items in the spare bedroom's tiny closet while her husband, Stan, watched football in the living room. Something between a smirk and a smile crossed her lips as she heard him swear at the television with the crowd's roar. She shifted a box of his random things, college football trophies and awards protruding, to a lower shelf and replaced it with one of the new-baby items she'd brought up from the basement where she'd stored it after the miscarriage. She smoothed the onesies on top, a warmth spreading through her; she was ten weeks pregnant again, though they hadn't told anyone else yet. They'd agreed not to until well past the first trimester … not after what happened last time.

Stan swore again louder, but this time she heard the sofa scrape across the hardwood floor and the lampshade next to the couch knock loose.

"Shit, shit, shit!" Stan grunted. "Get out of here!"

Pam frowned. Stan's heavy footsteps clattered towards the kitchen, then quickly reversed in her direction. A thrown magazine whacked high against the wall in the hallway outside the closet. She flinched as Stan shouted, "No, get out, get out!"

Just as suddenly, the door to the spare bedroom slammed shut, followed by a high-pitched clicking sound, then a small thump against the window. She thought she heard the rapid beat of something like wings, and a short scream of her own escaped her as she yanked the closet door closed. Pam fell to her knees and clapped her fingertips over her mouth.

She said, "Stan?"

"You in there, honey?"

"In the closet, yes."

"Is the door closed?"

"It is now."

"Good. Stay in there. Don't come out, don't move. I'm calling the exterminator."

"What is it?"

"A bat." He paused. "A big one."

Pam's eyebrows raised. "A bat?"

"Really big. Nasty looking. Came screeching right at me … I saw its goddamn fangs." Another pause. "Those things have always freaked me right-the-hell out. Absolutely, completely, no joke."

"Can't you come get rid of it? Trap it, open a window or something."

"No fucking way. Could be rabid. Stay put. I'm calling now."

She heard him retreat to the living room and the faint report of his cell phone conversation. Then he was up against the wall separating the closet from the hallway again. "A couple of hours," Stan told her. "Three max. The guy's on another emergency call, then we're next."

She sat down on the floor, blinking rapidly. "Three hours, you've got to be kidding. Do something. Just shoo it away."

"Impossible." His voice was firm, unwavering. "Not a chance."

The clicking sound moved closer, then the flutter again. She stiffened when another thump trembled the closet's door jamb. Silence followed. Pam looked at a football award of Stan's poking out of the box, one given for courage, determination, and grit. She remembered the pride she'd felt for him when he'd received it a half-dozen years before; he'd always made her feel so safe and secure. She placed her palm over her abdomen where she imagined the baby inside her to be, the life they planned to cherish and protect together.

She muttered, "My big hero."

"Jesus, honey. What do you want me to do?"

"I don't know. Something, anything."

More silence followed. She heard her own breathing, but not his. Finally, he said, "Listen. Do whatever you were doing in there. Try to forget about all this. I'll go out in the living room so I can keep my eye on the front door for the exterminator."

Pam squeezed her eyes shut.

"You'll be okay," he said. "Just sit tight and don't open that closet door."

Stan's footsteps clumped down the hall. The sound of the television crowd grew louder. A faint odor of mothballs wafted through the closet. The bat's rapid, tinny squeal click began again. The future opened before Pam like the mouth of a cave. She hugged herself, stared at Stan's box, and wondered what other myths it held.

# Did You Get Two?

## John Riley

"65 more miles," she said.

Mom stared at him. "Did you see the sign? 65 goddamn miles."

Dad was driving me and Mom to Grandma's house so we could stay a few days. It was a long ride. We were going to have to stop and sleep. I hoped we would stop soon.

I was on my knees on the backseat. Out of my safety belt. My door lock was pushed down.

Mom said, "You'll have less than nothing. I'll see to that. You'll be a beggar. 65 miles to the goddamn hotel. I hope it was good. Did you ever drive 65 miles to get some of it?"

Dad clung to the wheel with both hands. "Everything is not all my fault," he said. He waited a minute then said, "You have too many expectations."

I held on to the hand strap and leaned against my door. The moon had been out but now it was gone. The air was so hot in the car I had to fight to breathe. Mom had made me close the window so her hair wouldn't be blown out of place. She got it set just yesterday. I cracked my window an inch. Mom didn't notice. I sucked in a mouthful of air.

"Expectations," Mom said, and covered her face with her hands and began to cry. My insides filled up with hot water. I needed more wind on my face.

Dad kept both hands on the wheel.

Mom cried for a long time, quietly, like she was trying to hide it from me. Then she said, "Did you get two rooms? Tell me you got two."

There was no answer. I slipped my fingers around the door lock.

# Born a Bride

## Phyliss Merion Shanken

In the 1940s, Susie and her family weren't much different from others in her middle class neighborhood. By her fifth Christmas, she added a fashion doll to her collection, which arrived all decked out in a bridal gown, veil, and white slingback high-heel shoes.

By her eleventh year, her parents gave her a subscription to *Brides' Magazine*. At sleepovers, she and her girlfriends sat around for hours flipping through the pages. They pulled out stuff from her wardrobe and pinned them together to make bridesmaid costumes. They each stretched an undershirt over their heads to form a headdress. One girl played the flute as the bridal court lined up and strolled down the driveway aisle.

After a few years of this game, the girls, having paid no attention to the groom's role, fought over who would be relegated to that lowly position. No one wanted to don a bowtie and fake mustache and take her dreaded turn, but the beautiful bride needed a handsome escort, so they all had to do their share.

In the meantime, in school, they attended home economics classes, a prerequisite for graduation. They learned to sew and cook. Their babysitting classes were covert training for motherhood.

When Susie's real wedding day arrived, she was completely prepared. She and her friends no longer played with dolls or dressed up, but had spent many an hour plopped on Susie's bed reading *The Joy of Sex.* Making a V shape with their fingers over their reluctant eyes while spying the illustrations, they gurgled sounds of protest: *Ugh, Really? No way! Disgusting. Ugh.*

After all the planning meetings, money talks, consultations, and multiple bank checks written; after the shopping and gown fittings and invitations; after the arguments with the groom about his parents' invitation list; after whopping fights and fears of break-ups and power plays; after getting back together again and again, the day finally arrived.

The bridesmaids collected themselves at the beauty salon, getting their nails and hair done, and makeup applied (at the bride's family's expense). Susie found herself, as she had always rehearsed, walking down a staircase in the back of the church to the tune of singsong *oohs* and *aahs* by the assembly.

… A few months later, when the honeymoon was long over, an unexpected thought came over Susie. Maybe she should relinquish her "homemaker" pretense. Without her girlfriends to spur her on, Susie wondered: *Where is the real Susie?*

Like a candidate who spends years readying himself to win an election but doesn't have a clue as to how to do the job, Susie surprised herself by blurting aloud: "I'm finally here. Now, what do I do?"

# I'm separated but together

## Sharon Rockman

Meaning that early last Thursday morning, I went directly to my husband and told him it was over. Thank you for 25 odd years together. And there were good times and great times and chaotic times and traumatic times and beautiful children that we made together and a life that was sutured together like so many muscle layers following complex abdominal surgery. But he didn't take it too well because he didn't want to let me go, not so much because he loves me – and maybe he still does or he thinks he does – but because change is a frightening prospect for humans who commonly prefer adhering to the familiar grooves and furrows of their everyday lives.

And now I think otherwise of post-op healing as I do of love. Both turn upon the letting go, the letting grow, the blood letting.

And what of fear. Fear of loneliness? Feel of the power imbalance? It is stasis I fear. The stagnation of the swamp and the danger of its quicksand. To pull my legs free and then my arms and to walk away. That's my meaning of together.

# Surface Tension

## James Bates

He remembered it from biology class. Surface tension. It meant, *the tendency of water molecules to shrink into the smallest area possible*. He remembered something else, too, about a water bug being able to walk across the surface, which at the time he thought was pretty amazing.

He'd never been the best student and probably failed the science test back then, just like he'd done years later when their marriage failed. He'd shrunk, become smaller as a human being, while she'd grown and blossomed like the flowers he grew in his carefully tended garden. He'd stayed safe and secure in his IT job. She'd grown like the bright blooming lilies in that same garden, excelling as a fast-tracked manager in a prestigious marketing firm, making new friends, traveling both home and abroad and even joining a running club and completing a triathlon. She'd grown and he hadn't. Pure and simple. He'd taken the safe way, kept his head down and played it safe. She'd moved on like that water bug, moving ever forward, fearlessly into the unknown.

Sure, they'd tried, especially during those early years. They'd made time for date night once a week and together planned three getaway vacations each year. But now, nine years in, their interests had changed, and they'd drifted apart. Their marriage had died. He hadn't been enough for her. She'd given up and now was leaving; moving on.

He watched as she descended the stairs.

"All ready, Bill," she said, shifting her suitcase from one hand to the other. It didn't appear to be all that heavy. "I'm done packing. I guess this is good-bye."

He had nothing to say; knew her leaving was inevitable, yet he was now emotionally unprepared and stunned speechless by the finality of it all.

"But ... But ..." he finally mustered

"No buts, Bill. It's over."

He watched her eyes slip from his to some unknown, but for her, eagerly anticipated future. A future that didn't include him.

There was a twinkle there. And something else he hadn't seen for years. A spark. She was on fire with her passionate desire to leave him.

She picked up her laptop satchel from the table by the door and slung it over her shoulder. She kissed him on the forehead, turned, and walked out.

He watched as the door closed, leaving him alone. The reality sat heavy on his chest.

Man, how he still loved her.

Man, how he wished he could change.

Man, how he knew he couldn't.

He shuffled into the kitchen, filled the teapot with water, and set it on the stove. Some tea would be nice, soothing chamomile perhaps. Relaxing. Maybe. He sat down, looking through the window toward his garden but not seeing it. Time slowing to a crawl.

The water boiled, the teapot whistled, but he didn't hear a thing. He stared into space, remembering the remainder of the definition for surface tension. How it allows for objects to float on the water's surface. Suspended and driftless. Just like he felt now.

# Last Love

## Tony Warner

'Kind, sophisticated gentleman (70), widowed, terrible SOH, seeks charming lady of a certain age to be his last love.'

Gerard adjusted his tie, folded the double-Windsor knot he favoured, pleased its combination of muted greens and dark red nestled delightfully on his unostentatious pale grey shirt. He had played with wearing a suit, but dismissed the idea as too formal. The tie will go well with his tweed jacket and carefully ironed jeans. How strange to be wearing jeans as a fashion item. He can remember the days when any respectable restaurant would have refused him entry in 'working man's attire'. Today's restaurant was the best choice. Clean, with a good reputation and moderate prices; well within the budget of two independent pensioners.

Annabel chose a plain dark blue dress, enlivened by the silk scarf she had bought many years ago in Pisa. Black strappy shoes with low heels in case she had to walk any distance; her favourite brown nubuck floor-length overcoat. No rain in the weather forecast, but one must be prepared. The lizard brooch was rejected as too showy. She packed a paperback in her handbag to read on the train.

He was early, as he had intended. She was five minutes late, as she had planned. His appearance was reassuringly close to the photograph he had posted on the website. The restaurant was disappointing in its menu but reassuring in its prices. Their conversation sniffed around one another like dogs meeting for the first time. Each finding the other friendly and relatively harmless, it was allowed to move on to more general topics.

Annabel had family, as was to be expected, now dispersed to France and Australia. Grandchildren were briefly mentioned, to be passed over by names and ages. Gerard announced he had few close friends, while his family was similarly dispersed. His occupation? Years of unproductive boredom in accountancy and banking, which had left him comfortably off in retirement.

She told him of the amateur choir she belonged to. 'A huge shortage of men,' she complained. He smiled, described a disastrous concert he had attended at his local church. She told a long and involved story of a rehearsal for a Handel oratorio, which ended with the vicar sitting in the font, still full of water from an earlier christening.

Gerard laughed uproariously. Annabel noticed he had listened to her, sitting forward as if to catch every word, one finger stuck in his right ear. He did not do this when he spoke himself. They stayed longer than either had intended, made an arrangement to go together to a concert in the cathedral, shook hands politely and went their several ways.

As Gerard said afterwards, the concert was 'a mixed bag'. They discussed it in detail in the lounge bar of a nearby hotel. Annabel noted he still put one finger in his ear whilst listening to her. She found this disconcerting but felt their acquaintance too new and fragile to mention it. If he were deaf, she would need to make allowances. At their age, one had to expect a certain amount of infirmity.

The train was delayed. Animals on the line, the conductor said. Fearful of falling asleep and missing her stop, Annabel took out her book. Something was irritating her. It had been a bad idea to indulge in the free nuts on the hotel bar. First looking round, she delicately removed her false teeth, placed them in a sandwich bag she always carried for the purpose, and stowed them away in her handbag. A pity there was no trolley service, a sip of water or lukewarm tea would have been welcome.

Gerard drove home. He felt the evening had been a success, both in terms of the music (except for that execrable second violin) and the company. Annabel was a charming companion, except for her terrible diction and habit of mumbling her words. Even his old trick of pressing the hearing aid further into its orifice produced only a modicum of improvement.

The weather warming, they arranged to meet at the sculpture park near Annabel's home. She wore a light knee-length skirt, beige in colour, topped with a green blouse which she knew set off the blue of her eyes. Again, her faithful strappy black shoes, proof against the rough grass of the park, and a light cardigan, since one cannot trust the weather this time of year.

Gerard was on high form, reflected in his paisley cravat and dark red trousers. He told Annabel scabrous tales of the sculptors' lives, to which she responded with stories of their love lives and their offsprings' peccadilloes. Gerard listened politely, finger in his ear. They stopped at the café for tea and cakes.

In the middle of a conversation about Anthony Caro, she halted in mid-sentence, covered her mouth with her hand, turned a becoming shade of pink. Indicated the door to the ladies' toilet, flustered away. On her return, she was quiet, answering only in monosyllables, a napkin held before her face. Gerard found this endearing, but realised the situation could not continue.

'I did a lot of carpentry in my youth,' he began, 'making small items of furniture. Because I was no good at cutting the joints I always reinforced them with PVA glue. Useless on furniture. A friend gave me a tube of a commercial one called 'sticks like s★★t' (excuse my language, but that's its real name). Now, I've brought something which I've been meaning to show you when the time was right.'

Gerard reached into his pocket, producing a small tube of ointment. 'Shafak's famous dental adhesive. See what it says on the front: 'sticks like concrete.' You are obviously having trouble with your teeth; I suggest you try it. If you find it works, then please keep the whole tube.'

Who could resist such a caring and perspicacious gentleman? Shafak's famous dental adhesive cemented not only her teeth but also their whole relationship.

# Death Doesn't End a Marriage

## Dev Berger

Death doesn't end a marriage. The physical may not be present anymore. But then togetherness was always more than the physical. What remains is the ethereal, the intangible, the substance of memory that clings like a soft embrace.

What we remember is legion. Unspoken words; the special smile; the familiarity that never grows tiresome; noticing the first gray hairs and the quiet wrinkles. The flowers, the cards, the gifts that were exchanged, they leave footsteps but are merely stand-ins for the real words, the real touch, the real actions that shape and transform our lives.

The ceremony that brings two people together, the vows, the signing of the marriage license, these are the formal parts of ritual formalizing the partnership. But even without a ceremony of words, and often long before those words, the connection, the desire to experience the journey together on a joined path, these already existed.

All of us are jigsaw puzzles, trying to understand ourselves a piece at a time, and learning where the interlocking pieces belong with those we love. The lifetime it can take connecting the pieces in the give and take of life, these do more than shape us. They renew us, they inspire us, and yes, even sadden and bruise us. Sometimes the pieces fail us, deceive us, mock us. Were they wrong pieces? Or were they the right pieces provided at a time we were unprepared to accept? Does it matter? To live a life means accepting the pieces, no matter how jagged the edges.

There is no perfect journey. It is foolish to even want it for it denies what is real in the world. There will be wrong steps, wrong turns, wrong decisions. What matters is seeing the problems for what they are and letting them become the tiny lighthouses, guiding us from the dangers of crashing and splintering into pieces.

This is what I shared with him as he lay dying at our home, his eyes wide open with the shock of recognizing the end was near, his breathing difficult puffs of air. I was exhausted by his dying, crushed by the impending finality. Death becomes a river gathering speed until it drowns the life and releases the spirit from those it takes.

If you have some romantic notion that you can be a pillar of love that softens the blow of death as it carries away the person whom you vowed to love, you will lose that notion as you fall to your knees and wrap your arms around the shell of flesh and bone that remains.

Moments after he died, I stepped outside and picked white gardenias as a winter moon, white as death cast its light upon them, making them shine. These I placed on his body before calling the hospice nurse to come and finish the ritual, where death and the time it happened are recorded.

The body died. The marriage didn't. Not even the death certificate, the cremation, the memorial, or sleeping in bed alone stopped his spirit from wrapping his arms around me. We were still married but the marriage had taken on a different reality.

We were together, one walking the physical plane, the other walking in silence among the ether, and the mysterious unknown. The heart sees nothing wrong with a marriage between the living and the dead. You learn how to do it and even when another miracle of love enters your life, another union, another marriage, the heart records it all and you learn to live in tandem with all of it.

The heart is not a place with walls. It welcomes the mistakes, the successes, the time lost, the time spent. It whispers that death can come to the person you love, to you, but the marriage doesn't die. It is merely transformed and becomes part of the blood circulating within you, and the breaths exhaled.

These were the words I spoke to my daughter and her daughter on their wedding days. They were my gifts to him whose invisible remains rested within me.

Death doesn't end the marriage. The marriage doesn't die, not the ones where love was real.

# Grandpa's Interview

## Ivan Rehorek

Well, thank you for this opportunity, Santa. It has been far too long since we last chatted, hasn't it?

Oh my, what would I like for Christmas?

That's simple: a train set is what I'd like. With a tunnel of course, a station, a bridge over a river, yes, and a road crossing with a small house nearby, with a rose garden out front, a fruit orchard and a duck pond down the back.

The winds were gentle, and the stars reflected in her eyes every night …

There's a small copse of trees nearby, and a little hill with the remains of a tiny castle on top.

The river winds around, and the train tracks followed it, and went into the hill and out again and up to the station.

We spent many happy years there, in that cottage near the hill, watching the trains go by, sometimes full of children, sometimes grownups on their way to work.

Holiday crowds one time, soldiers another … summer gave way to autumn, the ducks all flew off, winter came and the pond froze over. Then it was springtime again, the ducks all came back, and soon they had little ones.

They all grew up and flew off, away into who-knows-where.

We were very happy there, for many many years.

But all good things come to an end, they filled in the pond, levelled the hill, the winds died, and then she did.

The seasons came and went as always, and every year I put a rose on the window sill in her memory.

I moved away, went elsewhere, found other friends … came back one time, there's nothing left now, the railway's gone, there's an overpass and a pylon where the house stood.

Well, you can't stop progress, can you?

So yes, train set is what I'd like, with a tunnel and a road crossing …

# And So It Begins

## Louise L. Pace

Milly twisted the diamond ring on her left finger and then threw back a neat shot of vodka. It was meant to hurt. Punish.

She closed her eyes and swallowed back tears and held on to her breath. In just ten minutes' time, everything would change.

She sighed, remembering that periwinkle sky delicately lit by a full moon and a lone star that twinkled in the north. The feel of the warm brown sugary sand under her tanned feet. It wasn't meant to be real—any of it.

She glanced through their kitchen window. This sky was creamy grey with heavy clouds like dirty thumb prints over paper.

Milly tilted her head and watched Jack relaxing on the sofa, carefree, flicking through TV channels, his work shoes kicked off. An empty crisp packet lay next to a half-empty pint of lager.

Seb had been a nightmare. A total creep. She shuddered at the thought of his cartoon teeth, his powdered skin, the navy sculpted hair and the comical brows that looked like the shadows of two dolphins facing each other in mid-air

But Kez. Jeez, his eyes unapologetically kind. His smile was genuine. Beautiful. He was so perfect he could have been immortalised in marble. She shivered as she allowed herself to remember absolutely everything about him. But now that chapter was closed. Or it had been.

It was just some low-budget Australian reality TV show. Never to see the light of day. An opportunity for some free fun during the separation. A working holiday if you like, but with benefits, drama and endless catfights. She would have been a fool to turn it down.

Jack never needed to know.

But now things were different. In five minutes' time, Jack would never look at her the same way. The anticipated pain was too much to bear.

Milly gulped a breath and swigged back another neat drink. It felt warmer now, her insides beginning to numb over.

*Why did Netflix have to buy the show? Why?*

Marrying Kez in a fake televised wedding seemed perfectly harmless and fun. Both of them beautiful, like Disney had drawn them himself.

It wasn't real.

That's what she was led to believe.

Two minutes from now, it would be all over. Another drink and she would care slightly less.

She walked slowly over to Jack, leaned in and kissed him on the lips. 'I love you,' she said with a sad smile, taking the remote from his hand and nervously switching over to Netflix. She scrolled through the shows and clicked on 'Save the Date'.

'I'm not watching this shite,' Jack sat up, his blue eyes blinking with confusion.

'You have to, I'll explain later …' she leaned in and kissed him again, possibly for the last time and while she knew right at that moment he still loved her, 'That's if you ever speak to me again.'

She wiped away a tear.

'I'm so, so sorry, Jack, I should have told you …'

His phone lit up as multiple texts poured through with furious urgency.

An unfathomable world awaited them.

And now it begins.

# Soul Mates for Fifty Years

## Diana Raab

This year marks the fiftieth anniversary of my husband and I knowing one another. We met in 1972 and were married five years later. It was love at first sight.

People often ask me what's the key to a successful long-term partnership. I say that as simple as it might sound, there are four main ingredients—being best friends first, communicating openly, helping your partner meet personal goals, and sharing a sense of humor.

As a writer and storyteller, I am fascinated how people meet. I believe it can say a lot about how the plot or relationship unfolds. Simon and I met when I was eighteen years and he was twenty. A few years earlier, our parents became instant friends while on vacation at a hotel in Northern Quebec. The following summer, when my mother called to say that I was dating a boy she didn't like, his parents offered me a job at their plant nursery sixty miles north of Toronto.

That summer, Simon's mother, Jeannine, picked me up at the airport in her light-blue Valiant. My dark bangs hung straight over my eyes, and my makeup modeled Twiggy, as I'd painted vertical black lines beneath the lower lashes to emulate the model's classic wide-eyed look.

When Jeannine spotted me at the gate, she scanned me up and down and smirked. She was probably wondering if it was a good idea to have invited this rebellious-looking city girl (aka New York hippie) to spend the summer, given that she had two teenage sons and two younger children I could have easily unfavorably influenced.

From the airport, Jeannine drove down the winding country road to their home. After some rudimentary car talk and long moments of silence, we arrived. I thanked her for picking me up, and proceeded to lug my heavy red Samsonite suitcase onto the porch leading to the front door. Within moments the screen door swung open. On the other side stood a tall, skinny young man with a large red Afro haircut.

"Nice to meet you. I'm Simon," he said, smiling, and then gave me the firmest handshake I'd ever received. I later learned that he was the eldest son and the manager of the store where I'd work for the summer.

Our eyes linked as if superglue joined us. Jeannine approached the door behind me, saying, "Go in. Go in," but my feet wouldn't budge. I wanted to stand there forever, my eyes fixed on his, but without any further ado, Simon held the door open with one hand and used the other hand to wave me inside the house.

From that moment on, I knew that Simon and I had a profound connection, and it took less than a week for me to realize that he was the one I wanted to spend the rest of my life with. He was my soul mate. Years later when I repeated this story to others desperate to find love themselves, all I could muster up was, "It felt as if we'd known one another forever."

Intuitively, I felt that he had the same adoration and desire for me that I had for him. I was drawn to his sense of humor and self-confidence. He seemed quite comfortable in his skin.

At work, he concocted a project that we could work on together. For two weeks we assembled hibachi barbecues. This tiresome job of putting screws in an endless number of holes seemed painless in light of my escalating love. The hours drifted by as I laughed at Simon's jokes and gazed at him with a sense of knowing and awe. I was love struck. After dinner when everyone retired to their rooms, we stayed up engaged in our mutual passion for crossword puzzles.

Two weeks into my stay, Simon was scheduled to leave for his summer vacation. He asked me to join him on his road trip to the Yukon Territory; I couldn't contain my excitement.

"My parents will never let me travel alone with you."

"But our parents are friends."

"It'll never happen."

"What if I write a letter?"

"You can try, but I doubt it; my dad is really strict."

Simon wrote my parents a compelling two-page letter, and after reading it, they called me and gave me permission to join him on the trip to the Yukon Territory.

The next day, we packed his orange Volkswagen Beetle with a matching orange canoe on top. We spent two magnificent weeks together, camping, fishing and canoeing. We returned home and continued a two-year, long distance love affair laden with love letters and phone calls. When the time came to apply for college, we chose neighboring schools. We knew we were too young to get married, but when given the opportunity, we wanted to be together.

One evening near the end of our last semester, he visited the apartment I shared with another student. He took my hand and led me to my room. He told me to sit on my bed, and he knelt down on my hook rug carpet beside my bed and proposed to me with an emerald and diamond ring which he designed. He used all his saved earnings of $500. After our wedding in New York, we moved to Montreal. He started a technology firm and I began a nursing career until summoned to bedrest with my eldest daughter. Unfortunately, I had to do that with my other two children and Simon was the most supportive husband imaginable.

Our three children are now in their thirties and they're in committed relationships and parents themselves. They've blessed us with five wonderful grandchildren and in spite of the unexpected ups and downs of a long-term relationship, our love is as strong as it was back in 1972. We hope that our children are as lucky as us. We often remind them, that love must be at the core of any relationship, like it was and continues to be at ours.

# Are You the Husband?

## Elizabeth Stanley

Rolling my eyes, I crossed my arms over my chest and leant back in my chair, determined to get as far away from my brother's best mate as I could. Well, from his questions anyway. Trish smiled, placing a warm, manicured hand on my bare knee beneath the table. My skin tingled. Once Owen returned from the bar, we could head home, snuggle up on the sofa and watch *Game of Thrones* with a bottle of Chardonnay.

'Yeah, but who's the guy and who's the girl?' Terry asked, his voice fuzzy with booze.

'I'm not sure I understand you,' Trish answered, sipping her Pinot. 'We're both women, obviously.'

I watched as she swallowed, her throat expanding. The gold necklace I gave her for our first anniversary shimmered in the low light. I'd bought the tiger pendant for her because it reminded me of the brave and fierce woman I had married. Trish hadn't taken it off since.

Terry scrunched his shoulders.

'So, who does the cooking then?'

'We both do,' Trish replied, raising her eyebrows.

Her eyes glinted at the barrage of questions. Questions we'd both heard a million times before. Trish was so much more patient than me, working as a Primary School teacher for fifteen years as she has.

My spirits lifted as Owen sauntered over, half a Stella sloshing in his hand. Plonking himself down on the chair next to Terry, his face glowed, his skin glimmering like a lake. He stuffed shards of poppadom into his mouth and grinned.

'Alrigh', I hope this pillock ain't upsetting my two favourite girls,' he said.

I shot him a death stare. The same one that used to work when we were kids and I wanted him to help me reach the good biscuits in the top cupboard. I may have been older, but Owen was always bigger than me.

'I mean women!' he corrected himself.

Trish chuckled, turning her eyes to Owen.

'Terry just wants to know which one of us is the husband, don't you, Tez?'

I bristled, but Trish just squeezed my knee lightly with trilling fingers, sending a flutter to my stomach.

Owen's eyes turned to moons and his mouth gaped, soggy yellow crumbs speckling his tongue. He slapped Terry round the back of the head, making him wobble on his seat. Terry grunted and rubbed his shaved head, but they both broke into smiles.

'What? You asked that? Not cool, Tez. They're obviously both gir – uh – women. They're wives.' Owen nudged Terry's shoulder.

The tension in my shoulders disappeared and I smiled too. Owen didn't really understand when I came out when he was twelve years old, but he'd always been my biggest cheerleader. A warmth spread over me as though I'd been swaddled in a blanket straight from the tumble dryer.

'Yeah, *and* they both wore wedding dresses,' Owen continued, slurping foam from his lager, waggling his eyebrows.

Trish nodded, her cheeks pink.

'That's right, and they were both white dresses!' she exclaimed, pressing her hand to her chest in mock surprise.

'White dresses with flower bouquets and veils,' I piped up.

I giggled into my vodka-coke as Terry's face screwed up and he rummaged around in his ear with a thick finger.

'Wait a sec ...'

Owen held up his hand.

'No mate, no, listen.'

Owen's eyes darted to me, and he winked. I bit the inside of my cheeks; I knew what my brother was about to say. Trish huffed a discreet laugh.

'If Elle was a bloke, right, if Elle was a bloke, you definitely wouldn't be my best man next week, Terry. Elle would.'

# The Artist's Take on Beige

## Rachel Canwell

The day her divorce came through Miriam turned her attention to the carpet.

That vast, impractical expanse of cream that *he* had insisted upon. And she had never wanted.

The same carpet upon which you could not eat, shag, breathe or even walk.

The same carpet upon which, one morning, she had found him crawling, commando-style on elbows and knees, picking up speck after speck of imagined lint and dust.

Miriam had stood in the doorway, silent, watching as he shrugged off his dressing gown, and began to shimmy naked across the floor.

Arse in the air, face low to the ground, his eyes keen, he had inched forward; picking at the fibres, like a chimp grooming his mate for fleas.

And she thought, "He really loves that carpet. He loves that carpet more than me."

That realisation ended her marriage. Coupled with the sound of his balls slapping against his thigh as he shimmied.

Not forgetting the messages on his phone. The ones from Janey in Accounts.

*

So now Miriam has the house. And the car. And the chairs, the crockery, the silver and the beds. His pension plan, ISAs, credit cards. And not a single debt.

And she has the carpet.

This morning Miriam squats in the sunlight, sweeping the deep pile with one loving stroke and silent, heartfelt thanks. Before walking into the kitchen. Where she pulls on decorator's overalls, snaps her latex gloves and opens up carefully hoarded stores.

She collects bottle after bottle, jar after jar, loading up the hostess trolley (also hers), humming as she works. When it is full, she pushes it, breathless and lightheaded with anticipation, through to the lounge.

Miriam has emptied this room in preparation. No furniture, no curtains, no TV, nothing else remains. Just that beautiful, impossible acre of vacuumed off-white; upon which she positions her trolley. Slap bang in the centre of the room.

Miriam breathes slowly, a long exhalation. A final moment to consider, to settle upon her first weapon of choice. This is her opening gambit, so long imagined. There is no rush, better to take her time; so important to get this right.

Ketchup.

Sweet, viscous, so delightfully, terribly, deliciously red.

With one manicured nail she pops the top, squeezes hard and laughing, begins to spin.

Vivid, horrifying and scarlet the sauce bursts forth. One long jubilant arc sailing across his pride and joy.

And the air is full with tomato, undertones of sugar and high wild laughter.

Throwing aside the empty bottle, Miriam reaches out and picks again.

Tabasco in one hand, in the other paprika; a two-handed draw.

She dances back and forth shaking her hands. Bracelets jangle in time with her heartbeat; loud, deliberate and incredibly fast. A splash here, a dash there. Spreading and blooming like flowers. New life bursting forth everywhere.

HP next. Then chocolate spread, peanut butter, followed by BBQ sauce, some marmalade. Christmas chutney, a forgotten pickle, French-style blackcurrant jam.

Behold, a constellation of condiments. A masterpiece of marinades.

Created by her own exhilaration and slightly shaking hand.

One final flourish, a sprinkle of masala, and she is done.

Surveying her work she takes out her phone. Spends several minutes taking photographs.

Just one second pressing 'SEND.'

# Home Sweet Home aka A Recipe for Gaslighting

## Delphine Gauthier-Georgakopoulos

***Preparation:*** *10 minutes*
It had been cooking for years, but he hadn't noticed the rotten apple.

***Ingredients:***
*Butter: 125g*
*Sugar: 125g*
*Cocoa: 3 tablespoons*
*Flour: 175g*
*Egg: 1*

Henry rushed home happy as pie. He had all the ingredients for a lovely evening: good news, a bottle of wine, and flowers for the wife.

"Home sweet home!" he exclaimed, closing the front door.

Susan stood in the kitchen, looking at a recipe. She grabbed and threw the ingredients on the counter. An egg fell. She bent to clean it, swearing under her breath.

When Henry breezed into the kitchen, his smile evaporated as he watched Susan banging and clattering around. What had he done wrong this time? Did he forget her birthday? Their anniversary?

"Hello, Love," he said.

"Ah, you're back."

She looked up, sighed, and returned to her recipe. He walked on eggshells towards the fridge and laid the wine to cool before placing the flowers on the table. She remained silent, frowning.

***Mix the butter and sugar in a bowl.***
***Add the cocoa, flour and egg.***

He glanced at her as she mixed the butter and the sugar with her wooden spoon. She threw in the bitter cocoa, and he felt the familiar knot in his belly.

"What are you making, then?"

"Biscuits for work. It's Josie's last day tomorrow."

"That's nice of you."

"Yes, well, I'm a nice person."

"But you don't like Josie."

"Yes, well, I'm a really nice person."

***Work the dough into a ball.***

She worked the mix expertly, hands moulding it into a ball. He sat down, tapping his foot nervously.

"So, the job review —" he said.

"Dear Lord, not this again! You've been rambling on about it for days. I told you not to get your hopes up. You're not manager material!"

"But I got the promotion!"

"Well done ..."

***Using two teaspoons, place small balls of dough 5 cm apart on greaseproof paper.***

"I got you flowers, and I brought wine … But we could go out to celebrate?" he offered.

"No, I'm tired."

"Alright. Maybe this weekend, then?"

"..."

"I'll call David to share the good news."

"He knows."

"What do you mean, he knows?"

"I told him."

"You knew?"

"Of course, I knew. Your secretary blabs! She called as soon as she heard."

***Cooking time: 10 minutes - 190°C***

"So, me not getting my hopes up, not being manager material? What was that for?"

"I never said that."

"You just did! Not ten minutes ago!"

"I said no such thing. Putting words in my mouth, now? That's new! Is it 'big cheese' talking?"

"Are you kidding me?"

"Don't let it go to your head. You might be the boss at work, but you're not the boss of me!"

"What?"

"I could have had a career too, you know."

"What stopped you then?"

"Marrying you."

# Marriage (In Three Six-Sentence Stories)

Robert Scotellaro

## Accompaniment

She follows me around playing a tuba, says it suits my disposition. I play a viola outside the shower stall as the sudsy water circles the drain at her feet. During canasta we play air guitar, for there's no accounting for the wiles of chance. The sitar she plays as I'm getting ready for work annoys me—hyperbole has always been an irritant. The musical saw I play as she's shaving her legs puts her nerves on edge, but in the sack, the cymbals are cherished, handed back and forth. And in the morning sometimes, we play the timpani, after that second cup of coffee, just to keep us on our toes.

## Newfound

I bring home the wrong suitcase from the airport. It has a monocle, a black cape, and a book of prestidigitation tinged with dark arts in it. It takes a bit to learn how to keep the monocle in, and a good deal of squinting is required, but the cape is fetching and goes well with the pair of black chinos I break out. I somehow feel instantly transformed / powerful and a bit, strangely, aristocratic, as the cat glares at me suspiciously.

Though a bit blurry, I read the book of magic through the monocle all day instead of going to work. I learn sleight of hand and how to levitate while gravity slinks somewhere out of reach, and when my wife complains, with a wave of my cape, I make her disappear—well, not really, but yes, really too.

## The Jester

My wife hires the court jester from an agency and says, with a more than fair amount of conviction, it will be far less expensive than couples therapy. He arrives wearing a checkered vest and a derby hat, not at all like I expected, and tells the corniest jokes which keep Susan in stitches. He brings his own food, which is nice, and once ate peanut butter straight out of the jar with a spoon as he and I discussed Nietzsche. As soon as he leaves, Susan gives me "the look" and we scurry up to the bedroom and it's like the old days. The jester (who is no fool) and Susan enjoy gardening and he says his bawdy limericks are good for "enhanced floral vibrancy" and that they give a blush to the roses. Reading in the parlor: *The Cycle of Microclimates in the Western Hemisphere*, I look up at the gladiolas in a vase on the piano, I just might start playing again, and he's right—they have never looked happier.

# Wearing Disguises

## Matthew Hisbent

*Frere Jacques, Frere Jacques.*

*Doo-be-doo. Doo-be-doo.*

The sound of the door chimes shattered the townhouse silence.

My heart leapt.

I glanced at the bedroom mirror; its surface segmented by chevrons of late afternoon sunlight, flickering on and off as summer rain clouds scudded across the jagged peaks and shadow troughs of the Old Town cityscape. Amy, wronged woman, or sneak, stared accusingly back at me. That infernal tune burrowed wormlike deep into my ear. Pressed under a relentless thumb. (The doorbell, not me, but then again, who was I kidding?)

The purloined letter burned like acid on my fingers, daring me to open the lightly perfumed envelope. I feared the scarlet words might herald the second death of my marriage. Admittedly, it had been languishing on Death Row, temporarily reprieved but hopeful of a full pardon, while we tested the bubbling, fomenting waters with tentative toes. His pleas for forgiveness had weakened my resolve just long enough to allow him back through the front door. The children had been pleased. I had been wary. The scrap heap is a terrible place to be, and whilst there may be plenty more fish in the sea, I fear not for me. If one fish is poisoned, perhaps they all are. Yet I wanted to believe and for the moment, a truce sustained, separate bedrooms in operation.

The burning itch had started as Victor and the twins were departing to swim. Like herpes, it came on suddenly when I was stressed, this time precipitated by my urge to snoop around Tom's room, Victor's Elba for the moment. The twins, Tom and Lindy, were my life, the issue of Victor's first assault upon my virginity. He never felt the need to try too hard or too frequently again. The twins were now nine years old and had pushed his earlier betrayal into the background of their forgiving minds. Not so easy for me to forget the redhead, the little sports car or Victor leaping in before they drove off. I'd vowed that if he had left me for someone poorer, uglier, and positively skeletal I would kill him for my shame.

Till death us do part.

I stared at the envelope. My rock was an uncomfortable perch, but the hard place might mean hell for the twins.

*Frere Jacques, Frere Jacques, doo be doo, do be doo.*

For a moment I thought perhaps Victor had returned with the twins but had forgotten his key. My mum always said that no good came of snooping. Maybe not, but I had suspicions and an itch and maybe even a desire to find something. A photo, a lock of hair, a diary even. All I had found was a single page in an unsealed envelope, white with an ornate Florentine design inner, the faint whiff of a lady perfume rising on the currents of air. Every fibre in my body screamed 'read it, read it' but even as I hesitated that damned tune had rung out for the first time.

Insistent. Accusing. Demanding attention, the essence of Victor.

I was torn. Take the envelope or replace it? Prudence nagged. If Victor discovered it gone then our marriage was broken beyond repair, and I would have gifted him the moral high ground. Yet how could I be normal around him always wondering what the note might have revealed?

For better or for worse.

The rock made for an uncomfortable perch, but the hard place might be too tough on the twins.

I put it back in the small inner pocket of the black hold-all and zipped it closed. Exactly as I had found it. Walking slowly down the stairs I had time to take a couple of deep breaths and smooth my jeans.

In the opened doorway stood two half-drowned strangers.

Smiling bravely behind the rain-plastered hair, the slumped shoulders and the water dripping upon the stone steps. Soaked through and shivering. The rain was abating now thankfully but my entrance had no cover above three small steps to the street. No place for them to hide.

Young and handsome, blonde, and fey; younger versions of Victor and me.

Spooky.

They were dressed lightly for summer, little thinking of a sudden downpour. Their discomfort was tangible.

"Yes, can I help you?" I asked, cold and formal. Unwelcoming. There might yet be time to read the letter.

"Mrs Stein?" Handsome asked. I detected Wales in the accent. I nodded half-heartedly, cautiously. "We've come about the house."

"What house?" I asked, confused, sounding dumb.

"This house," the fey wee thing explained in a reedy, piping voice. I stared at them.

"What? This house? Why?" Hair trigger temper. My Achilles heel.

"It is for sale, isn't it?" he asked, but suddenly he didn't sound so sure or confident.

"Do you see a 'For Sale' board outside?" I demanded, more sarcastically than they deserved. I was beyond taking prisoners.

"We couldn't see anything with the rain battering in our faces," she answered very quickly. "That's not how we found out about it. Your husband mentioned it to me at the University. That's where we work." She fell quiet, realising that I obviously knew where Victor worked.

"He said it might be coming on the market soon," Handsome chimed in. "We are looking for a house in this area." He paused, reality dawning slow. "I think we might have jumped the gun. Yes?"

*Oh yes.*

I waited, nodding slowly, venom building behind the dam in my heart.

*Belief fading quickly.*

I didn't smile as I said good day, steadily closing the door upon their miserable faces, a mirror to the anger ravaging mine.

I would read the letter, though now I did not feel the necessity.

Already I was thinking about the bonfire I would set to Victor's vanity and how I would toss the fading remnants of our marriage onto the flames.

Then I would inter the ashes.

*Frere Jacques, Frere Jacque.*

*Ding ding dong.*

# The Search for Prince Charming

## Barbara Schilling Hurwitz

Evie squealed with delight watching her new princess dress twirl about her as she spun circles in front of the full-length mirror. Loose pink sparkles clung to her cheeks, and her mother snapped the keepsake moments. Someday, Evie imagined, she would be a real princess living in a castle where she would host a magnificent ball, and at the end of the evening, she'd sit upon her golden throne pondering her choice of princes with whom to live happily ever after.

Years gone by, Evie morphed into Evelyn, a single woman who traded social time for career building. After one mind numbing day she sat alone on her plush white sofa sipping wine wiggling her tired pink painted toes. While she maintained her princess-like beauty, turning heads as she passed, there was no prince in her life, no little girl to pass along the child-sized trousseau of ball gowns stashed in her parents' attic. It had been too long since her mother had passed while still pining for grandchildren to photograph, and her father had expressed his regret of her unfulfilled dreams. "Enough," Evelyn told herself. "Only one time around in this life," and she was not going to go through it alone any longer. "Match.com to the rescue."

Lunch dates followed. Meet ups for cocktails, speed dating, and blind dates. None that offered Evelyn the relationship of her dreams.

Try Catch or My-Date, Swipe-Left, her friends suggested but nothing proved successful.

Then one evening, a friend who trolled the sites for her phoned. "I found him. The guy for you! He responded with the pseudonym and emoji of Prince Charming to mine of you as Cinderella. He's everything you are, hardworking but longs for a companion. He's athletic, enjoys fine food, wants to travel ..."

"Too good to be true," Evelyn said, "but ok I'll meet him."

"Good, I've set up your date for tomorrow, 7:00 PM at Tess's on 49th Street.

Evelyn arrived a few minutes early, and precisely on time, her eyes met Prince Charming's.

"Dad," she said, "what are you doing here?"

# Mintie Paper

## Leone Gabrielle

Asleep in a house never locked, I snuggle into my man. Tightly wedged in a mash of pillows and one dog. Something falls into my ear. A bug. I think a bug. Dribbling at slug speed. Into my ear. Human fingers too thick to follow. I tell myself, get up. I turn around. This damp slow snowing thing, an unwelcome bouquet like yard-dogs barking, like light lightning in summers dry. Night laments, trapped in tight corners. Closer and closer. Itchy. Echoes my ear inhales.

Sensitive are canal hairs. Red warning memories, primary school lessons, on what not to poke into an ear. Concealed in my girl box are tweezers. The girl box by the wardrobe. Where I dress in sight of my languid man. I live only with male company who have no need of private instruments for womanly whiskers. The box holds hairbrush and mirror. Lives next to the underpants and bra box. Cardboard Aldi boxes that used to hold apples. Red and green.

I pull from my ear this crawling vex. In the beak of the tweezers, a paper Mintie ribbon. Like the ones I used to make on long journeys. Ripping delicately a wrapper into the longest long ribbon possible. This is the bug, demanding to be withdrawn. Gently, I tell myself to converse with this long shelling story, a story tied on a thin torn ribbon.

My Alabaster sits up. He sits up in our dark lounge room, a hunched mass waiting to steady his balance. A new habit I assume brought home from the pulmonary sessions at ambulatory care. He stands up. His long oblong body leans towards the bathroom. Cutting the dark with lanky strides. Snow white limbs meeting underpants. In his wake I roll like a ninja cat. Soundless, for the laundry toilet. Our dog disturbed, stands bewildered. Then bustles his shovel nose back into the waves of our single bed.

A light informs me, from the open toilet, that my son is up. His phone's torch, loud. I hear him drinking at the kitchen sink. Finish my quickened wee. He, wearing yesterday's uniform, replaces me. In the sleeping lounge I feel out the girl box. Digging the tweezers backward. Scrape the hairs of my inner ear. Alabaster in passing asks 'what are you doing?'

'Nothing.'

I race back to our bed. On the side of gravity, pressed into his back and the wall.

Asleep. I read the dreams written on that ribbon wrapper. Imprints like scent on fresh laid cement. A path led by the perfume of a story. I am realising how sad I'd feel to be as deaf as my loveable man. Missing the calls of night airs that tango, their word-heels pricking my skin. This memory ribbon melts like a Mintie in my mouth, after slowly, slowly sucking.

# Squatter

## Chuka Susan Chesney

When we were first married, we lived in a commune with forty pages of rules we never bothered to read. When we moved in, I was seven months pregnant. It was okay at first. We had a bedroom suite off the living room.

But after we had the baby, things got weird. The lady who ran the commune told us she didn't like all the baby stuff in the living room—playpen, burp cloths, and stroller. She said we could only change the baby in the garage. So we went and lived with my mom for a month. A lot of our stuff was still in the bedroom at the commune. The lady told us we had to clear out since we didn't live there anymore. She said we no longer contributed, so we found a cottage and moved.

Then we realized we'd left my frozen placenta behind in the freezer.

My husband called and the lady's boyfriend answered.

"Hey, dude. We left Brie's placenta in the freezer. Can we stop by and get it?"

The lady's boyfriend replied, "You're not supposed to come by anymore."

My husband said, "Yeah, but Brie really needs the placenta."

"Yeah, well, we're not supposed to let you in. Besides, you didn't pay your food bill last month. Pay and you can have the placenta."

"But we didn't even eat there the whole month. We were staying with my mother-in-law."

"Well, you were technically living here — your stuff was here, so you need to pay for food."

"Are you telling me you're going to hold the placenta hostage until we pay for food we never ate?"

"Yeah."

"Okay, I'm going to call your employer and let him know you're holding our placenta hostage."

"Whoa, Dude, no, chill, you can have the placenta."

"When should we come by?"

"Right away."

We drove over to the commune. I got out of the car and rang the doorbell. Boyfriend came to the door, holding a paper lunch bag neatly folded at the top.

"Thanks," I said.

"Bye," he replied, and closed the door softly. That's one of the rules.

No noise.

# Maybe Next Time

## Raquel Levitt

"Jesse came to see me last night."

"You mean you had a dream about him."

"No. I mean he came to see me."

"Jesse's dead, Mom."

"Please don't talk to me like I'm stupid. I know he's dead. Physically he is dead. Spiritually, he's very much alive."

"What did he say?"

"Not a lot, really. He smiled at me and held my hand. It was as if we were communicating with our souls, like we used to, letting our eyes and the warmth of our hands tell each other just how much we still love each other."

Jesse was the love of her life, the man she met when she was thirty and married to my dad. He came into her life like love tends to do, out of nowhere, and knocked her for a loop. She claimed to have loved my father and was therefore confounded how someone else could walk into her world and shake the foundation of her marriage to its core, but somehow Jesse did. She fought hard against her feelings, or so she says, for my dad's sake and eventually mine, and although she succeeded in not crossing any physical boundary of infidelity, emotionally she failed miserably.

Jesse connected with my mom on some sort of higher or deeper level; something my dad apparently couldn't do. He lived in our town for only two years but it was long enough to prove to my mother that people can communicate with their hearts and minds, no words or kisses necessary. Eventually, Jesse got a job offer in another state and moved away, but his memory took up permanent residence in her mind and for the next twenty years thoughts of him almost drove my mother over the edge.

Something I admire about her is that she never let on that she was having a moral crisis, that there were certain times a year when she would dream about him and her yearning would last for days. It was during those times she obsessed about him, fantasizing what life with him would have been like. She admitted to emotionally pulling back from me and my dad for several days at a time, apparently unaware or not caring that neither of us noticed. She said she would have to fight like hell to get out of "the clutches of where I wanted to be as opposed to where I was." When she admitted that, it felt like a punch to my gut or a slap to my face or any other cliché referring to hearing something unexpected and hurtful from the one person who should know better. Mothers aren't supposed to have desires. They aren't supposed to fall in love with someone other than their husband. They aren't supposed to reveal their secrets to their daughters.

The first time she spilled her guts to me was the night of my father's funeral while she and I were sitting at the dinner table surrounded by casseroles and flowers. I quickly ran through the typical responses: shock, disbelief, and then self-righteous anger. "You're thinking of another man on the day you bury your husband of twenty-eight years? Nice, Mom."

"I'm sorry, Sweetheart. I figure now that your father's on the other side, he knows everything. No reason for me to hide anything anymore."

"You're just feeling guilty," I said. "You're telling me this to feel absolved."

"No. I'm telling you this because I want you to know the soul's capacity to love is bigger than our society is willing to accept. It is possible to love two people at the same time."

*Bullshit* I wanted to say in defense of my newly deceased father but I didn't. "Whatever makes you feel better," I said as I patted her hand. The way she stared into me at that moment made me understand clearly. She was telling the truth. "So out of decency are you going to wait a few days before you call Jesse?" My mom didn't answer. She stared at me a little longer and then withdrew her hand from mine. She then stood and walked upstairs. There had been a perceptible shift in her eyes from tenderness to pain. She didn't need to say anything. I had said too much.

It was as if she had transferred her obsession to me because for weeks afterward, I thought of Jesse. I waited for my mom to tell me she had tracked him down and that he was divorced or had never married due to his inability to get over her, but that never happened. Finally, I couldn't stand it any longer.

"Are you going to call him or do I have to?" I asked her.

"What on earth are you talking about?"

"You know exactly what I'm talking about."

"Sweetheart, Jesse died two years before your father died."

"Are you kidding??" I didn't understand. It just seemed cruel. "Why didn't you tell me?"

"What does it matter?"

*It matters because you're still in love with a dead guy.*

"How did you hear about it? I thought you never contacted him."

"I didn't. I received a letter from his best friend. He sent me the obituary and a note saying 'I thought you'd want to know.'"

"So, you knew his best friend?"

She shook her head. "No."

"Well, then how did he know to send it to you?"

"Jesse must have told him about me."

I was frustrated and obviously more upset about the shitty circumstance than she was. "It's so unfair that you spent years of your life loving someone in silence and never getting the opportunity to tell him."

"I told you, Sweetheart. I didn't have to tell him. He just knew."

"But aren't you angry that you'll never be with your true love?"

"Maybe next time, I will."

She said 'maybe' but her eyes told me she was certain of it.

# Driving Lesson

## Hedva Anbar

- Right, I said. RIGHT. Why are you indicating left? That's the fourth time today. Yes, the fourth. I've been counting. Lucky the road's almost empty. That's because everyone believes the weather forecast and they're scared of getting caught in the storm. Well, that's one lesson I've learnt, the weather forecast is ALWAYS wrong.
- MIRROR. How many times have I told you? You have to check the mirror every time before you signal, change direction, slow down and stop.
- What gear are you in? You should be in fourth. We'll never get there at this rate. I hope they keep the room. They don't keep rooms forever, you know.
- Windscreen wipers! I know exactly what you're thinking. Why have I picked a route with dark narrow undulating roads? Wouldn't it be easier and quicker on the motorway? Yes, it would, but learner drivers aren't allowed on the motorway.
- MIRROR.
- Slow down. You have to drive extra carefully in a downpour. Slow down, I said. SLOW DOWN. Don't you know by now that you mustn't overtake on the left? You'll never pass your test at this rate. What a fool I'll look. I know just what they'll say. A driving instructor for seven years and can't even teach his own wife to drive.

- Left at the next turning. Left, I said. LEFT. Why are you indicating right? That's the fifth time today. Yes, it is. I've been counting.
- Don't just sit there like a sack of potatoes. You'll fail the test if you stand still when it's safe and correct to proceed.
- Brakes. Clutch. You're coasting again. You should be learning on a computer operated car that you just tell it where you want to go and it.
- Accelerator. MIRROR.
- You almost grazed that car.
- CANCEL THE INDICATOR. I know what you're thinking. We'd get there quicker if I drove. But I don't need to drive. I KNOW how to drive. YOU'RE the one who has to learn to drive. And if you're going to pass your test first go you need to practise whenever you have the chance.
- Don't stop. It's your right of way.
- STOP. Can't you see he's trying to get out? Never forget – consideration and courtesy are the key qualities of a good driver.
- Straight through the water. That's right.
- What gear are you in? You should be in third. At this rate it'll be after midnight by the time we get there. I'd better phone and let them know we're on our way. Damn. No bloody signal. Not you, the phone. They won't keep the room. No chance.
- Careful, there's some sort of obstruction on the road ... looks like a fallen tree.
- MIRROR.
- Look how close you are to the curb.
- YOU'RE TOO FAR FROM THE CURB.
- Right. Right, I said. RIGHT.
- Accelerator. Accelerator, I said.
- Why are you braking?

– Stalled? Try again. Try again. Let me. Must be the rain. Out of petrol? Damn. I must have forgotten. Understandable given how hectic it's been, what with ferrying your aunts and uncles from the station to the church and from the church to the hall and from the hall to the station ... You should have reminded me. Why didn't you remind me? Still no signal. God knows where the nearest open filling station is. I don't suppose you brought an umbrella? I can't leave the car in these clothes. I'll get soaked through and catch a chill and before you can say Jack Robinson I'll be in hospital with pneumonia. We'll just have to spend the night in the car. Don't worry. We'll be all right. It's very comfortable. The seats tilt all the way back. And I've got rugs ... a flask ... some great music. Quite romantic in a way. I bet we'll be the first couple to spend the first night of their honeymoon on the road in a car with dual controls. Shame there are no blinds ... but that doesn't really matter, does it? There'll be no peeping Toms in weather like this.

# Guilt Edged

## John Maskey

"Is THIS it?"

Frank had hoped for a better response. It had cost him a fortune.

"It's great inside," he said. "Come on, I'll get the bags."

"It looks nothing like the photograph you showed me," said Rachel, making no move to get out of the car. "It's a bit gloomy."

"Jesus, Rachel. Give it a chance will you? This is our anniversary break. I've gone to a lot of effort."

"Don't go off on one. I just thought – "

But Frank was out of the car and walking up the steps of the hotel before she could finish.

Rachel hung back but as she watched Frank step inside the hotel she gathered her luggage and followed.

Inside, the hotel was luxurious. Their feet sank into the carpet. Chandeliers twinkled, casting beads of light on gilt-framed paintings on wood-panelled walls. The large gull staircase made her momentarily fantasise about being Ginger Rogers, not with Frank as Fred Astaire, but Tom. Frank danced with the finesse of a man wearing diving boots.

"I'm sorry," she said, squeezing his hand as they walked up the stairs. There was more gilt on the balustrade, and more guilt building up in Rachel. "I was a bitch just now."

He smiled. "This is our room."

The lock clunked as he inserted the card key. He pushed the door open and let Rachel in first, wanting to savour her reaction.

"Oh. My. God."

A four-poster bed dominated the room, while a plush Chesterfield settee added *olde worlde* charm. Matching wing-back chairs sat in the bay window. A bottle of champagne resting in an ice bucket and two glasses stood on a mahogany table.

Rachel joined Frank as he opened the bubbly. She took her drink from him and they clinked glasses. She looked out at the sapphire sea and sipped, taking Frank's hand in hers.

"What are you thinking about?" he asked.

The answer was Tom. And how she would love to spend a weekend here with him. They would emerge from the bed only to marvel at the expansive ocean view then jump back under the covers.

She needed to be careful about what she said. And try not to think about Tom, especially during sex.

Frank deserved a good anniversary weekend. Seven years of marriage had been good, largely. She would tell him about Tom, but not now.

Later, perhaps after Christmas. 'New Year, new start' was the phrase people used. This weekend would be a celebration of what she once felt for Frank. She still loved him in a way, just not like before.

"I'm thinking about what a lovely treat this is," she said. "Thank you." They kissed longer than usual.

Frank smiled.

It pleased him that Rachel was happy with the surprise he had laid on. She deserved a memorable weekend. It eased the guilt he had felt since meeting Carolyn. He would tell her, but not now.

Later, perhaps after Christmas.

# Happy Wedding. Are You Out of Your Mind?

## Paul Beckman

A cabin really. You want to carry me across the threshold of this termite and bug-infested log cabin? What called to you that said, "charm"? Was it the dank mattress as thin as a duvet or the flickering gas light that could burn us up while we slept? If we could sleep. Oh, I have no doubt that you could sleep. Was the fact that you couldn't find a Motel 3 around why you had to settle on this? Of course, I'd like a drink, yes, leave the bottle, Jameson's Irish unless they only have moonshine. Do you have any idea how much my parents paid for the wedding or just the flowers not to mention the band and the open bar and all your friends from kindergarten on up? No, you wouldn't have any idea because not coming from money was our hindrance for all these years. Cheetos? What's the matter, was the country store out of pork rinds? This calls for another drink. No, let me pour my own. It's no wonder you said our honeymoon was a surprise. You might have said it was an embarrassment. I feel itchy just being in this so-called cabin and my allergies are beginning to act up. It's after four in the morning and no I can't close my eyes and get a little sleep. I'm afraid they would stay shut from fear. What, you want me to get up from this fine bean bag chair and come stand by the window with you. What makes you think the sun coming up will make a difference on our wedding night? My cousin, Sarah, told me she had a feeling and begged me not to go through with this. Because I loved you. Still? I can't think that hard, yes, pull me up from Mr. Beanbag and I'll stand by the picture window with you. No, I don't want to walk out on the deck and sit in an ersatz Adirondack chair. Okay, but bring the bottle and I'll hang on to my glass. What's the sun doing between those clouds? Hmm, these colors. Of course, I know it's coming up but when I look straight out, I see it reflecting off something. Okay, I'll give you that. It is beautiful. Breathtaking even. How big is that lake and does anyone swim in it besides creatures that go glug in the night? It's all part of this property? Well, yes, but if you took your start-up public you could have sold some lakefront land and built us a proper house. Why are you taking my hand? Where are we going? The back door? The one with spiders and stuff. Yes, I've gone this far, and I'll follow you up that path behind the hill. Wow! Now that's a house that a girl wouldn't mind being carried across its threshold. I'm coming, don't rush me. But I saw the sun over the lake already. No, not from that house. Is it VRBO?? What time is check out? This is the most gorgeous view I've ever seen and yes now you can carry me across the threshold. Oh my, look, a view of the lake from every window. Yes, I could be comfortable here. Why do you ask? You bought the land and designed this house? What about the cabin? Oh, as a reminder.

# First Attempt

## Jan McCarthy

Joanna West read all the books that tell you how to live happy and fulfilled, but failed to put the experts' advice into practice.

She saved hard to move to the city from her parents' place on the coast, found a job in domiciliary care and put herself out there, dating random men. One wet Saturday afternoon, however, waiting at the bus stop, she was confronted by an impressive array of muscles and tatts with a not un-handsome head perched on top. Tom was a builder working on a fixer-upper two doors down from her place.

He said he'd been watching her, which normally would have freaked her out, but he only seemed to want to talk about his plastering exploits and flair for replacement floors. It seemed a more promising start to a relationship than picking up guys in bars and clubs. At least Joanna was sober when she gave him her phone number. They courted for six months. He was predictable: flowers, chocs, high street jewellery. On the anniversary of their first meeting, he presented an engagement ring that had belonged to his granny and asked Jo to move in with him. She let him persuade her. While hers was boho shabby chic with an upstairs neighbour who practised tap-dancing at 3am and a heating system with IBS, Tom's was all sleek lines and high tech.

He'd done a complete refurb himself and sold Joanna their new life together like she was destined for paradise and he was the archangel to fly her there. She'd never seen a robot vacuum cleaner in motion, or played with voice-activated lights. It needs plants and cushions, she told him. He'd often mocked her fluffy cushions and cacti collection, but said she'd make the place feel homier, it was something women knew how to do. He kissed her on the nose and told her she was cute.

She knew she was inclined to go for comfort over excitement, but wasn't that the sensible approach to life? Her friends were off exploring the planet, posting photos from Bai Sao, Blue Lagoon, Railay, doing bar work to fund their travels. But what would they have to show for it once they were back, said Tom. Nothing saved in the pension pot. He'd already opened a joint savings account and sorted out life insurance. Wasn't the future more important than the present? She silenced her inner adventuress and settled down.

Tom seemed determined to get Joanna pregnant, which was only fun when she wasn't on nights. Having failed to knock her up by Christmas, he decided it was because she wanted a house with a garden, for nesting purposes. She'd get pregnant once she had a proper place.

The crumbling rural ruin was within budget, but a tough renovation project she couldn't contribute to, so it wasn't long before he took up moaning as a second hobby. When Joanna went to stay with her mother for a week to give her ears a rest, she was advised that was just men all over. Males judged themselves by social status, money and property. Be grateful, Mum said. Men with practical skills are like gold dust. Suck it up. You made your bed.

The following Sunday, Joanna and Tom were invited to a barbecue. Tom's old mates from his home town of Ely were meeting up. It was an annual event, but Joanna's first time. She'd been too nervous before. All the women in the photos Tom showed her looked like *Love Island* candidates, more plastic than flesh. She'd found a way to duck out in previous years, but this time he sprung it on her the day before and she was too taken by surprise to think of an excuse.

Ushered into the garden, napkin-wrapped vegeburger in one hand, glass of OJ in the other, Joanna soon grew tired of following Tom around. The man was too busy talking cricket with his mates and hugging fake boobs to introduce her. She grabbed a bottle of vodka and an ice bucket and looked for somewhere green and shady.

A no-fly zone encircled the bench where she sat, slumped under a mimosa tree like a doll nobody wants to play with. None of the women came over. They huddled in their bikini tops and short shorts drinking Prosecco while the men grilled meat and drank beer from the bottle. Joanna stuck it out till ten, caught a cab home. Tom rolled in much later, turned on the TV, stayed on the couch. Neither of them had anything to say in the morning.

Monday lunchtime, popping to the pharmacy for yet another over-the-counter pregnancy test, Joanna was surprised to see Tom, smartly dressed and sitting at a pavement table of the café opposite. Joanna watched from behind a display of condoms as Norah-next-door appeared from inside the café carrying two glasses of wine. Joanna checked the test kit in her hand. A single line. Thank god. I've been conning myself, she thought. It's gone cold and it was only ever lukewarm from the start. As if she needed more of a shove, Tom and Norah's heads collided in a face-suck that made the two blue rinse biddies at the next table purse their lips in disgust.

She had four hours before Tom would return. While she thought of what to put in a farewell note, she packed her car with suitcases and boxes. Every cushion, every houseplant – all the extras Tom said only attracted dust – Joanna scooped up until there was just enough room to drive comfortably and get the hell out of Dodge. How much of a nothing their whole life together had been.

She'd dump her stuff at her mother's. Tolerate the I-told-you-so's. And then she'd see where Angie and Tasha were at, grab her passport and a bikini, and vanish.

# Invisible Labor

## Hillary Campos

She held still, not even daring to breathe as the crying began in the next room. If she squinted (she couldn't risk reaching for her glasses), she could just barely see the glowing numbers on her alarm clock: 3:13am.

She was not getting up.

She could feel her husband stirring. The mattress moaned under his weight, giving her just enough time to breathe deeply and curl up even tighter into the blanket. (She didn't want him to hear her moving!) She had already spent the last nine months in a sleepless, miserable daze. Getting up to pee multiple times each night. Getting up to adjust herself when her arms grew numb. Getting up to adjust her lumpy pillow. Getting up because she'd been kicked in the bladder (again).

She was not getting up.

The baby surely wasn't hungry. She had just fed him. (Hadn't she?). She was always feeding him – just a leaky faucet of milk constantly on call. Every outfit had to be coordinated with feeding. (Would she be able to easily pull this shirt up or that dress down?) Every appointment had to be carefully scheduled. (Could she make it to the store before he needed to eat again?) Every meal had to be carefully considered. (How would he react if she ate dairy or tomatoes or spicy food?) She couldn't even have a glass of wine without thinking of him! She was nothing more than a servant to a tiny, imperious master.

She was not getting up.

Perhaps if she just nudged her husband slightly. She gave him a quick elbow to his side and an "accidental" kick to his leg. Nothing too noticeable, but something sharp enough to pull him out of his REM cycle. (God, she couldn't even remember what a REM cycle felt like!)

She was not getting up.

The crying intensified to a persistent wail. It was truly amazing that such a small creature could create such a racket. And still, he slept like a rock. No, she was the one sleeping like a rock – since, after all, rocks don't actually sleep. (What was the purpose of that useless cliché anyways?) He was sleeping like a hibernating bear – undisturbed and unaware.

She was not getting up.

And now, to add insult to injury, her husband was snoring. Deep, long inhales. Grumbling, gargling exhales. Each cacophonous breath stoked the rage that was burning inside her. Was he trying to shove it in her face that he was sleeping soundly while she was lying awake? Each rasping snore felt like a sharp slap in the face. (Maybe she should literally slap him in the face! Ha!)

She was not getting up.

She sighed, hoping that he would hear her frustration and desperation and anger in that one breath. When he didn't move, she sighed again – but louder. All of the midnight diaper changing and burping and feeding and rocking and bouncing and singing. All she wanted was one night (just ONE night!) where she could stay in bed. Was that too much to ask?

She was not getting up.

Waah. Waah. WAAAAAHHHH!

Surely, he was not sleeping through this commotion. Jesus! It was shocking that the neighbors hadn't called the police to report a noise ordinance violation! It's a good thing they'd never had a house fire – they all would have burned in their sleep while this oaf slept through the shrieking fire alarms and the shrill engine sirens! (And he said he was a light sleeper! Bah!)

She was not getting up.

She was not getting up.

She was not getting up.

The sun rose, and little streaks of light peeked through the blinds. His eyes fluttered open and focused on the clock: 8:06am. "I think that's the first time the baby slept through the night," he yawned, turning over to face his wife.

But she was not there. She was already up.

# Choices

## Ronald T. Hardwick

'That'll be eight pounds, please,' says the taxi-driver.

Peter Harris feels in his pocket.

'Keep the change.'

'Ta, Guv.' The driver pulls away with a cheery wave.

Peter steps out into the cold, grey dawn. It is one of those bleak winter days in which it will never be truly light. A steady drizzle falls on his bare head, and he is obliged to turn up his collar against the cold.

The decision Peter has taken surprises him – until now he's felt he's too weak a person to go through with it. He drags a suitcase on wheels behind him as he steps through the graceful Georgian porte-cochere of the railway station and enters the train shed proper. He glances up at the clock, under which a myriad of lovers have met for well over a century – the time is six-ten. He has twenty minutes to wait for the arrival of the London train.

'Which platform for London?' he asks a uniformed guard.

'Platform seven, over the footbridge and past the first-class lounge.' The guard points the way with his flag.

Peter nods and walks towards the turnstiles, sets down his case, removes his spectacles, and cleans them. He tends to do this when he is apprehensive. He is apprehensive now. He sees 'open' on the coffee shop door.

'Cappuccino, please,' he asks a young black man serving behind the counter.

'Three pounds sixty,' says the young man, and Peter pays him. In exchange, he receives a cardboard beaker, with a plastic top, full of scalding hot coffee. He returns to the concourse and finds an uncomfortable perforated metal bench upon which to sit. He has trouble punching a hole in the plastic top and almost spills the coffee down the front of his overcoat.

A parcels truck rumbles by, light flashing, squawking like an anxious blackbird. An elderly gentleman seats himself next to Peter.

'Truck's nearly empty – they don't send parcels by rail like they used to when I was a lad. It's all by road now.'

'Plus ça change ...' says Peter.

'What's that?' asks the old man.

'Everything changes; nothing remains the same.'

'Too true,' says the old man.

Peter nods to him, stands up and walks towards the wooden overbridge. A diesel engine thunders under it, hauling a heavy load of cement wagons. The bridge shakes with the weight of the freight on the rails.

Peter ponders on the twenty-five years of strife his marriage has endured – a wife who never took the trouble to understand him and two greedy and selfish children, all living in a small terraced house on the bad side of the city.

His job is as hopeless as his marriage, selling insurance to people who have no interest in buying it. His boss, Mr Thomson, told him a week ago:

'Mr Harris, if your figures don't improve, I'm afraid we're going to have to let you go.'

Peter knows his figures will never improve. Thank goodness for the internet, which has given him the chance to escape all that misery and torture.

'Je ne parle a great deal of Francais,' he mutters to himself.

A northbound train slides into an adjacent platform and half-a-dozen folk, wrapped warmly against the cold, disembark.

Outside the station another cab pulls up. A woman of early middle-age rummages in her handbag and carefully hands over eight pounds plus a fifty pence tip.

'Last of the big spenders,' says the cab driver as he speeds away. She purses her lips at his rudeness, then adjusts her hat. She is a plain woman, but there is something in her posture that suggests she is formidable, uncompromising. She marches into the station, scattering a flock of pigeons scratching around the marble floor for crumbs. She sees that the exit door from the platforms is open and sprints through it before a woman in a red cap can close it.

'There you are,' she says to Peter, 'thought you could get away on your own, did you?'

'Pauline,' says Peter, jaw dropping.

'I think you'd better come home with me,' she says, hands on hips.

'I'm leaving you,' says Peter.

'You're leaving me, are you? A man who can neither make a bed, iron a shirt or cook a meal? You won't last five minutes.'

'I have to do this.'

'What about me? What about the children?'

'They're hardly children.'

'You still owe us all something after everything we've given you. We've been married a quarter of a century. That must mean something to you.'

'Long and wasted years.'

'What?'

'Nothing. A song title. Bob Dylan.'

'I've done my best. If you board that train, there'll be no turning back – you're out for good.'

Peter takes his spectacle case from his pocket again, opens it and rubs the lenses of his spectacles till they gleam like diamonds under the station lamps. He looks at his watch. It's almost half-past six. Pauline bars his way – defiant, challenging. His feet seem to be nailed to the floor. He tries to move, to push Pauline aside, to force his way over the footbridge onto the platform, to board the train, to escape to a future of happiness and fulfilment. He can't. He stands, transfixed. A passenger rushes by and gasps to his companion – 'Quick, or we'll miss it.'

The train screeches to a halt. Passengers disembark. The guard stands, flag unfurled, waiting for permission to move the train onwards. He receives the signal, nods and waves his flag. Peter watches the train pull away from the platform. His eyes are clouded with tears.

Pauline puts out a hand, and says, softly:

'Come on, we'll get the bus home - it'll be cheaper than a taxi.'

Peter grasps her hand like a little boy clutching an ice-cream cone. The pair leave the station and head towards Benjamin Street, where their bus is waiting.

# Signals

## Fabiana Elisa Martínez

A rising flare from beneath my sternum. Like the distant fleeting stars we used to admire, both of us mesmerized by their impetus and silence, against the orange sunsets at the Cape from Corina, our tiny sailboat. When I still believed in him, my husband, and my heart sang immune to erosion and pain. Like the real omens, those that swerve our existence on the path of life, mine comes from inside.

I move my hand to my stomach to contain the feeling, the mix of dread and abysmal curiosity. My daughter must think I am going to be sick and immediately puts her arm around my shoulders and lowers her head to whisper in my ear if I need to get up, walk away, breathe. I vaguely refute with my left hand, the one adorned now by two wedding rings, mine inside the orbit of Henry's. I straighten up, feel the impious touch of the pew on my backbones, and inhale the incensed dusty air in which musical notes still vibrate.

Pastor Rowling is complimenting Henry's life with a decorated speech I cannot follow. Neither am I able to explain to my daughter, busy in the labyrinth of her confused tears, that I welcome my abrupt movement because it is the first life sensation I have seized since the news of Henry's accident.

The signal inside me is pristine, clear, and transparent like the fado songs I used to hate and now understand. Like an advanced echo of a pain that has the power to make you stronger. There is a presence in this church, some disturbance in the atoms that surround us, some unintelligible dispersion of the notes of the hymns that our family and friends and neighbors sing and will continue singing until the end of the funeral. I do not need the walls to crumble, or the clouds to roar, or the flowers on the coffin to wither faster, to know that something I am not brave enough to face is waiting for me on the left aisle.

With suspended eyes, I watch the slideshow that Maggie has created by herself, frustrated by my distance. I see again, through the veil of a callous soul that has been trained not to look at the past, images of happy family moments that were only blissful at the very beginning of my marriage, when we raised the sails of Corina, and disintegrated one doubt at a time on the cobblestones of Lisbon and the silent hallways of our house in Concord. My fading smile in all those pictures weaker and weaker, like the phases of a unique moon destined only to wane and finally disappear into the black sky, never to be seen again by the green eyes of the man I used to love so much.

Even eternal funerals end. There is always thirst and hunger and tempting rays of sun emanating signals to the brains of those who dare to remain alive. Mrs. Holland, the roughhewn administrator and real queen of the church is instructing the visitors. A gigantic mother goose in the care of adult ducklings in search of peace and the condolence cookies that follow burials and Good Fridays.

Maggie helps me stand up. I stumble to the left, a solitary bride now, dressed in black, more pushed than embraced by a daughter who is too old to care about peacock feathers anymore, who forgot the musical language she learned before English, and never guessed the dark secrets of a father who always had other things to do.

As I pass the rows of pews, I touch their dark wood in a solemn gesture of abandon. I am a new Orpheus who already knows that our beloved will never follow us. The narrow path of tiles unfolds underneath my feet like a chessboard. The silent cry inside my bones intensifies. Some people extend their hands to me. Only one lands three fingers on my knuckles and demands with terror that I turn to its owner.

Our eyes lock. We both have shared shadows and breezes on different sides of one ocean. We both have held a tight rope of sorrow. We are tired and just realized that we have stopped being the two catheti of a right triangle that was very wrong. Nobody here knows who she is, except for me and except for the one who lays in the front, prisoner of the cedar and velvet of a coffin that will never open again. She cries as silently as the far stars. I do too. She is beautiful, with her short hair and her square jaw, with the same dignity her grandmother must have had at the same age, but with less determination. I wonder if she can imagine how much I know about her. We were forced into a sisterhood that I honored. I was able to decode in the end the reason for her in my life.

Maggie pushes me forward. Pressed, not knowing which is the incantation for the world to stop just ten seconds so I can contemplate my nemesis and my savior for a small eternity, I grab Andréia's hand. I squeeze her delicate joints and try to steal from her the warmth of all the Portuguese suns that caressed her skin as Henry did. I still have time to feel the last call from a universe that makes sense despite all of us. I touch the tip of her deformed finger, another legacy of the woman who raised her and protected me while I sat under the rain with my baby under the eaves of an ancient castle in Lisbon. My rival utters a drowned word that I do not comprehend. It does not matter anymore. I nod and walk away from my dead husband, his puzzling beautiful lover, and all the trembling shadows of the one I will never be again.

# A Way to Get Through

## Christine Collinson

They find a picnic spot on the hillside with enough shade to temper the late summer heat. "You set the rug down, I'll fetch the basket!" Malcom calls as he returns to the car. Sarah, shielding her eyes from the gold-glare, looks out across the valley and sighs. The last picnic of the year perhaps; the first year since VE Day, nearly passed.

For a while they eat in unbroken quiet, surrounded only by birdsong and the gentle stir of the breeze. "This fresh ham is excellent, Sarah. The butcher's come good again." He brushes stray crumbs from his beard. "How far away it all seems on days like this."

She dabs the corners of her mouth with a napkin, then replies. "Yesterday, I met up with my friend from town. Miriam, you may remember. Lives off Rushton Street. She saw you coming out of a shelter one time, with a lady."

He jerks his hand as though swatting an invisible gnat. "That could've been somebody else. Easy to make a mistake in a crowd, in a brief instance."

"She swore it was you, on God's honour."

"Standing beside a stranger!" He laughs.

"With your arm hooked through hers."

"She's making stories, your friend. Give it up now, Sarah."

She looks straight at him with grey-flecked eyes. "I found a pearl earring, down the back of the chaise-langue in our room. That first time we stayed at the house again."

His shoulders stiffen. She doesn't need to keep looking to know it. Already knew it. That single earring, a pearlescent drop of guilt. She'd tried to picture the face beside the pretty lobe, the colour of the hair, the shade of complexion. Did the woman's dress suit her colouring or mar it. Couldn't; ceased to try, to care.

"One earring, really! The housekeeper could've mislaid that."

She snorts. "Her wage wouldn't buy one-hundredth of a pearl. No need to try that line with me, dear."

He strokes his moustache like always when he's nervous. "Are we, are we still alright, darling?"

"Oh, Malcolm. Don't you remember the chap you sent to do the garden while you were in town?"

He stares at her, like a man lost to the undercurrent.

She begins to pack up the basket. Wedges of Victoria sponge and some leftover plums, beginning to garner wasps. "You needn't look so aggrieved. We all had to find our own way to get through."

# How a Broken Bone Can Reset a Marriage

## Arlene Schindler

In marriage vows there's the "for better or for worse" that people kind of skim over on their way to the exchanging of rings, a wedding toast, and cake. My friend Edie got married at 63, and six months later, her husband had a heart attack. What a grueling thing for newlyweds to deal with. So, I questioned if a "late in life marriage" was a good idea.

It turns out, I married a year later than Edie to a man who was 65 and never married before. I called him a "fresh from the box newbie." My friends marveled. They forgot that before we were even engaged, we'd dealt with his cancer surgery and three months of treatments that took us to living in another city. We were pros at adversity.

Then, last month I tripped on a raised piece of concrete on a busy city street that sent me flying into the air and crashing down. I fell hard onto the concrete. Attempting to break the fall, I seriously broke my right wrist which caused a truly horrifying distortion of my hand's relationship to my arm. Additionally, I sustained significant soft tissue injuries in both the left wrist and arm. My chin hit the concrete causing a huge black bruise resembling a goatee and a nasty swollen chin knot that still persists. My face and right knee had cuts and bruising as well. Breaking one arm, fracturing another with soft tissue damage ravaged both arms and my face. Not pretty was the least of it.

This has been one of the most challenging experiences of my life. I now have use of only my left thumb and index finger. I can't lift anything. I can't dress myself. I only drink from straws.

Terry, my husband, is a good nurse but there's been lots of pain, physical and emotional. He has had to dress me, close and open the bathroom door for me, do all the cooking, the dishes, and the laundry.

And he's had to bathe me like a baby. It's not romantic, more like going through a car wash.

Terry hoses me down in the shower every 3 days (but I have to ask, otherwise I'd grow fur and crust). I think he takes special joy, hosing me in the face.

I'm in my third cast. Soon I will have as many casts as the road company of *Hamilton*.

This incident made me very aware of how fragile life can be after sixty. If I wasn't doing Pilates four times a week before the incident, might I have broken a knee or a hip? As generous as my girlfriends are, offering everything from hot meals to donating blood, who would have lived here day after day, to make sure I had straws for every beverage, took the right amount of pills at the designated times, or bathed me? Would a roommate have been as dedicated?

Whatever mystery there was in my marriage, it's now sadly gone. This is truly a test of someone's patience. I give my husband points for never grousing, always a smile, even when I'm moody or irritable or going through opioid withdrawal. (Really not pretty.)

Who else would be so devoted? How patient can he be and for how long?

When men are sick they behave like preschoolers, demanding and whiny. Women are usually more mature, plus they think about the wear and tear on their caregivers, usually saying something like, "You deserve a break." Men put on socks the way they put on condoms, loose in the toe, then pull the rest all the way up. A childless man like my husband excels at unhooking a bra with two fingers in two seconds, but putting shirts and jackets on someone else is mystifying.

On a good day, once he has bathed and dressed me, there's a moment when I can get him to share a minute waltz, a few dance steps, holding me close. Because of my cast and sling, I can't quite put my arms around him, but this brief time, holding one another reaffirms why we are together.

All things considered, I'm grateful for my husband. Our marriage is tested many times and, in many ways, even without cancer or a broken arm, as I'm sure many other relationships will attest to. Our "for better or for worse" vows are renewed every day, whether we are aware of it or not.

Besides my fall, Covid hitting many loved ones, plus other life challenges, I decided to sage our home to remove negative energy and clear it for prosperity. I had Terry light a sage stick and I proceeded to go from room to room clearing the energy. He saw me spending time by the toilet and was perplexed. I explained, "In Feng Shui the toilet symbolizes money. You keep the toilet lid closed to prevent money from leaving your life." I continued through the rest of the house to all the rooms. When I used the bathroom later, there was a dollar bill hanging out of the toilet. That's when I realized I'd married the right person at exactly the right time.

# Another Chance for Together Time

## Tim Law

It's finally here, that one precious weekend a year when the two of you get the chance to escape. Escape from the pressures of work, distractions of home, and of course the kids. Your three delightful offspring have gone to Grandma's or Aunt and Uncle's house or the home of a friend to stay. For two incredible nights there's only the two of you, nothing else matters except the chance to reconnect.

The trip is a long one, only two hours in the car but it takes all day what with the stops along the way at wineries (many of those) and of course the beach. You both love wine and the platter you choose at that third winery (the one with the great name) has an incredible assortment of local cheeses, cold meats and the best pitted olives you have ever tasted. And the beach, that is a must on your list of stops. You both met at the beach, much younger then and slimmer too. Regardless of how the years have changed you, your summer escape always includes a swim in the sea, laughter, freedom, simple joy. You both smell like salt and spray when you hop back in the family van and hit the road again.

Eventually your destination appears, normally around mid-afternoon. You've given yourselves enough time to unload your bags and bring in the bottles of wine bought through the day. There is a short period where you explore the house. An open fireplace at some, a spa for two always; it is still too warm for either though, maybe after sunset. The air conditioner is a blessing, turned on as you walk in. Immediately you feel relief from the hot car and the sizzling day.

Soon enough you find the bedroom and all of those wonderful feelings of freedom and escape twist and turn into remembered love and rediscovered lust. Alone, no phones, no kids and no distractions. With your eyes only for each other you satisfy twelve long months of pent up desire. Sure you've had moments throughout the year when the sparks of passion have ignited. Away from it all is where the sparks become a blaze and then an inferno. That is why you have two days away, to reconnect. Passions rise and fall only to rise again. In between is time for deep and meaningful discussions about the serious things you normally can't because little ears listen and phones buzz and flash. There is no television, no droning on radio announcers, nothing to numb the senses. This time an old gramophone and a collection of vinyl become your background. The classics as well as one or two of your favourites. One of you likes Rock and one likes Pop so through love and an unspoken respect you switch genres regularly. You even try one or two of the records from yesteryear. As you both imitate playing the pin whistle flute you cannot help but fall into fits of laughter.

It's a well-stocked kitchen. You peer into the depths of the giant fridge, thinking of the feast you plan for breakfast. As the hour drifts close to eight you hunt for pots and pans and together some sort of meal takes form. All you seek is fuel to help you regain your energies. The passion is there and it sparks again in the kitchen while dinner cooks, sweet smells waft through the house. You return to the stove just before it burns, like culinary heroes you've saved the meal that threatened to be over before it began. More laughter as blackness is scraped from pots, dirty pans left to soak. More talk as the meal makes you sleepy. More kisses, more caresses and then with a knowing smile and a playful wink you return to bed.

As the hot summer sun rises on a brand new day you welcome it with a coffee and a smile or perhaps a glass of champagne to go with breakfast. The whole day is ahead of you with no responsibilities. All that is on the cards is togetherness. Memories are shared and new ones made. Another weekend escape is almost over and yet there still remains many more hours of one another to enjoy. More wine is drunk, more records played. The spa is nice, but the bed is nicer. It is your world away from reality where you can recall a time before commitment and sneak some moments to feel that same feeling again. For those two days there is bliss, satisfaction and the feeling of utter contentment. This is why you ache for these two days each year. This is why you continually promise yourself another two later on.

The drive home is far different. Your mind is a whir with all the responsibilities (that dreaded to-do list) you left behind that now rush towards you with the return trip. You talk and laugh and listen to the music pouring forth from the radio. There is that song you heard and you both laugh at the shrill toot of the flute, a shared memory of a too-recent moment of silliness. A reconnection has been made. You consider another dip as the beach flies by, a way to truly cement the passion and respect rekindled over two magical days. But you realize you are already late and two days is all you get.

Not wanting to push your luck you hurry back to the real world. You stay for coffee with those who have taken care of your kids, showing your appreciation. Kids climb aboard the van to stamp the fact the weekend is officially over and soon enough your house, the place where you shelter for the rest of the year, becomes your horizon and then your world once more.

That is until next year comes around. Another adventure that awaits your planning. Another time to reconnect. Another cottage to visit in the heat of the summer. Another chance for together time.

# Alarming

## Andrea Marcusa

The alarm breaks the night quiet. It wakes her with its harsh noise. She is a light sleeper. Every fifteen minutes it shrieks and then announces, *Low battery!* She has no idea about the source of this sound. From where this pushy, demanding woman's voice blasts. It could be the smoke alarm in the hallway, the Wi-Fi box in the closet, or the second smoke alarm in the kitchen. But between the AC whirring and her husband's C-PAP machine for his sleep apnea chirping all night long, the alarm noise is scrambled.

As the night wears on, and the woman's voice badgers, she wonders who belongs to this voice. Where the sound engineers found it. Or generated it. Its tone bossy like her mother's. Urgent, overbearing. *Sit up. Tie your shoes. Eat your vegetables. Drink your milk. Brush your teeth. Go to bed. Don't bother me. Low battery!*

She keeps her eyes shut. She curses at the sound and asks the dark room why smoke alarms always run low on batteries in the middle of the night. She wonders who will find the voice, get out the ladder, locate the correct battery, buy one if there are none, feed it to the alarm and silence it. Of course, it will be her. Her husband is a deep sleeper. Her husband does not respond to this commanding tone like she does. He barely hears it. She has given up using it on him. He has had too much practice with his mother, rest her soul.

The battery will be changed. The woman will be silenced. Her husband won't hear a thing.

# Impasse

Len Kuntz

Time, on your tongue, must taste like acid, or arsenic, as you slow-swirl it in a bitter glob across your molars. It'd be okay, if it wasn't creative non-fiction. We've only months and weeks left, yet you keep punching holes into everything until it all seems fabricated, like a toupee, Gulliver's Travels, or a trapdoor with an itchy spring under the rug.

My phone is as dull and dead as a blade I can't use, so I shatter it in the barren sink, listen to the shards spit, rattle and groan in the garbage disposal.

If you're wondering, the dog's been seeing things and clawing your name on the bedpost while your parrot's run out of harsh insults to hurl.

But what I'm wondering is, didn't I kiss you like the world was formed just for us? And didn't you kiss me back with a tremor in your throat? Didn't that all matter more than any kiss, more than what we're both regretting now, as The Reaper takes two steps forward?

# Tiptoed Path

Trisha Ridinger McKee

Laney found herself tiptoeing through her own house, speaking softly to her husband Thomas, as he mourned the death of his mother.

It was a far cry from the barbed comments and snarky responses that usually reverberated through the crowded rooms.

"Can I make you something to eat?" She lingered in the doorway of his home office, not sure how to approach this man, her husband of thirty years. He sat in the middle of boxes, piles of papers, and general chaos. From the outside, their home was the envy of the neighborhood, but inside Laney felt trapped by their possessions. Possessions that seemed to multiply and breathe, taking the very oxygen Laney gasped for late at night.

Thomas did not meet her gaze. "I'll make something later."

With a nod he couldn't see, she left, skirting around stray antiques and boxes. As she stumbled around the corner, she inadvertently caught her reflection in the mirror. She was still tiny yet curvy, auburn curls cascading down her back. But her face was wrinkled, leathery from all those years basking in the sun, achieving that perfect tan. Once the homecoming queen, she now had to face that her prime was long past her. Her best years had been wasted, stifled, with a man who loved his possessions more than anything else.

★

Thomas stepped into the hallway, dodging the antique grandfather clock and boxes of comics. Laney often screamed about the clutter, but to him, this was comfort. This was how they could afford such a majestic house. This was how they could afford that pool she spent so many hours lying beside. The pool she had insisted on having and yet never swam in. He wondered what the water in the pool felt like, if it would be bitter cold, not accustomed to a person in it.

They had bought this house twenty years ago with visions of parties, drinking on the deck under tiki lights and heat lamps, laughing around the stone fire pit.

But Laney first claimed to not want people traipsing through her house and the beautifully landscaped yard, and then in later years, she stated she was embarrassed by the packed house.

There was always a reason. Something that solidified the distance between them.

He remembered how lively, how utterly engaging she had been at nineteen. And she had been enchanted with him. At twenty-five years old with a career already in place, he fascinated her. Everything he had said, everything he did, she thought was sophisticated and sexy.

Even when they had discovered she was pregnant after only one month into their whirlwind romance, they had been thrilled. He had never thought that Laney would soon feel so trapped.

And he had not expected to find his wife so vapid and fickle. Her bewitching beauty that drew him in had been used as a weapon over the years, spurring fits of jealousy and insecurity until he forced himself not to care. Not to notice.

As if sensing his thoughts, Laney stepped out from the many shadows. "Thomas, you have to eat."

It took a tragedy for his wife to show concern. Still, he knew it was simply to stifle her own discomfort.

But he forced a semblance of a smile. "I know. I'm going to the kitchen now."

He reached out to rub her shoulder, not missing how she tensed up. And he realized he was okay with that.

Laney rushed into her bedroom, forgetting to tiptoe.

When it became too much, when she was faced with the emptiness of her life, Laney retrieved the box from the closet. She no longer tried to hide it behind the family photo albums. She no longer cared to.

Lifting the lid, she stifled a cry as she gazed at pictures of her youth. Of a boy who had once loved her, idolized her. Dan, her high school sweetheart, her first love. They had been the envy of her high school. And she had dumped him, thinking there was better out there. Thinking an older man was the answer.

Laney thought back to the last time she had seen Dan with his wife and three children. She relished the fact his wife had gained weight. But now she remembered how Dan had turned to his wife and gazed at her, actually locked eyes with her. Laney lost her breath at the memory.

A rage surged through her trembling body. She considered storming into the hallway and destroying those damned boxes with the funky smelling old items her husband could not live without. She wanted to slam each piece against the wall until there was nothing left but shattered pieces. Because he did this. He ruined her life.

She caught her reflection in the mirror above her dresser and stopped. There was no sign of that homecoming queen beneath the layers of crinkled skin and age spots. With a soft sigh, the rage dissipated.

It would do no good. Their paths had been set and traveled.

She tiptoed to bed.

# Self-absorption

## Kendra Jackson

Once upon a time she had had a solid form of her own. She had been an individual entity, with her own life, independent of anybody else. She had had her own personality, her own friends, even her own last name. She had been as solid and as insoluble as a rock.

Or so she had thought. She had forgotten that solids could be dissolved by liquids, that even rocks could be worn away by the sea … given time.

If she had thought about it, she might have considered marriage to be an alloy. Two separate entities, combining to make something that was stronger together than apart. But she had been naïve, like all her friends, assuming that their eventual husbands would be all the things they'd hoped for. They had hoped for Mr. Right, but many of them had settled for Mr. All Right even if they hadn't realised it at the time.

At first, marriage had felt like all that she could have wished for. A loving husband, a beautiful wedding, and then home to a little house that was just their own. She saw travel in their future, cocktail parties, and evening gowns. She couldn't wait to add an R to her title.

Now though, she wished that she had taken her time, thought about all the alternatives available to her as an individual.

Now though, she's Mrs. Woman, ostensibly half of a pair, but in reality, she has been absorbed fully into his life. Some days she feels like the victims in that horror movie that he'd taken her to while they were courting. She'd wanted to see 'Some Like It Hot' instead of 'The Blob', but had deferred to his wishes. At the time, it hadn't occurred to her that she was setting the pattern for their lives together.

Every day she prepares the breakfast. Cereal and milk in the summer, porridge with honey in the winter. Always with a steaming cup of tea to start him on the day. She watches as the sugar cubes dissolve into the water, melting as quickly as her individuality had on the day she'd said, 'I do.'

By the time the ink had dried in the parish register, she knew that she would forevermore be inextricably linked to him. It would always be 'Mr and Mrs,' she would always be 'Mrs.' His label upon her as permanent as any brand.

Every day he eats the same meal at the same time. A perfunctory kiss on the cheek from him, an exhortation to have a good day from her. He'll tell her to have a good day as well, but it's hardly necessary. Her days are always intermediate, neither good nor bad, they simply are.

The passing of the seasons are marked more by the changes in her shopping list. Cereal, oatmeal, tea bags, sugar. Her wicker shopping basket sees more variety than she does on a daily basis.

He arrives home at a quarter after six each day. She fixes him a drink with two ice cubes from the large tray. One day when she'd pulled out the small tray by mistake, she'd wondered if four small cubes would have the same amount of ice as two large ones. Once upon a time in her previous life she'd known how to work it out, she'd taught students the formula to work it out. But lack of use has atrophied her memory of such things.

Now she only needs to remember the important things.

How long to cook the oatmeal on the stove, how much gravy he likes poured over his mashed potatoes, how many ice cubes he takes in his drink.

He talks at her while he drinks, tells her stories about his day and who he's met. The names of the people have no meaning to her, but he's speaking more for his benefit than her own and he doesn't really expect much of a response.

When he's finished his drink, she gives him space while she finishes preparing the meal of the day.

Meat and two veg. The gravy boat on the table with its Royal Doulton markings they were given as a wedding gift. It had travelled more distance in its life than she has in hers. The mashed potatoes on the plate slowly lose their form as the gravy seeps around them.

Every day the pattern on the plates fades just a little more.

Every day the pattern of her life becomes more and more ingrained.

Every day the liquid absorbs the solid yet again.

She can see the future stretched out before her. Another five years, another ten, silver, pearl, and ruby, maybe even gold. Always deferring to his needs, her routine always an echo of his. The monotony crushing her.

And so, one day at quarter to six, she steps out of her routine. She opens the oven and adds gas to the equation, knowing that one way or another, today the pattern will be erased.

# Soup

## Jackie Davis Martin

Helen shuffled cans of black beans and pumpkin puree and tomato sauce around, knocking one can off the wire rack, predictably. The cans, of course, didn't fit this way and she knew the whole damn cabinet had to be cleaned and sorted, but she shuffled and pushed nonetheless, the tins of spices tumbling right onto the floor in front of her.

"I have chicken-rice and vegetable-beef, the Progressive stuff," she called to her husband. "Which do you want?"

Harry called back that neither one sounded good.

Okay, then, she thought, you figure it out for yourself. What should she have? She'd bought Ramen at Walgreen's last week—the gummy noodles having an inordinate appeal suddenly—and had brought the cellophane packages home—four for a dollar—how could you beat that? They used to be ten cents each, Harry said.

Well, everything used to be something else, that was true. Including them.

Harry hadn't wanted the Ramen, although, once she'd fixed it, he regarded it with longing, sitting there with his cold cuts and mustard, making bread-less sandwiches.

She shoved back the tins of spices—young Laura, the other day, said she didn't know spices came in cans: how old were they? Didn't they lose their punch?—and discovered one of those cardboard cups of dried soup, popular, she supposed, with secretaries and teachers who could put them in a microwave. This instant cup was labeled Split Pea. Surely she didn't buy that? Maybe her son gave it to her, getting rid of his overflow from time to time. "You can probably use this stuff," he'd say.

She read the directions—far too fine, far too small. Why would anyone put small beige print on a pale green background? The creative directors must all be young, with perfect eyesight. Design was all. Directions didn't matter. Not that it was difficult to guess at. Add water (how much?), place in microwave (how long? with or without lid?) and stir. The pea soup had an added step—a flavor packet. Good lord, could she ever use a flavor packet. She'd like to add it to her whole existence, her marriage, spice it up. The flavor packet was to be sprinkled into the dried whatever-it-was (peas? there was no resemblance, either in color or in texture, even considering they might be dried, to the original peas) and then add water.

So she did. She put the emulsion-in-a-cup into the microwave and waited for the bell. Something like onions wafted into the air and she tapped her fingers abruptly on the microwave, as though reprimanding it. She hadn't wanted onions; she'd been willing to try Split Pea (as opposed, she supposed, to Whole Pea) soup but there had been no mention of pea-and-onion soup. And how could any of this be trusted? Were there peas in there at all? Maybe just flavor buds made to taste like peas.

There was a thought: *imagine the taste of peas.* Harry would say, Are you kidding? They have no taste.

*Imagine it anyway.*

Now either the real or the chemical onions, dried into the pea-powder or the flavor packet, took over the kitchen with fragrance. She removed the steaming cup and stirred. It was the consistency of wet cement, not that she'd ever worked with wet cement, but she'd watched the men slather and sculpt the new sidewalk squares out front, and a rather unpleasant shade of green. Still, she'd take the dried soup company's word for it and eat it according to the recipe. Recipe. There was a word worth thinking about considering this product.

She scooped the green paste from its steaming cardboard container into a gleaming white ceramic bowl where it assumed more dignity. It had to be scooped, like watery mashed potatoes, but, to her surprise and pleasure, it tasted just fine. Who knew?

"What smells so good?" Harry asked, drawn from his reading in the living room. He stood at the kitchen door.

"Pea soup. That dried stuff."

"Pea?" He squinted. "Was it reconstituted or something?"

"I guess. I added water."

"Is there any more?"

"No."

Harry studied her white bowl, glanced briefly at the cupboard. "Maybe I'll have one of those other ones after all, the ones you mentioned earlier?"

"Easy enough," she said. "I'll open a can."

"I can do it," he said. "But can I just have a taste of that? You just added water? Who knew?"

# Grow Old with Me

## Dawn DeBraal

I was seventeen when I met him—fresh out of high school, working at a TV store. Tim lived on the third floor of the Continental Hotel, and I lived on the fourth floor because the rent was only forty dollars a month. He'd moved from a different apartment after a box fan was accidentally pushed out of the window, crashing to the sidewalk, and he'd been asked to leave.

You could hear his loud music from the stairwell as I walked the flights of steps to my room. The elevator never worked the entire two years we lived there.

I was nineteen, and he was twenty-three when we married. We bought a twenty-five-foot motorhome with the plan to see the United States. We were carefree spirits.

Working construction takes you to many places. The first year we were married, we moved eight times, living in friend's driveways, parking lots of power plants and ordnance plants, and campgrounds. Gas was scarce in the 1970s, and at four miles to the gallon, we weren't going far in the gas-guzzling box we lived in.

In the winter, we moved into an apartment after coming home and finding water running out the front door from a broken water pipe.

We have been married for over forty-five years, and life with Tim has been an adventure. We bought an old hobby farm in 1983. It was nothing but fields surrounding us. We've planted trees under which we now stand. We raised two children together and watched them leave the nest and become decent human beings. We have two grandchildren, one of each.

We've gone through sickness more times than we care to count. Now that we are on Social Security, health has come up more than we'd like. We fight these battles together. I still see that charismatic, funny redhead when I look at him. We have grown separately and together. It's what holds us here in this marriage—the willingness to allow your partner to be themselves and to support their dreams. I was so young when we married, not realizing I'd chosen the right person to share my life with. I hope he feels the same.

# The Day a Spider Landed on My Marriage

## Ray Morrison

I was the first to spot the spider inching along the ceiling above the sofa where I sat beside my wife. In hindsight, I should have simply suggested that my wife step out of the room while I disposed of the bug. But I didn't. As Aimee watched *Seinfeld* I sat mesmerized by the tenacious, determined march of the spider above our heads.

But my failure to warn Aimee was not my worst crime.

The spider, whose tiny disc of a body could not have weighed more than a fraction of an ounce, didn't merely float down from its perch on the cracked plaster above. Rather, it dropped like a Navy Seal, rappelling rapidly on its silken thread to land squarely on Aimee's chest. My wife emitted a shriek so piercing I reflexively dabbed at my ear to check for bleeding, and she flew off the couch with such speed that she flipped the coffee table 360 degrees.

It was my response to that moment that sealed my fate. I did not rush to stomp on the offending beast, or grasp my terrified wife in a reassuring hug, but rather burst out in a peal of laughter so forceful that I was paralyzed with convulsions and blinded by tears.

For three days afterward, my wife would not utter one word to me. Not one. I'd try to apologize for my inexcusable dismissal of her arachnophobia, but when I did, she'd merely continue walking or reading or cooking (for herself only), pretending she couldn't hear me. It was as though I was Patrick Swayze and she Demi Moore in some alternate un-love story remake of *Ghost*. I'd learned my lesson, I told Aimee that third night as we slipped beneath the bed sheets. She nodded, giving me a look I was certain meant that she didn't believe me, but would generously give me the benefit of the doubt. She then kissed my cheek, rolled over and went to sleep. The following morning as we each got ready for work, she chatted about her day as though we'd never had a spat at all.

Back on the day the spider landed on my wife, Aimee and I had been married for little more than six months. Tomorrow, we celebrate our fifteenth wedding anniversary. I've just arrived home from the jewelry store where I bought my wife a diamond pendant that the saleswoman assured me Aimee will adore. Over the years, we've developed a tradition. On the night before our anniversary, we each set our gifts on the dining room table, as a playful tease. No peeking, no shaking of boxes, no hefting weight to gauge possible contents is allowed.

I carry the jewelry box, professionally wrapped in white paper with a plum-colored ribbon, to the dining room. There, already waiting in the middle of the table is my gift from Aimee. It looks, to no surprise, exactly the same as the gifts I've received each year for the past fourteen years. Wrapped haphazardly in old newspaper is a small cylindrical tube standing no more than 10 inches tall. It's hard not to smile at the sight of it. For I know that no matter how excited and delighted Aimee will be tomorrow morning when she flips open the velvet box to see her pendant, it will not exceed the pleasure I will receive from tearing off the newspaper to reveal a shiny new can of RAID Spider Killer.

# Taking a Break

## JA Rose

Jonno is used to getting his way, and if things aren't going his way, he's not averse to forcing things so they do. Like taking a break from Serena and the kids. She's seven – no eight – months pregnant and he needs some peace and quiet. She's been getting more and more hormonal the fatter she gets, and the housework is more non-existent than usual. This morning he had to make sandwiches for the kids' school lunches before he could leave for the workshop, which made him late due to the traffic congestion and the red lights he hit at every effing traffic light.

He's got a couple of weeks' leave due and he's decided to take one now. He'll go crazy if he doesn't; do something that will land him in big trouble with the law. That would complicate life even more than giving the wife the shits with his clearing off down south for a few days.

'See ya next week, Mondo,' he waves to the salt-and-pepper-haired man working on some riveting near the back of the shed. Mondo doesn't look up but gives him a two-fingered wave and grunts something indistinct. The boss left half an hour ago to see about a contract with a potential customer. Knows Jonno will be there next week: he's been a rock-solid worker up to now, reliable; a problem solver. Willing to stay late to get the job done.

The traffic's getting heavy but it's still flowing well; it won't be in another twenty-five minutes. Green light at the traffic lights – first time this week. Green lights all the way home. It's a sign. Jonno is sure of it. He's feeling lighter with every step towards the front door.

Serena and the kids are in the kitchen eating nuggets and chips. The place is spotless. Four huge suitcases squat nearby in the hallway. Hang on. What the …?

'Mum and Dad will be here soon J. I think the kids and I will take a break until after the babe is a couple of weeks old. You don't mind, do you? Didn't think you would …'

# Waking Up Somewhere Else

Louella Lester

Wally drove the family to a new place on the continent every summer, waking up early to get a good start on the road while the family still slept in the back of the camper van. Each night, the children discussed where they might be when they awoke—a U-Pick strawberry field, a gas station, a farmers' market parking lot—and they revelled in the never-ending choice. But for Gladys it was different. Or rather, it was always the same.

Gladys spent most evenings, vacation or not, prepping the next days' meals. Plucking organic chickens until the feathers made her sneeze. Scooping pumpkin seed until her fingernails turned orange. Chopping turnips until her wrist suffered pins and needles. All because Wally refused to eat fast-food or even the odd store-prepared meal. If Gladys complained, Wally smiled and handed her a bunch of radishes or a pail of peas. "You knew about my family's blood pressure issues when you married me. I've always been careful with my food. That's how it is." And that's how it was, always.

As the children grew, Wally started to enthuse about the trips he and Gladys could take once they all left home. "We won't have to worry about serviced campgrounds," he said one day, after dropping a sack of yellow onions on the counter. "We can explore real wilderness sites." His wife ripped open the sack netting with her knife and selected an onion. Saying nothing, she peeled and sliced and chopped it up for a batch of onion soup.

She chopped so many onions her tears dripped into the pot as she stirred. "It's a bit salty," said Wally after he ate the first spoonfuls, but he had a rare second bowlful. And this got Gladys thinking.

Every day, after that, she peeled and chopped yellow onions, tears dripping into sauces, stews, and casseroles. Wally gobbled up the meals, commenting more and more often, as his tastebuds grew used to the salt. "Honey, these are delicious veggie burgers, your cooking has really improved." And Gladys, slicing onion for the next meal, smiled through her tears.

That first child-free summer, Wally said he didn't feel like heading out in the camper van. Said he was feeling a bit tired. "Let's stay home, it won't be the same without the kids, anyway." So they stayed home. And when, one night, their visiting son mentioned the saltiness of the goulash, his father, tucking into an extra-large portion, told him he was imagining it.

A few summers later, after the memorial service and the scattering of Wally's ashes, the attendees stayed for the luncheon Gladys had prepared. Many spoke of their surprise that Wally, such a health-conscious man, had not outlived them all.

They also said the luncheon dishes were all so perfectly seasoned.

# Track seven — Love me forever my darling until we are as dust

## Joyce Bingham

Today is a good day. Jonnie wakes up smiling.

He lifts a lock of my hair and kisses it. I close my eyes in pleasure as he rolls out of bed, leaving me in the warm sheets, crumpled with last night's making-up.

Dressing, I select the pale blue dress, his favourite, the matching necklace of silver he bought me when we married.

I smear a touch of lipstick, brush and style my hair, smoothing the unruly curls he dislikes.

We meet in the kitchen. A calm day of communal breakfast in our spotless kitchen.

I swept up the broken plates during the night. There was a small splinter in my finger this morning. I teased it out in the shower, dropped it, the beads of blood merging and flowing with the splinter down the drain.

He kisses me before he leaves, coffee mingled with yoghurt. As the door closes, I touch my mouth where his kiss lingers, revel in the tingling and warmth. Perhaps I'll bake a cake. Make his favourite meal. Buy some wine. Keep the good vibes going.

I'm in the mood for music, not the radio, the annoying DJ and the quizzes. Real music. I creep into Jonnie's study. My fingertips caress the ridges of the covers of his vinyl collection. So many to choose from, I want something joyous to match this day of bright sunshine. I close my eyes and my fingers select.

How clever were my fingers picking 'Love songs'? A single dew-dropped red rose on the cover. I ease the record out of the sleeve, a note falls out, thick textured paper, and in violet blue ink, 'To my darling Jonnie, track seven, all my love M, xxx'. The writing is cursive, dynamic and flowing free.

I place the record on the player. Carefully count seven tracks. Ease the stylus down. I must not scratch it.

A slow rhythmic beat. Sensual and steamy. Martha. Unmistakably Martha.

She wore perfume you could taste, red sequined dresses of fire and multi-faceted jewels. Bright red lipstick and huge eyelashes, every day. A whirlwind, a she-devil in love with life, heading up the corporate ladder.

Breathing hard, I stand still. I spy myself in the mirror, the pale blue dress wan, the pearly pink lipstick feeble and aging.

The tempo of the music increases, the drum solo vibrating through the soles of my feet.

In the kitchen, I pile up the used breakfast crockery and cups on the table. These are all that remain of the dinner set Jonnie smashed last night.

I swipe them to the floor, the smash reverberating in my head, drowning out Martha's haunting music.

Crockery pieces spin across the tiled floor. I kick off a shoe and kneel to pick up his broken bowl and our chipped cups and with each pulse of the drum, I grind the smooth surfaces into dusty fragments with the heel of my shoe.

# Proposal

## Judith Shapiro

A simple name, Joe. I've always planned on something more exotic, at least two syllables, preferably three. I imagine picnicking in a park in Barcelona or Milan with Renoir or Constantine, wine, bread and romance. Joe, one syllable, barely any letters. I'm not meant to marry a Joe.

It's a perfect September day. Tourists have returned to the city, the beach uncrowded, wide open. Bare feet, playing chicken with the waves as they reach the shore, daring them to soak us. Casually, he leads me from the water's edge onto dry sand. It's nothing like in the middle of the summer when it burns like hellfire. This feels like a hug, a tickly warm sand caress.

He kneels, and I think, wait, am I being proposed to? It's not like I need a dancing flash mob, strangers applauding under the arch in Washington Square Park, or graffiti on the overpass. But this is a surprise. I suppose being proposed to on the beach, feet cradled by warm sand is pretty much as good as it gets. Other than his tiny name, there isn't anything wrong with Joe. In fact, there are many things right.

Pros: He doesn't watch football, ensconced on the couch staring at the television all day Sunday in a pile of greasy junk food crumbs. He's kind, funny, quirky. He loves my cat. The first time he spent the night, when I came to get in bed, my cat was kneading and drooling on his chest. He doesn't have a pet of his own so we can get a dog. Or more cats. I figure he'd be a great dad, so good with my cat, imagine him with a human of his own. He keeps the knives hidden in the cabinet. He's a grown up. He washes his whites and darks separately. He seems to love me, so much so that he's about to ask me to marry him. I wonder where he stands on picnics?

Cons: He uses thick, fluffy toilet paper. The roll runs out so fast I use practically half of it for one poop. It's embarrassing, like I'm a huge pooping toilet paper hog. Also, it leaves linty white stuff on my cooch and I don't shave down there so it gets all stuck. He doesn't mind that I don't shave. (Pro) Does he buy it because it's fancy or because it's cheap? Maybe he grabs whatever's on the shelf without a thought. Can I marry a man who I don't know something this fundamental about?

Neither pro nor con: He plays video games. He almost always wears a hat. Usually a baseball cap, but sometimes a fedora. He's not even bald, like he has a full head of hair. The hat can stay, but it is a confusion.

Will he fight me on baby names? I have my ideas. If it's a boy, so far I've listed Lucien, Alistair and Rafferty. Rafferty because it means one who will prosper, not because I like the sound of it. I kind of like Jasper, known as the supreme nurturer, one who brings tranquility and wholeness. I'm not sure though. It sounds like he's the butler instead of the mansion owner.

For a girl there's Evangeline, bearer of good news. Angelique because it's awesome. Justine, because, just because. Picking out names is the fun part of being pregnant. I don't know if there are any other fun parts, except sometimes walking down the sidewalk, or in the mall I think, huh, I'm pregnant and I feel special.

My first night at his house, I wanted to surprise him with my fancy oatmeal for breakfast. He had everything – organic oats, cinnamon (also organic), Himalayan pink salt, raisins, and almonds. When I searched for cinnamon I found his spices, bunches of them. Cumin, coriander, basil, oregano. He even had bay leaf and arrowroot. What the hell does he do with arrowroot?

I couldn't find a knife so I bit the almonds into pieces. He loved the oats, or at least he said he did. I never told him about biting the almonds and he never asked. I still make oatmeal. It's our thing, a ritual. I bring my Swiss Army knife to cut the nuts. My dad gave it to me for my 16th birthday. It has everything – tweezers, scissors, a corkscrew. My prized possession. I can see him doing that, giving our kid an amazing knife.

I've always thought co-parenting seemed appealing though. Parents get time off. Freedom. Summertime at the beach without, "I have to go to the bathroom," the minute you get there. "Pee in the ocean." "I can't, it's poop!" Nope, he's got the kids and you're lying under an umbrella with a cooler of beer, extra spicy salsa, and guac and chips. No worries about losing your kid in their polka-dot bathing suit that blends in with the thousands of others. But he doesn't want to co-parent. He wants us to be married and raise this kid together.

I make a mental list of things to discuss: 1. Toilet paper. 2. Hat. 3. Picnic. 4. Arrowroot. 5. Almonds?

I look up. How long has he been there on one knee? A nanosecond? An hour? I want to say yes, but I can't choke it out. Sure doesn't seem earnest enough. Finally, I look into his eyes. They're hazel. (Pro) Maybe our baby will have hazel eyes, or even better, green. "Of course," I say. He smiles, and I'm pretty sure lets out a sigh. Toilet paper is negotiable, hat, arrowroot can wait. Almonds, maybe forever. "On one condition," I say, as he visibly clenches. "You go on a picnic with me."

# Salsa

## Rita Wilson

I'm at a fundraiser for the local chamber of commerce with my husband. It's at an estate called Rosalea Farms. I'm happy to have the chance to put on something other than my usual tee shirt and shorts, and I'm dressed in a blue-green sweater set and black cigarette pants. I had my blonde hair highlighted in the afternoon, and I'm feeling pretty. It's a perfect summer night. The oppressive humidity that has pressed on the city for the past two weeks has been blown away by the previous night's thunderstorms and left in its wake a perfect sky with big cumulus clouds and a soft breeze.

A limousine shuttles us down a long driveway flanked on either side with green fields and tall pines. A man in a light brown suit greets us with peach sangria, and we saunter past pastel linen tables full of items available for bid at the silent auction – coupons for hotel stays, dinners, or dance lessons, and large gift baskets with candles and wine wrapped in cellophane, or cigars and golf balls. We walk over to the large barn, where succulent samples of food from local restaurants beckon us. We load plastic plates with red and black tortilla chips with duck comfit, and mahi mahi with coconut rice and mango. We sip the Moscato wine, served deliciously cold with its crisp orange and lemon notes. I scan the crowd, but I don't see anyone I know. I lean towards my husband with an observation: "So many of these men have beer bellies."

He looks down at his own and replies, "I've lost nine pounds," but I'm sure it's the same nine he keeps losing, then gaining back. The women look nice in their summer dresses and sandals, and I compliment a woman on her long dress that appears to be trimmed with intricate beadwork. Close up, I realize it's just a design.

A six-piece salsa band has begun to play in front of a makeshift dance floor. My husband sees a man he knows, and we walk over to his table to say hello to him and his client. We stand around a high-top table covered with a light rose tablecloth and a glass jar centerpiece containing sand and shells and wrapped with straw on the mouth of the jar. The music stops and the MC announces that they will be giving salsa lessons and encourages the crowd to come to the dance floor. The three men at the table look at each other. "Come on," I say to my husband. He looks uncertain. The other men laugh.

"Uh, no, that's ok."

"Come on, it'll be fun," I say, and nod toward the dance floor. He furrows his eyebrows and shakes his head no. The men look down. "Suit yourself," I say, and put my purse and wine glass on the table.

Sixteen or so of us congregate on the small floor made of 12-inch by 12-inch wood squares snapped together. The instructor high-fives all of us in a circle, then has us form three lines, all facing the stage, and he demonstrates the basic salsa step. He has us count one-two-three-four-five-six as we move first forward, then back. I'm glad I'm wearing low-heeled black sandals. I notice the tall, brown-skinned man next to me, or rather I feel his presence. The instructor shows us how to move side to side and tells us to put our hips into this. The man next to me is easing closer with each side-to-side movement. He is wearing sunglasses and a close beard, and his mouth is full and wide. He is wearing a striped long-sleeved shirt, jeans, and teal suede loafers. He pulls this off, somehow. The instructor stops the music, and the man leaves the dance floor. I'm disappointed, but I turn my attention to the instructor, who now has us line up across from each other – men across from women. There are only six men, and about ten women. The instructor steps in, and one of the women moves across to the men's line. The man in the teal shoes steps into line directly across from me. "I have my partner," he says. He smiles and points to me, and I smile back. The instructor explains how the women will have to start backwards for this to work. Then he tells us to join hands. My partner is holding a bottle of beer in his right hand, and he takes my right hand loosely with his left. He introduces himself as Lee. "Rita," I say. The band plays a slow salsa rhythm, and we dance. Forward, back, side to side. Lee sets down his beer and takes my hands. We all follow the instructor's commands, and then Lee and I break formation and he twirls me around the dance floor.

"You've done this!" I say.

"I'm Latin," he explains, and I try to follow his lead, but he is far better than I am. The instructor pauses the music and asks everyone to get back into line.

"Uh oh, we're in trouble," Lee says. We dance to another Latin song which I do not recognize, but Lee does, and he begins to sing and spin me around.

"My husband is going to have a fit," I say.

"Because you're dancing with me?"

"His loss," I say.

The lesson finishes and we applaud. Lee takes my hand. "I enjoyed dancing with you. I hope to see you again."

I walk back to the table where my husband is now standing alone. He does not have a fit. But he doesn't say anything, either. "Where are your friends?" I ask. He shrugs.

"I saw you out there," he says.

I sip my wine and say nothing.

"Nobody else was doing what you were."

"Nope, they weren't," I say. "You should have come with me."

"I know," he says. I wonder if he is aware of the difference between knowing and *knowing*.

# When Fathers Shake Hands

Annie Bien

Guanian woke early. She kept her eyes shut. She would imagine him next to her, instead of looking at him. Even as the years had drained away from them, his brows had never furrowed when he slept. The war had taught them both to sleep quietly, to press their faces into a rolled coat serving as pillow and silencer, leaving creases on their cheeks rather than the risk of a gasp aloud when sweat and blood-soaked men raged, carrying that smell of rot.

When they arrived in Hong Kong from cold Harbin, he never learned Cantonese but spoke his unfamiliar Yangzhou dialect. Everyone claimed they didn't know it, but somehow, they continued their conversations with him in Cantonese, he would reply in Yangzhouhua, and they all laughed and worked together becoming friends. People always liked him, perhaps it was his deep-set eyes, or his mellow voice, or how he listened.

They all loved her for being his charming wife. She spoke Cantonese, English, and Russian, being raised in cities where European concessions changed their daily life after the fall of the Qing dynasty.

There were women who wished he'd turn his head their way, she saw that. After all, they came from a culture of concubines. She tried not to think about that traditional custom, or of the romance of choosing your own partner like the romance novels she read in English. She did think of her father repeating the story of how he and his colleague had agreed that if their expectant wives gave birth to a boy and a girl, the babies would wed. Their fates were set.

She pressed her head into her pillow to hide herself from her thoughts. She remembered once a few months ago, he had said to their niece, "Well, MeiMei, your Ganma and I would love to visit you in America, but your Ganba's health is so bad now, I'm lucky to be alive. Do you know our combined weight is 170 pounds? I'll leave it to you how to divide it. Ganma and I wear our wedding rings on our thumbs now but it's still loose, see? I've run out of holes on my belt so even the tailor sighed and said, 'never mind.'"

At first in Hong Kong, even with the windows shut tight, the silence of their apartment could still produce noise in her head. She would awaken to hear screaming, and discover it was her screams. Then she'd feel his hands cradle her cheeks, "Guanian, you were dreaming. We're safe. We're home."

Now she smelled lilacs, and remembered that late spring day in Harbin, 1925, just after they married. They had walked into the park across the bridge over the lake to look at the carp. He had buttoned his coat, tucked in his scarf, then placed a lilac posy in her coat buttonhole. He extended his arm for their promenade.

Cold sunlight bathed them in brightness. Others were out too, voices chattered around them in Russian and Chinese. They didn't speak. They hardly knew each other. They stepped onto the bridge. She pointed to a large orange carp, tail swishing. They heard a large crack of wood, like the sound of a fir tree. The bridge had buckled under them, screams and shouts. They plunged feet first into the lake, ice cracking beneath them, his arm clasped hers.

She didn't know how to swim. She didn't know him well enough to know if he did. Her body shook and her teeth chattered as her coat ballooned with icy lake water. Her skeleton rattled. She cried and her tears froze. She gasped, "Jiancang, it's the end ..."

She heard him. "Guanian, I'm holding you. Something struck my leg ... Can you undo your bun to spread your hair? Maybe they'll see us ..."

She felt his hands around her waist. She pulled the wooden hair pin out. Her hair tumbled, undone.

"Okay. Relax, look to the sky, lie back. See if you can float with your hair loose like you're on a bed of flowers. I'll hold your hair and won't pull you down, the shore isn't far ... someone will see us."

Her long hair spread like tentacles across the water ... she looked up to the sky ... she heard him groan, and then shouting.

When she came to in the hospital, she heard someone crying. Again. He had a cast on his leg. He reached his hand toward hers. "We survived. My love, if it were not for your composure and beautiful hair, we would have drowned. Thank you for saving my life so I can be with you."

She always believed an arranged marriage meant financial security and if fortunate, some meager affection. But that day went beyond her expectations. The silent walk, the cold lake, the collapsed bridge, the choice to float or sink, the choice to survive together. And he had called her, "my love."

She dreamed an owl had flown by her last night, caressing her face like his hand. She listened for his breath. How she wanted to see his unusually long lashes. How they fluttered when he was dreaming. Sunlight slipped through the drapes. He always rose before the clock chimed. The clock chimed. No movement.

She opened her eyes.

He lay next to her in his cream-colored linen summer suit with white shirt, barefooted. His eyelashes didn't flutter. He lay very still. In his hands, he held a lilac posy and an envelope. Inside, she removed a postcard of the Harbin bridge. He had written a note:

*My love,*
*This is when "It's the end," meant the beginning of "we."*

# Mommy Loves Daddy

## Robin Cantwell

"So you see, if you press this button right here, the device will link up to our mobile app, and hey presto: you just got yourself a front row ticket to your favourite furry friend's entire universe."

"I thought this was a tracking device for my cat?"

"Oh, Sir, it's so much more. Not only can you follow where your cat goes, you can literally see what your cat sees, thanks to our fully-patented collar cam. I give you: Cat's Eyes."

This is a strange conversation for several reasons. Firstly, I don't own a cat. Second, it's my wedding anniversary, and instead of taking my wife Shirley for dinner at The Ivy or drinks at The Plaza, she and I have taken it upon ourselves to spend this most special of days at the biggest trade show for pets in North America.

As I back slowly away from the gentleman on all fours trying to demonstrate the unique user experience of Cat's Eyes, I instead do some tracking of my own, hoping to catch my wife through the packed booths beyond. We've barely spoken all day, of course. We went through the usual morning rigmarole of me handing her my 'Happy Anniversary!' card while she smiles politely back and pretends to read my heartfelt words within. But now, as I clock her strolling down the pooch aisle, I contemplate how I've been relegated to fourth in line for her love:

Her first love, of course, is reserved for our darling daughter, Beth.

The second, as I have reluctantly grown to accept, is for our Rottweiler, Ludwig.

The third, to reveal a crucial plot twist, is for her lover, Jacques.

I sigh as she chats to the vegan doggie treat spokesman at the opposite end of the shopping mall. There it is: her fake, nasal laugh usually reserved for my parents. Ah, and here comes the playful biting of her bottom lip, a mating call openly used to flirt with men in front of me. I recognise all her sly little moves now, rehearsed like a stand-up routine, ready to call upon whenever she so desires—the same way they must have done for Jacques all those sordid months ago.

I check my watch. My pulse starts racing.

3:00pm. It's time.

Shirley's brief flirtation is interrupted by the vibration of her phone. I hide behind the parrot cages and watch her smile at her touchscreen in a way only secret lovers do. She breaks into a giggle, then her face hardens as she searches for me through the crowd. She wants to check that the coast is clear for a covert rendezvous with Jacques, the man of the hour, the apple of her eye, the re-invigorator of her libido. Little does she know that I'm waiting in the wings to expose them once and for all.

It was a year ago today that I found out about her affair. I arrived at her workplace in the hope of surprising her, armed with a bouquet of roses and two tickets to 'Swan Lake'. As I grabbed the door handle of her corner office, I heard squirms of joy erupting through her muffled moans of pleasure, accompanied by full-throated grunts from an unknown man, who was quickly identified by screams of 'Oui, Jacques, Oui!!!'

From pictorial evidence I've managed to carefully curate through my Instagram burner account, Jacques is a real man's man, blessed with the body of a Rodin masterpiece and the silver fox hair of Clooney in his prime. He's been my obsession ever since. When Shirley calls to say she'll be back late from work, I'll sit there, hunched over my laptop in the fading light, a devil's halo glowing around me as I try like mad Captain Ahab to harpoon myself to his whereabouts in a pointless attempt to discover if my wife is actually up against a deadline or up against the wall, his burly hands wrapped passionately around her.

I follow at a safe distance as she steps onto the escalator to the Level Two toilets, where, according to her clandestine conversation in the kitchen last night, they're scheduled to meet. I'm approaching the crime scene when I realise I've imagined this moment a thousand times over, but never what to do next. Do I … punch him? Do I … burst into tears? Or maybe I should just help myself to a Cat's Eyes collar and watch my worst nightmare unfold from the comfort of my iPhone.

As I run through the various scenarios, my phone rings. It's Beth.

"Is everything okay?" I ask, distracted by my wife slipping inside the restroom.

"Dad, what's the Netflix password? I'm logged out again."

"It's MOMMYLOVESDADDY, all caps."

"Ugh. You guys are gross."

And with a hiss of disgust, she hangs up.

As I stare with glazed eyes at the bathroom door before me, I think more about that golden day when we set up the Netflix account — how Shirley and I were still madly in love. How the troubles of the world felt a million miles away. Then I switch, back to the here and now, trapped in a moment that'll decide the course of our lives. If I enter, the family collapses. If I walk away, I will be forced to live in the shadow of another man, and stomach it for the greater good.

Then comes a tap on my shoulder. It sends a cold shiver down my spine.

"Er, do you mind?" he sneers with that all-too-familiar-grunt, shuffling past me as he steps eagerly inside. Then he stops, his mind unable to place who I am, how he knows me, the significance of my untimely appearance. He turns, and looks me dead in the eye.

"Have we met?" he asks.

"… Don't think so?" I reply with a puzzled look and a lump in my throat, before I retreat, back to the safety of the animals below.

# Monumental

## Alex Reece Abbott

"Group's gathering. Better get going." Seeing his husband's downturned mouth, his ritual of support, Declan kicks the gravel path, shooting shards towards the Great Circle.

"Cold, eh?" Cormac's sigh lands between them. "Go, or you'll miss it."

Declan stares over Cormac's drooping coathanger shoulders at the peat-stained Boyne, where Finn McCool ate the Salmon of Knowledge.

Cormac crunches his lemon-drop like it's a chunk of granite off the monument's facade. "Goodbye Daddy, en-joyyyyy!" He bends to the stroller and takes Grace's podgy arm in her dinosaur onesie, making her wave to Declan. "We'll be fine – you won't be long."

Queuing with the tourists, Declan studies the massive, overturned saucer, a beacon iced with white quartz, that rests in the crook of the swollen river. As he nears the entrance, he sees a weathered slab, a Neolithic kerbstone, the front carved with swirling, interlocking circles.

He stoops to creep into the burial chamber, edging along the narrow passageway lined with standing stones. The interior of the world's oldest existing building is smaller than he imagined, and surprisingly dry and cosy. Supported by jutting stones, the ceiling is high – maybe twenty feet – and the walls are patterned with spirals and chevrons. Welcoming the warmth after the gnawing December wind, he wraps his arms around himself, basking in a rare sense of connection. Newgrange. He feels he could live here.

Guido, the beaming guide, sports an uber-Celtic red beard. He reminds Declan of a smug, panto leprechaun. Using a sixty-watt bulb, he demonstrates how the tomb's alignment allows a shaft of sunlight to penetrate the roof-box. "Lights the floor, then the whole chamber for seventeen minutes during the midwinter sunrise."

Built a thousand years before Stonehenge, older than the Great Pyramids, this remarkable time-telling device steals Declan's breath. He grins, savouring the moment.

"The sun has shone into this chamber since it was constructed and probably will forever," says Guido. "Thanks to grooves in the roof-slabs, rainwater never breaks through."

Declan examines the empty stone basins, where ashes and bones of the dead were once placed. This complex, beautiful building is a lot of effort for storing some bones. Maybe Stone Age people had more in mind than marking the start of the new year.

Stroking his long beard, Guido signals a rehearsed realisation. "The tomb may have served as a powerful symbol of life's victory over death ... remember ... their average life expectancy was forty. Forty! Perhaps it's a house ... where spirits were going to live ... for a long, long time. Special people ..."

Special people. Like you've never said that before, thinks Declan, wishing Guido and the others would all feck right off and give him a minute to himself, leave him to wonder.

It hasn't been much of a honeymoon and – tomb apart – it's possibly his worst-ever birthday. Then again, according to

Guido, if he was a Neolithic farmer, he'd be dead by now. Harnessing his gratitude and serenity, Declan imagines joining people thousands of years before, waiting in darkness at the ancient tomb. Waiting for the seamless ending of the longest night of the year, waiting for dawn to break.

Guido ushers the group out of the tomb. Emerging into the light, Declan blinks. The grass dome of the cairn roof is lusher, greener. The quartz walls glow. The dancing river glitters in the winter sun.

He spots his husband of seven days, huddled with a slack-jawed, wide-eyed baby hippy-chick, a twenty-first century Janis, all swirling tie-dye, dangling beads and velvet, faded and crushed. Waves of patchouli rising from The Janis almost overpower the stench of self-pity rising off Cormac, who is oversharing again – this time his epic, boring history of self-diagnosed, untreatable claustrophobia which has forced him to wait outside with Grace.

Declan fights the urge to turn around. For a moment, he considers rescuing The Janis ... but don't adults put on their oxygen masks first?

"Sake! Not even anywhere for a *latte*." Cormac adjusts his rucksack. "Hi hon, any good?"

Declan nods and hoists his daughter onto his hip.

Cormac releases the brakes on the stroller. "Tick that one, eh."

Grace yawns at Declan, cherub lips puckered into a sullen nap-time pout, blissfully unaware of how much he yearns to sneak back into the tomb alone, to see in the dawn of a new day, and how much he yearns to share the space, share the moment with someone special. He plants a noisy kiss on her milky baby-head and breathes the future.

# One Catholic's Tale

## Lisa Costa

There was no diamond on my finger, nor did my parents have money for a big wedding. I bought the first dress I tried on at South Hills Mall. It was decked with Chantilly lace, much like my communion dress, and had a long matching veil. Laura was my maid of honor and Jenny was a bridesmaid. Derrick's brother-in-law, Vince, was the best man and his friend Danny was an usher. Derrick's parents hosted a home-cooked rehearsal dinner.

I calmly entered Saint Bernadette church on November 11, 1975, ready to walk down the aisle. As I stood in the vestibule on an otherwise cold, gray, late autumn day, a ray of sunshine shone through the stained glass and lit up the floor in front of me.

"It's a sign from God," Cindy, my future sister-in-law, said.

The processional music began to play. I thought about the sign as I walked slowly down the aisle to Derrick and Father Graham waiting for me at the altar.

"Beautiful," Father Graham whispered when I reached the altar steps.

I smiled.

"You are without a doubt the slowest bride to walk down that aisle," he joked.

After Mass, the out-of-town relatives descended upon my parents' house for an old-fashioned wedding reception. There were sandwiches and beer and a yellow sheet cake with white frosting and gold foil decals.

We drove to Laurel Springs Mountain Resort for our honeymoon. The cold, icy night had made the path up the mountain slippery. Derrick had trouble controlling the steering wheel, but I felt safe with him.

Once in our cabin, we drank champagne from fluted glasses that had the words "bride" and "groom" decals. The champagne made me sleepy and before I knew it morning came. I looked at the majestic mountains outside of our window and felt as if I didn't belong in the room. After a buffet breakfast of pancakes, ham, fruit, and juice, we walked around the resort. We stopped in a small store where Derrick bought me a fake diamond necklace, and after a light lunch, returned home.

"I'm back," I sang as I walked into the kitchen of my parents' house after the brief honeymoon.

"Did you have an enjoyable time?" Mother asked as she spread brownie batter into a pan.

"Yes, it was nice," I replied.

We stayed over for a night. It was strange to have Derrick sleep in my childhood bedroom with me. As I lay in bed, I looked at the gold band embedded with small diamonds on my left hand. It was comforting to be in my childhood bedroom, but I rose early and began to pack my things for the move.

Our new apartment was on the third floor. We walked up the steps carrying our overnight bags, planning to bring the rest of our belongings inside the next morning. As we reached the door of the apartment, Derrick stopped and put down the suitcase.

"Want me to carry you over the threshold?" he asked.

I nodded.

He unlocked the door, pushed it open, and picked me up.

"Here you are, married lady," he said and carried me, giggling, into the apartment.

In the bedroom, I pulled out a silky white negligee and matching silk coat from the overnight bag.

A tiny blue ribbon threaded through the waistline of the negligee.

"What are you wearing?" he said.

"It's a negligee, it reminds me of my wedding gown," I told him as I touched the silky fabric.

He laughed, remarking that the wedding was over.

I drove home one afternoon, almost eighteen years after that night, to see my friend and neighbor, Kara, looking at the impatiens in her front yard.

"Hi, Kara."

I waved to her and walked over to look at the blooming flowers, full of color.

After a few minutes of conversation, she said to me, "I heard him yelling at you."

Kara's words were another sign. It was time for honesty.

"I'm looking into divorcing him," I said.

"Do you have an attorney?" she asked.

"I made an appointment with an attorney I found in the Yellow Pages, but I wasn't happy with him."

"I'll be right back," she said and disappeared into her house.

A few minutes later she arrived with a business card.

"My attorney's name is on the front and my therapist's name is on the back. Go to both. Don't lose this card. You'll need it."

I put the card in my dresser drawer then decided it was time to tell my family I needed a lawyer.

# Dry Dream

## Tom Hazuka

I've been thinking about Ann today. I suppose it's not that weird to have an old lover pop into your mind, though she's been out of my life for what, eight years? Nine? And it didn't end well. Maybe the best that can be said for our split was that each of us wanted it as bad as the other.

It wasn't nostalgia that brought Ann back. Sure, we had lots of good times before things fell apart, but pining for those days is not part of the equation. Life is far better now. I love Rebecca, she loves me, and I want to keep it that way.

No, what brought Ann back was not nostalgia, but two words: dry dream. Why those words knocked on memory's door is a mystery; I only know that they did, yesterday while Rebecca and I were making love. If it had been during any other time I doubt they would have stuck. But during sex with your wife on a Sunday afternoon? Of course, I remembered. And of course, I said nothing to Becca.

Ann came up with "dry dream." She was always inventing clever stuff like that, puns and such. I don't recall the context or when she first said it, but it soon became her catchphrase for anything that seemed promising but would likely go wrong. It was equally useful to describe something that had already failed.

I used "dry dream" too, on occasion, and eventually so did most of our friends. Somehow, though, it always felt like stealing. For better or worse, the phrase belonged to Ann.

It came back to me this morning on my drive to work, "dry dream" a mental retort to some politician prevaricating on NPR. I might have even said it out loud, at least in a whisper. Then at the office I did something unusual for me: I checked for Ann on Facebook, feeling not sleazy exactly, because it wasn't, but maybe a bit like I was reading someone's diary without asking. I sipped my cooling coffee and told myself it was Facebook, for crying out loud; if I'm reading her diary, it's because she left it open on the kitchen counter.

She wasn't on Facebook, at least under the name that I knew. There were a dozen or more with her name, but they were definitely not my Ann. "My"? I took that as a sign and didn't google her name—until lunch. It was a waste of time. It's weird how a particularly unique, interesting person can get lost in a herd sharing a common name. I'm nowhere near as interesting, but my unusual name pops right up in an Internet search. There aren't that many of me around.

I wonder if Ann has ever googled me. If so, she obviously decided to stay disconnected. That's probably for the best. Let napping canines repose. Lame, right? Not clever like something Ann would come up with.

Rebecca usually groans when I make puns, and I don't blame her. I'm no wordsmith like Ann, and my feeble attempts often embarrass me before they're halfway out of my mouth. Not that Becca's any great shakes in the inventiveness department, which is fine. I didn't marry her to entertain me, I married her because I love her.

I never wanted to marry Ann.

Of course, I was younger then; I didn't want to marry anyone. I did want to have sex a lot, though, and Ann was a kindred spirit in that regard so we got along great until our expectations of each other extended beyond getting naked as often as possible. To be honest, it was mostly Ann's expectations that grew; getting naked as often as possible was still enough for me. But I was with the person who invented "dry dream." She was just with me.

Rebecca knows about Ann, a few facts like I know about Jeremy, Bruce, Dave #1, Peter, and Dave #2. Not that it matters, but for the record my law practice is going gangbusters and I make more than any of them except possibly Dave #1, who inherited Daddy's company. That's not why Becca loves me, but let's face it, it can't hurt.

The next chance I get, I'm going to say "dry dream" to her. Probably she'll roll her eyes: "Seriously, Michael? What does that even mean?" Maybe, though, just maybe, my wife will love her plagiarist husband a little more than before, even a little more than she thought possible.

# Helpmeet

## Susy Churchill

A thin film of dust clouded the window: Saharan sand, apparently. The dahlias still glowed in the border, and the grasses were in full flower, tassels swaying in the breeze. Mists and mellow fruitfulness: autumn has its joys, but signals winter's imminence.

Alice placed the final folded tee shirt in the drawer, and slid it closed. Her youngest would be home at Christmas. Empty nest: she'd been warned, thought she was prepared. She and Colin had joked about possibilities: salsa class, that delayed holiday. What is a marriage for when the kids have flown?

Words from the wedding service trembled on the edge of memory: mutual support, be a helpmeet.

Companionship mattered – they were still friends. Surely there should be more? They had renovated the house and garden – was it time to renovate their marriage? What would that even look like?

Assess the basic structural stability: sound. Liking, respect, trust, shared values – tick, tick, tick. So much works really well – what is this emptiness? 'Change – always unsettling – give it time – you'll adjust.' Friends' words floated. The house felt empty without teenage energy bouncing through it. Did she want to inject more of that energy? Sports bags, dirty mugs, legs draped over furniture? A smile slid across her mouth: probably not. But perhaps a different type of energy was needed?

A group of swallows arrowed through the sky. They were late leaving – must be the last of the year.

She and Colin had talked about travelling, but work, concern about their carbon footprint, more bureaucracy since Brexit …

*What do you want, Alice? A comfortable life – well, I have that. To feel connected to Colin – I have that, too.*

Fun – they had slid into middle-age without noticing. *But I don't feel old, and we're both fit and healthy! Why did we stop doing fun things? Because they're not fun anymore: theme parks are noisy and tacky; so many leisure activities involve ferrying equipment from one place to another, and I'm happy to let go of ferrying! What else do we enjoy? Maybe we should do that dance class. Am I going to stuff our lives with hobbies?*

Passion, excitement, novelty. Do something different. Maybe they should take on a new project? Distractions were fine, but surely there was something deeper? Curiosity, creativity – where had they gone? *It isn't diversion I want, but a sense of purpose.*

Smoke from a neighbour's bonfire drifted across the garden.

They'd simplified and decluttered over the last couple of years. The books they no longer loved, chipped mugs, Gran's lace tablecloths and antique china. *Do I need to discard my view of marriage?*

*If renovation means restoring to full usefulness, I'm back to the same question – what is marriage FOR when your children have gone? Childless couples can have good lives. Is being lovers and companions – supporting each other in the everyday minutiae of life – enough?*

# Happily Ever After

## Joan Leotta

After forty-five years of marriage, I can honestly say that one of the many rituals that brings us joy is our tradition of movie viewing at home, primarily on the holidays but also to create in-house date nights.

You could say that we were fated to be intertwined with movies and viewing them outside of the theatre. 1977, the year we became engaged and got married, was the debut year of *Star Wars*. We missed the first movie in the theatre and had to catch up. Over the years, our collection of movies and our streaming options have grown.

The connection between repeated at home viewings of the same film, began with our first Christmas in 1977. We wanted to watch the Dickens' *Christmas Carol* but had missed the televised showing. So, we rented the movie and then watched it. The same thing happened with *It's a Wonderful Life*. That first year, we also watched *Miracle on 34th Street*. However, in succeeding years, input from children and the desire to watch something new added *Home Alone* (1 and 2) and *The Santa Clause* to our Christmas viewing. We had to spread out the movies over several days. We decided to move *Miracle on 34th Street* to Thanksgiving.

The year before he died, our son asked if we could add *Die Hard* to the Christmas line-up since the movie takes place at

Christmas. And we did. We owned these movies in VHS and then DVD and now, when we add a movie, we usually check streaming services before purchasing.

Easter has variable viewing—from *The Robe* to *Meet Me in St. Louis.* The Fourth of July is another holiday with more than one regular—*1776*, *The Music Man*, and *Yankee Doodle Dandy* (the story of George M. Cohan).

When we are at loose ends, or feel the need for a lift, we head to our store of movies and pull out *Auntie Mame* or *My Fair Lady*, or the *Sound of Music.* If we want a dose of childhood, we own the original *Prince Valiant* or *The Phantom.* And then there are the rom coms, (*While You Were Sleeping,* and *Sleepless in Seattle* are two favorites). The Sherlock Holmes series (with Sir Basil Rathbone). There are more, but a long playlist is not the point. The point is that while watching, we sing along with the musicals, quote our favorite lines, laugh again and again at the humorous sections, and tear up at the sad parts—every year. We are suckers for a good film, especially ones related (at least to us) to the holidays we get together for, cook for. And if a family member is absent, he or she can participate in the ritual with us from afar, a technique that really came in handy during the pandemic.

When I wish someone was near, I pull out the DVD selections that we watched together, *In the Heat of the Sun* (a PBS series) for my son, and *Downton Abbey*, or *Brother Cadfael, or Foyle's War* for our daughter. It's comforting to know I'm bathing myself in entertainment we both enjoyed. And when my husband needs to be away, my movie of choice would likely be one of the rom coms or *Fiddler on the Roof.* And yes, the *Star War* series is among our favorites—the original first three. Our list of films we love grows as does our collection. Watching them over and over is like inviting old friends to visit.

We never really set out to make movie watching a ritual, but it is a hallmark of our marriage. My cousins ask me—what movies are you watching now? when they call to wish us a Merry Christmas. People coming for a BBQ know that a movie viewing will be included on the Fourth. We add to the repertoire for a holiday as appropriate, discussing any additions for several days. After all, it's a serious matter to us.

We've added the tradition of gifting each other favorite films on holidays, Christmas, and birthdays. This year our daughter will receive the new *Downton Abbey* movie. Last year one of my husband's gifts was the complete set of *Castle* (tv show) DVDs.

Happily ever after for us is not *in* a film, or living in the unreal world of films. Watching these movies together is our happy time. Our in-home movie nights have provided us with hours and hours of entertainment in each other's company. Happily ever after indeed.

# Celestial Irony

## Howard Brown

If you've read the other stories, you already know most of what you need to know about my background. But somehow, I doubt that's been one of your top priorities. And I don't have time—or the words to spare—to bring you up to date. So, you'll have to fly blind.

This one is about marriage. And I know a thing or two about the institution, having been down the aisle three times.

My first bride was Missy Talliferro. She was the secretary assigned to handle my work when I first started in the District Attorney's office in Memphis. Adorned with a petite figure, hazel eyes, dark shoulder-length hair and a wicked smile, she was a fox.

"So, you're the new guy they've been telling me about," she replied when I introduced myself. "I hope you're an improvement over the last two."

And apparently I was, as we were soon seeing each other regularly, a bit too regularly perhaps, as within a few months, she announced she was pregnant. I couldn't say I'd ever really been in love with her, it was infatuation at best. And even that had begun to wear thin. But I was born a bastard, never known my own parents, and been raised by my grandmother. And that was something I didn't want for a child of mine. So, we married.

Unfortunately, it didn't last long, no longer than it took for her to miscarry, and inform me she wanted a divorce, as she was still in love with the married man who'd actually been responsible for her pregnancy.

Number two was Ellen Martin. Ellen was quite different from Missy; not loud or brassy; attractive, but in a more understated, subtle sort of way.

I'd been introduced to her by my grandmother, of all people. Grandmother and Ellen's mother played bridge together and, after a few glasses of sherry one day decided to play cupid. So, Grandmother set up a dinner party to introduce us.

I was mortified, yet given Grandmother's domineering nature, there was little I could do to avoid it. However, Ellen was a pleasant surprise. She was a librarian, fluent in three languages, well-travelled, equally well-read, and a brilliant conversationalist, all traits that made her absolutely fascinating to me. We began dating and there seemed to be a real synchronicity between us. But I was a bit too precipitous, soon pressing her to marry me. She was hesitant, telling me she thought we should just let things remain as they were for the time being. But, blinded by infatuation, I persisted and she finally gave in.

I should have known something was amiss from her initial reticence. Because within a year, she began to express ambivalence about her sexuality, uncomfortable in the traditional, heterosexual role she was playing. We went to marriage counseling, saw a therapist, but it was all for naught.

Because, in the end, it was abundantly clear she preferred women over men. And so ended marriage number two.

My third marriage was altogether different. The District Attorney's office where I worked usually gathered at the P&H Café for happy hour on Friday afternoons. And on one of those occasions, a colleague showed up with an old Central High classmate of mine, Kate Bascom. Kate and I had known each other back in the day, but never dated. Frankly, I'd thought she was pretty much a skinny little nobody. But when I saw her that Friday at the P&H, she appeared to have blossomed quite nicely during the intervening years.

Kate's escort was soon involved in a game of pool, and that initial round evolved into a second game, then a third. And watching Kate from across the room, sitting alone at a Formica-topped table, you could literally read her irritation growing by the minute, until she finally rose and headed for the back door.

I followed, caught up with her, and offered her a ride home. And though I half-expected her to keep right on walking, to my surprise, she accepted.

When we reached her apartment, she invited me in, poured us each a drink, and we began to reminisce. Turned out she'd had a crush on me in high school (of which I'd been totally oblivious), we'd both been married and divorced twice, and she was now an English professor at Rhodes College, William Faulkner being her field of expertise. I later managed to sit in on a couple of her classes and was totally enthralled by how she brought the man and his work alive for her students.

I won't bore you with all the details, other than to say we soon fell in love and married. And that third time around seemed to be the charm, as they say. We bought a house, settled in and began talking about starting a family. Then, a year or so later, she began to suffer back pains, eventually diagnosed as pancreatic cancer, which killed her just a few weeks shy of our third anniversary.

That's been quite some time ago. Still, I curse the celestial irony that could bring two people together—both of whom had been devastated by unhappy relationships—let them begin dating, fall deeply in love, marry, and then cruelly rip them apart. And I continue to find myself asking: *What the hell did I ever do to deserve this?* Apparently only the gods know; but unfortunately, they've chosen not to say.

# Starting Over

## Ann Liska

As Rena steps out of the shower, she hears the phone ringing. The answering machine picks up, her daughter's voice.

"Mom, are you there?" Linda says. "It's almost ten …"

Rena hits the speakerphone button so she can towel off while talking. "I'm here, Lin."

"What are you gonna wear today?" Linda asks, her voice excited.

"Oh, I don't know. That yellow tunic thing, I suppose," Rena says. She looks down at her legs. Shave or not?

"Oh, good! That looks so great on you," Linda says.

Rena doesn't particularly care if she looks good or not. Her daughter's enthusiasm is already wearing on her, and the day hasn't yet begun. She is going to do something today that is almost certainly a big mistake. She is going to remarry her ex-husband.

Rena hasn't really examined this decision, made impulsively after James' latest medical crisis. And she won't be examining it, in future. Rena's reasons are strictly pragmatic. James is the father of her children, she bears him no ill-will – indeed, since the divorce they've got along better than they ever did, married. If he gets back on decent health insurance, he might live a while longer.

And, anyway, it's not like there is anyone else. About love and marriage, Rena has no illusions left.

Rena has shaved her legs after all, and even put on a little make-up. The courthouse in their small town is close enough to walk if she'd allowed enough time. As it is, she pulls up to the parking lot at a few minutes before ten.

Linda, Gary, and the twins in their stroller are waiting in the small lobby. Linda's dressed up in a frothy pink concoction. The twins, too, are decked out in baby finery; Rena recognizes the little outfits from their Easter picture. Baby Renate, like her mother, is a vision in pink tulle, although it looks a bit more appropriate on a child. Little James is wearing a tiny white suit with a pink vest.

Rena dutifully bends over the kids, fussing and cooing in a way that never seems natural to her, but that Linda seems to expect. Rena's mother would have already swooped down and removed both babies from the stroller to cuddle them. How her mother would have loved them! But Rena doesn't do this. As long as the babies are content to sit in their stroller, she wouldn't dream of disrupting them – soon enough, they'll be clamoring to get out.

Linda's holding a bouquet of white and yellow flowers. So that's why she'd wanted to know about the dress. She hands them to her mother. "You look great!" she squeals.

Rena sometimes wishes they'd given their daughter a serious name, one that would make her act like a serious person.

As Rena takes the flowers, Matt and his partner, Steve, walk in. Rena hasn't quite grown used to this partner business, although she likes Steve well enough.

James, of course, is not here yet. This among other reasons is why she wasn't too worried about being on time. James is always late, everywhere he goes, and anyway, there is only one other couple waiting in the slightly dusty, stuffy lobby, a pair of teenagers who can't be over 17. The girl is slumped in a plastic chair, her hand over her mouth. They have no one else with them.

Rena takes a packet of saltines from her purse and hands them to the girl. "Take tiny bites," she advises in a low voice.

"Daddy's not here yet," Linda says, fretful. She's no doubt calculating when the twins will need to nurse again, but also, she's probably thinking of all the close calls of the past few years, the times when the hospital called everyone together because James had a one per cent chance of living until the next day, or something like that. After a while, such things came to seem routine. Rena has wondered if, when the day does come, any of them will really believe it.

"He'll be here, Lin," Rena says.

"We'll go see if Dad needs help," Steve says. He and Matt head back outside, and return in a few minutes, following James in his motorized wheelchair.

"All the handicapped parking was taken. Assholes," James says.

"Daddy, that's rude! Maybe they're all really handicapped," Linda says.

Rena wonders again where this sunny child came from. Neither she nor James has this personality, yet here it is in their daughter.

"Hello, James," Rena says.

"Hi Rena," James says. He smiles up at her, his face so much – smaller – than she remembers, as if it had been years since she'd last seen him and not just a few weeks. His smile is grisly, his gums always bleeding from the diluted rat poison he takes, thinning his blood and keeping him alive.

The justice of the peace opens the door to the small courtroom, which sees more arraignments for Driving While Impaired than weddings. Looking at the teenage couple and then the rest of the group, he asks, "Who's going first?"

James nods his head to Rena, and they all file in. Linda has extracted a few blooms from Rena's bouquet and given them to the younger bride. "You can't get married without flowers!" she announces, then herds the two in along with their motley party.

For the first time, Rena feels nervous. She can still change her mind, she thinks. Then she looks at the kids, their touching hope – have they forgotten what it was like? It must be true that kids always want their parents to stay together, no matter what.

"Do you, Rena, take James to be your lawful wedded husband?" the pudgy justice of the peace intones in a bored voice.

Rena looks past the justice's shoulders. A worry line forms on Linda's face.

"I do," Rena says. And she smiles.

# Press Conference

## GP Hyde

*They sit there with their phones out ready to record every word, the bastards. Let 'em. I hope Suzanne sticks to the script. That's what we agreed so if the silly bitch does as she's told, we'll be all right. Alec, the PR guy, has managed all this well. 'Have an open press conference,' he said. 'Clear the air. Best way, mate. I'll draft statements for you and Suzanne. I'll make sure the questions are orderly and don't go on too long.' And here's Alec now, calling for order and inviting me to the stage. He gives me a friendly pat on the back and murmurs 'Remember – stand up, speak up, shut up.'*

Good morning, everyone. My wife and I are going to say a few words to clarify our current situation. I will take a few questions but then I would ask for privacy so that Suzanne and I can work through this challenging time.

First may I say that of course I understand the pain and the shame I have brought upon my family. I regret the mistakes I have made but I stand before you today, determined that with the support of my wife, I will move forward to make a better future for my family and for the party I love.

I went to see the Prime Minister this morning to offer my resignation. I have to tell you that he has refused to accept it and has requested that I remain in my post for the good of the country. This I have chosen to do so that I can make amends by continuing to contribute to the excellent work of this Government.

*I have to sit here and listen to the sanctimonious rubbish that Alec has set him up to say. He's got a script. And I've got a script. 'You impudent bastard,' I said. 'Here you are again controlling the situation, controlling me. Literally putting words in my mouth.'*

*'Press conferences can get turbulent,' he gushed. 'Like when sharks smell blood. It's always good to have a well-crafted statement to work with. Yes, yes, I know you've said you don't want to read from the script but remember, this is your first time in front of the national media. The TV lights are blinding, it's stuffy in that media room. We want this to go well. Don't we?'*

And yes, of course, I understand the feeling that I have let down not only my dear family but also the people I represent in this great country of ours. I issued a full apology this morning and intend to heal this pain and hurt by redoubling my efforts to serve my constituents, my party and my country. I understand their concerns and I pledge to allay them.

*And now I 'shut up.' That wasn't too bad. Alec gave me a nod and smile as if to say well-done. The hacks seem to have bought it. They all seem a bit bored. I've not been the only one recently. There've been several naughty boys who've been caught out playing away matches. Alec has been busy. He's the 'go to' guy for this sort of thing.*

★

*Concerns? What a prick! He showed damn little concern when it came out that he'd not only been knocking off his secretary but also some woman he'd pulled in off the streets. Three of them. 'Sandwich Man' – that's what the paper labelled him. And they'd splashed it all over the front page with the headline 'Stuck in the Middle'. Inside they'd plastered two full pages with photos, the hotel staff, anyone they could persuade to share some gossip. And all of this rubbish was capped with the headline 'Family Man's got Time for Everyone!' They even had clips of the action on their website. Hidden cameras. 'It was just a bit of fun,' he said after we'd sat and read the paper in silence. 'It was consensual. No one got hurt. It was just the once. But that was it, Suzanne, I swear.' But I was hurt. Deeply. Badly.*

*And now that smarmy PR guy is calling me forward to read my script – the part of the loving faithful woman. Yes, I've got a script.*

Good morning, everyone. I hope it is a good day for you. For me, I've had better days, better years even. You've heard my husband talk about the pain he has brought upon me and my children. You've heard him talk about an apology. You've heard him talk about how the PM has refused his resignation. So it's a case of 'Let's get back to normal, how things used to be.' Yes, I wish I could.

My husband was a decent caring man. We were a happy family. I could tolerate him being away in London and away at conferences and overseas trips. He was serving his country and his constituents. But last week he was in all the newspapers and for very different reasons. He's said it was a moment of madness, he was led on, it won't happen again.

But what no one knows is that his secretary at least had the decency to ring me and apologise. And I can tell you now that this has been going on for three years. Three years in which he has become a lying, conniving, cheating shit.

Yes, Alec, you may have turned off my microphone but I'm going to speak louder and longer. That's what anger does. It gives you a voice that allows you to speak up and be heard. So I can tell you now that it's not going to be business as usual. You've gathered here this morning and heard how the best PR in the business has tried to smooth things over. I can tell you that right now the best locksmith in the business is changing the locks on my family home. And that's where I'm going now to start a new normal life.

# Paradise

## Jonathan Pett

'These binoculars are brilliant!' I shout from the office balcony, to Kirsty, eating breakfast on the terrace below.

'Miles, you spying on Isa and Jack's terrace again?' Kirsty stuffs another chocolate croissant into her mouth and slurps her coffee. 'Don't you have to go and work on the roof in Paradise or something?'

'I can't hear you. I might be able to understand you better if you stopped stuffing yourself for a moment. Why don't you go for a swim? Shed some of those French pounds ...'

'Miles! Get off my back. Come on, I've got to work this morning.'

Yup, I think to myself, I pretend to work on the roof in our poisoned Paradise and you pretend to have a career in front of your ten-year-old PC.

'Paradise' is the name we gave the house we've been restoring in the countryside. This place which we bought smiling and complacent ten years ago, is, of course, going for irony in a big way.

This ironic, satanic, symbolic, head-in-the-hands place for me and Kirsty. Our poisoned paradise. The symbol of our bitter, failed, ruined relationship.

I was 31 when I found Kirsty playing on a tennis court, all flapping white skirt and attitude. Back then I didn't know what the hell I was going to do with the rest of my life. A friend had a place in South West France and invited us down for a few days. That's when we decided to stay and buy Paradise.

In Bristol, we hardly knew or saw each other, we were so pumped up with our own self-importance. It sort of worked like that. In a strangers-passing sort of way.

Down here we are confronted with each other and our love on a daily basis.

Maybe it's all because Kirsty and I met when we were already in our thirties, shelled in, marked, experienced. We weren't young innocents discovering life and each other and working out each other's problems over the years. We have never truly talked about anything deeply difficult, disturbing. Bleeding out over the sofa to each other, exposing our dirty souls, our pathetic childhoods. This is not our thing.

'I can see Isabella's pants.'

'What???' Kirsty's up like a shot. Yup, the chocolate croissants have been stuffed in her mouth. Bottom leaping off one of our expensive North African cast iron chairs we bought when we actually had some money. Pounding up the stairs. Coiffured, 90s TV series style hair flying. Up to the window.

'What about Jack's?' she asks, breathless.

'Probably doesn't wear any.'

'Let's have a look,' she says, grabbing at the binoculars.

'Don't you have to work or something?' I say, holding the binoculars away.

'Miles, what the hell do you know?'

I adjust the focus a little and, as Kirsty grabs them from me, I look into her saddened, jumpy green eyes, starting to like their soft flirtation, the need to conquer me a little.

'Miles, you can't see a bleeding thing through these things,' she sighs, looking through the binoculars, shrugging.

'Oh, give them here.' I grab the binoculars and re-adjust the focus.

Hand them back to her.

'Look, you old perv, I've got to work,' she says, but doesn't move from my side. Or hand back the binoculars. She's still not satisfied with our bitchy banter.

'No, you don't. You'll just put on all those old records of yours ...'

'Vinyl, Miles. Don't show your age. I knew you weren't right for me when we went to a club and you called it a disco.'

I grab the binoculars back. The strap snags around her wrist. I tug on the strap until it snaps free.

'Miles, that really hurt,' Kirsty says, rubbing her wrist.

I watch her, as she wanders over to her desk, flicking at a pile of papers. I clap the binoculars to my eyes again.

'You know, I can see Jack stepping out onto the terrace.'

'Miles, shut up. I'm working,' is the predictable response I was after. Followed by, 'Oh, alright. I can't concentrate, anyway.'

Kirsty shimmies back over. She does ... still ... shimmy. That was the first thing I ever noticed about her. Her shimmy. Shimmying around on the tennis court. In that white skirt. That little white skirt.

Sometimes I think I may still love Kirsty ... in my memories of her.

'Let's have a look,' she says. So easy, so fleshy, so naive, so open, after all these spiteful years.

'He looks really unfit,' I tease.

'Give them here,' she says.

‘I was just thinking about you in your little white tennis skirt.’

‘What are you talking about?’

‘Shimmying around the tennis court. I thought I loved you when I saw you that day.’

She looks at me questioningly, almost vulnerable.

‘That was before you opened your mouth, of course,’ I can’t help myself saying.

I hand the binoculars over to her. Of course, there is nobody on the terrace and if there were you’d see a dot. But we play. Waiting around, for a bit more hurt, before she spends her day listening to her old records, sorry vinyl, pretending to work, and I go off to Paradise.

# the anniversary present

## Lance Manion

This will show you exactly how messed up their marriage was. Neither of them could remember who originally came up with the idea of how to celebrate their 30th anniversary. Maybe it was just a natural progression, as long as you are comfortable using the term "natural" to describe something so messed up.

The writing was on the wall for everyone to see. Well, the cake anyway. Every year they put a number of candles on it equal to their years of marriage plus one for luck. This year there were thirty candles. There was no candle for luck. Did they each feel somehow that a candle for luck would be unlucky?

It wouldn't even be fair to say they hated each other. I mean, it would be accurate to say they completely loathed the very sight of each other, but not fair. Fair seems to indicate blame and the terrible truth is that each one of them individually would have made someone else a good spouse. Not a great spouse but not a bad one either. Not as bad a spouse as they made the other anyway.

I guess it's judgmental to say a truth can be terrible in the first place. The truth is just the truth. And the truth was that they had kids so divorce was never an option. They were stuck together and they both knew it. Each heard the gavel smacked down and the sentence handed out in their own way. A sentence that always seemed to stretch out just a little further.

At first, there seemed to be a light at the end of the high school tunnel. Get the kids off to college and then they could go their separate ways and enjoy what dwindling years lay before them.

Then came the realization that they would need to stay together until each child started a family of their own.

Then came the realization that having the grandkids splitting time with each of them on holidays just wouldn't work.

Then came the final realization that they were truly fucked. Realization ... resignation. Whatever.

Perhaps it was when their family and friends asked them what they really wanted for their 30th anniversary that the idea came to them. Each had been thinking it since their 5th anniversary. Maybe it was as late as their 7th but it had been there lurking in both of them for a long time.

So after the last of the well-wishers had departed they sat at their kitchen table. He placed the gun on the table.

You would think that at a moment like that there would be more drama but there wasn't. It was almost without any animosity at all. He put in a single bullet and spun the chamber.

Neither of them really cared how it turned out, just as long as it was finally over. That might be the hardest part to believe, but it was true.

They each produced their notes and placed them on the table in front of themselves. Written on the paper was a well thought out explanation of what drove them to suicide. There were little hints about the sad state of their relationship but what was the point of dragging old demons into the light at this point? Instead, they described a general malaise mixed with a fear of aging. It would make perfect sense to both loved ones and the authorities.

Did I mention that neither of them really cared how it turned out just as long as one of them was dead?

You might think that his gesture of asking if she would like to go first might suddenly ignite some small spark of sympathy or even allow them to rediscover some small bond between them, but clearly you haven't spent thirty years wishing nothing more than to hear the tragic news of your partner's sudden and unexpected demise, only to see their stupid face still breathing in bed next to you night after night.

She deferred. He took the gun, placed it to his head and squeezed the trigger.

Click.

He did so without any hesitation and was almost sorry to hear the firing pin hit an empty chamber.

He handed the gun over. An act completely devoid of malice. Robotic.

She looked at him and for a moment it appeared that she would speak, but then thought better of it and simply placed the gun against her forehead, closed her eyes and pulled the trigger.

Trigger is a funny word. It means to cause or generate or elicit. What it meant for the bullet is different than what it meant for the man. For the bullet it meant beginning a short journey through her cranium. For the man it meant putting away his letter, dialing the police in mock horror and starting his life again.

She was smiling.

He smiled.

# Miss Directions

## Gary Zenker

It's the same argument every time the two of them are in the car together with me.

"Don't listen to her, she's telling you the long way. Turn left here and then go straight," my wife commands. I don't offer any thoughts out loud because I know that tone of voice all too well. I fiddle with the dashboard sound controls to shift the entire music balance to the back speakers. My mate becomes testy when she has to compete with the radio.

"Make a U-turn at the next intersection," the other woman's voice announces from the back, refusing to acknowledge my wife's comments or presence. I grip the steering wheel and see my knuckles turn white. I should be watching the road.

"Don't listen to her," my wife instructs again, staring forward. This is a mistake, I know it. But it's too late. Is there a part of me that subconsciously believes I deserve it?

"You know I'm right," my wife intones. And with those four words, I know what's coming. All of it. Proof positive of her rightness. "I was right about the roof leak and that we should have fixed it before the fall." She doesn't mention the sheetrock sagging and then falling on her grandmother's teapot collection; the sideways stare she gives is enough. "And the washer, the tree in the back yard that nearly destroyed the living room, the finger paints that you gave the kids ..." All couples use shorthand phrases that represent entire stories mostly so they can fit more examples into a single breath for maximum impact.

Then it gets really personal. "I was right about your mom's boyfriend, and that woman from work who was flirting with you, and ..."

Of course, there's stuff she's been wrong about, as well. She was wrong that my sister would like the painting we bought for her birthday. You would think that the fact it isn't hanging anywhere in my sister's house might be a clue. It apparently isn't. And she was wrong about which direction to store all the records I'd had since being a teenager. They are all incredibly warped and unplayable, just as vinyl has made a comeback. And she was wrong about how long you can drive a car before you change the oil. Boy, was she wrong about that. $6000 wrong. There's more but, as I look over at her, I'm convinced that she gained the ability to read my thoughts. I immediately switch to thinking about the music on my iPhone and other things that will land me in less trouble.

All this time, the other voice is wisely silent. When it finally does speak again, it stays annoyingly on topic. "Turn left on Ash Avenue." Couldn't she focus on anything else?

"Wrong. There's always traffic there," my wife corrects. "It's backed up this time of day. And the Christmas tree leaning too much … half my ornaments broke that year. I was right about that. And …"

I begin to hum lightly to myself but not lightly enough.

"Are you tuning me out?" This time she turns her head to me when she speaks.

"No, of course not," and I am telling the truth, kind of. I may be trying to tune her out, but since I'm not succeeding, my answer seems at least not to be a full-out lie. "You know, there's nothing wrong with a second opinion," slips out without really thinking.

"Make a left turn at Orange Street," comes the voice from the back precisely at the wrong time.

"Orange? Who the fuck would turn on Orange? That's a tiny neighborhood, for God's sake. And remember the time we went to Reading. Her directions rode us in circles …" I do remember that incident, although I think the two of them talking over each other was part of the problem. I don't offer that up.

"You're right," I nod to my wife. I entertain visions of purposefully driving into the guard rail and flipping the car down from the overpass onto another car and into a fiery wreck or, if I'm lucky, a full fuel tanker. The thought is calming. I catch myself smiling in the rearview mirror. She looks at me and scowls.

"Go straight," my wife directs.

"Turn left at Maple," the voice from the back counter-instructs.

"Straight," my wife insists.

"Turn left here," the voice insists back.

"Don't listen to her. Go straight," the wife nearly screams. I jerk the car over onto the road shoulder and put on the hazard lights. There is a moment of silence nearly as scary as the previous din.

"This isn't a big deal. We're just going to the supermarket ten minutes away. Which direction do you want me to go?"

"Just go straight four blocks, then turn left at the light."

I pull away from the curb and exactly two blocks later, run into stopped traffic. Blinking red and blue lights and a downed electrical cable. With cars quickly stacked behind us, there's no space to turn around. Trapped.

For my own safety, I only look straight ahead. I turn up the music to fill the uncomfortable silence. And then I hear that little sweet voice from the back say one last thing. "Heavy traffic ahead. Recalculating."

I say nothing. Silence at the right moment. That's how marriages remain marriages.

# Frayed duet in 6 keys

## Rachel Weld

I try to head it off before the stairs. Argument #5 is a tricky one, all the whys and wherefores of twenty years, polished and pithy. He shuts the bathroom door.

Maybe I could subtly morph it into Argument #4. That one usually raises a smile by the end. Funny, isn't it, how arguments can have theme and variation. Same two people, same issues, opinions.

'Here it comes.' (Usual opener.) 'You're going to make it No. 6 again.'

'It's a good one, No. 6.' (My retort.) 'And I nearly always win that one.'

'No one *wins,*' he guffaws. 'Slippery little sucker you are, too.'

I yank open the bathroom door and address his back and planted feet.

'*Sucker?* Trying to be cute NEVER changes anything, does you any favours, etcetera, etcetera.'

'I don't need favours.' He has to shout over the torrent.

'Really? Last time No. 2 erupted, a favour was all that saved you.'

'You're pretty cocky when you get going, you know. Next time …'

At that point, the cat jumps in the window and squeals a thudding entry between us.

'Keep it in the bowl!' I yell, shielding the poor animal.

Even the cat is sick of that argument (No. 3).

# Disgrace

## Daniel Dioguardi

Before she returns to the room, I take off my ring and slip it into my duffle bag.

There's nothing surreptitious here; Allie had voiced her frustration to me before checking on Tori in the bedroom. Though she knows I am married, and has known since the moment we knew each other's names—*He's married* our mutual friend Nina had cautioned Allie upon introducing us and catching how Allie's face changed at the sight of my smile—she by this time two and a half months into our affair has grown embittered. Not out of ethics or empathy—there was none of that from either of us—but rather out of ego.

It is no longer about sex; now there is love, and Allie, justifiably, is afraid of feeling the most terrible of hurts—that which can only come from love. She wants me to herself.

I want her, too, but I also want everything else.

My six-month-old marriage already bores me. Not tedious exactly, just dry as dust. Not that this came as a shock. The chemistry between Kay and me was always more quaintly intellectual than it was physical. Familiar, yet undeviating. Sex one time since the honeymoon. Bought a nice house in the suburbs, ate vegetarian, ran in Central Park, went camping, went to work, cut the lawn, watched our shows. Sure, we infused the basic beats with a bit of our own whimsy that was on brand for us. But it was all tame, all same.

Thing is: I dig the domesticity; it anchors me in an existence in which I never quite had my moorings. Gives me something to do and someone to be.

But just a part, not enough.

My marriage (and the relationship which led to the marriage) lacks the crushing, relentless love that has developed between Allie and me. Something with real power behind it. Grabs hold, pulls you down. Quicksand. I often describe it as a brick through a window, quick and destructive, shattering everything I thought I knew, the barriers I built between the worlds I occupied.

Metaphors upon metaphors, piling up like lies.

It is New Year's Eve and I am with Allie in Tori's Philadelphia apartment. I am hoping to have sex with both of them. While I put away my ring and play out scenarios in my head, Kay is back in New York with her parents. At this point she knows my head is all muddied up, stuck either up in the clouds or deep in the dirt or both depending on the day. She gives me space; she cares about me. I tell her I'm going to ring in the New Year with my friend Buck, clear my mind.

A successful marriage, an uncle once told me, emerges from perfecting the art of lying. I take it he meant both lying to one's partner as well as to one's self. I don't know about all that. I don't want to lie, and I'm not even sure I realize I'm doing it. Certainly never thought I'd be *this* guy, lying often and poorly.

*Sorry, love. Missed the train home.*

*Sure, love. Go watch* Survivor *at your parents' house. I know how much it means to them. Why don't you just stay over?*

I didn't know the term *gaslighting* then.

Allie, Tori, and I step out into the stiff, cold Philadelphia night. I'd never been out on New Year's Eve, not since I was a teen anyway when my mom, dad, sister, and I would shoot East a click to a party thrown by their friends. We're talking cocktail weenies and Dick Clark. Home by 12:15. Not exactly a night with Gloria Vanderbilt. Never knew what the fun folks were up to. Anyway, thought I was too cool for that jazz, whatever it was, and now it's crept up on me.

I'm afraid because I'm no good around people, and worse around those I don't know. Allie, Tori, and I take a cab to Center City where we each grab an Old Fashioned at some dim lounge before walking a block or two under the highway to meet Tori's friends. They chat around me as I twirl my wine glass and look down at the table, looking for direction in the grain. The moonlight shatters the window, cuts right through the neon.

Lizzie is in the group and she's kind, she's cool. She talks to me, and laughs. Lizzie is a big girl, convex like an offensive tackle, and skin shrunken with years of anxiety. We each toss our credit cards on the table and Lizzie gathers up all the leftovers to give out to the unhoused and hungry lining the block.

Credit cards are to Allie a vital social marker. Which card to use and how and when to take it out is to Allie consequential to her appeal, to others' perception of her; it's all part of the show. I don't even think I know what credit cards Kay has.

Lizzie has heart; she has empathy. A year or so after this night, Lizzie and her boyfriend will be found dead in his apartment from what appears to the authorities to be a ritualistic dual suicide.

Later that night, Allie and I have drunken sex on Tori's sofa. I'm loud, hoping Tori will hear and join. She doesn't. Afterwards, Allie says *When you go home, don't forget to put the ring back on.* She cuts like a thousand killer blades.

Because weddings are dumb I made mine into a performance art exhibition, a chance to show the folks in my world what I could do. Make everything stick except the marriage. Thing is, I don't know I'm playing out a story until it's too late. I want Allie and the jazz and the power and I want the domestic comfort I have with Kay but without Kay and without having to tell Kay that I'm trying to replace her. Want clowns and chewed glass. Tell myself I'm doing this for me; I need to do it. It's like a romantic promotion. Deserved. I tell Allie let's see how we can have it all.

# Wild Kingdom

## John Carnegie

It took Willis less time than he had expected to set up the new television. The empty box and the Styrofoam packing were spread around him on the living room floor, and he sat on a footstool in front of the set. He held the remote control in his hands and pointed it at the screen, watching the picture change.

"Honey, come here and look at this."

"I'm busy," Annette's voice answered from the kitchen. "What is it?"

Willis lifted his walking stick from the floor and stood up stiffly. These humid days were the worst.

"It's beautiful, honey, you can see everything." He shifted his weight on the stick and paused to change the channel again. "It's like being at the movies."

Annette entered the room, drying her hands on a tea towel. She stood beside Willis in front of the television and watched. Willis put his arm around her waist. He tickled the changer across her belly.

"What's it doing?" Annette asked, slapping at Willis' hand.

"It's chasing the goat."

"What for?"

Willis gave her waist a squeeze then let her go. He shuffled over to the couch, dropped onto the cushions with the changer in his hand, and pressed the volume button. The living room filled with jungle sounds.

"Alligators eat goats," Willis said, and then, "Watch this! He's going to get him!"

On the screen the alligator began to suck the goat into its mouth. The goat struggled to get away.

"That's disgusting," Annette said and turned to look at Willis. "That's really disgusting. Did you do that on purpose?"

Willis turned the volume up some more as the announcer described how long it would take to digest the goat. By this time only its hind legs were visible.

"Watch! Why aren't you watching it?" Willis leaned to one side to get a better view around Annette's behind.

"I'm not watching that. It's disgusting," said Annette, and she returned to the kitchen. Willis turned the volume down and lit a cigarette from the pack in his shirt pocket. He blew smoke towards the ceiling. The goat was dead now, and Willis switched channels again. There was supposed to be a basketball game starting.

"Honey? Can you bring me an ashtray?" Willis called.

He heard something clatter in the sink. Then he heard running water.

"Is that alligator still there?" Annette yelled.

"No, the alligator's gone."

"What's that?" she yelled.

"The alligator's gone and so's the goat."

The running water stopped and he heard Annette speaking normally now. "Well, I'm not coming out until they're gone." A moment later she was in the living room with an ashtray in her hand. Willis touched the Mute button and the sound disappeared.

"You did that on purpose, didn't you?" she said. "You know I hate that kind of thing."

Willis looked up at her. "Did what?"

"With the alligator."

He grinned. "Aw, come on, I wouldn't do that to you."

Annette sniffed and sat down on the couch with Willis. She placed the ashtray beside him.

"Oh yes you would."

"Honey, I love you," Willis said, putting his free hand on Annette's shoulder. "I wouldn't do something like that."

"Then why don't you watch something nice for a change? We just got the television. Can't we watch something nice now?"

She pulled away and stood up, but she gave him a small smile, and Willis smiled back.

"Are you done in there?"

She nodded, "Uh-huh."

"Are you staying out here?"

She nodded again. "Well, I'd like to."

Willis opened his palms to her. "Then we'll watch whatever you want."

Annette sniffed again and looked at the screen. An announcer in a burgundy sports jacket with gold buttons was talking to the camera. "What's that?" Annette asked. "Is that a basketball game?"

Willis shrugged. "I don't know. I was just fooling around with it."

"Because I hate basketball."

He looked up at Annette, his face blank. She appeared to be thinking it over.

"Maybe we could have a drink and watch something together?"

"Whatever you want," Willis repeated.

Annette reached her hand down and squeezed his. "I'm so happy about this TV," she said, and disappeared into the kitchen. Willis heard the fizz and clatter of beer bottles being opened.

"How about a sandwich, too?" he called out. "I could use a bite."

Annette called back, "We've still got some of that ham. How does that sound?"

"That sounds great, honey."

Willis switched off the Mute and turned the volume low so only he could hear it. The pre-game show was just ending and the players were trotting onto the court.

"Honey, you won't believe this thing. It's like we're actually there!"

"I'll be done in a second," he heard Annette call.

"Really," he said, "It's something else."

He stubbed his cigarette out and shifted the ashtray to the coffee table, then he settled himself back into the cushions. A ham sandwich sounded good right about now.

# Basildon Can Be San Antonio

## Emma Phillips

Friday night was Paul's. He may not have the hairline that he used to, but this corner of Basildon could still be San Antonio; he could feel it. He knew.

Nowadays, a six-pack came at a price. Mandy let Darren keep his weights in the shed, but it was cold down there pumping iron in November. She wouldn't let him bring them in though, since that time one of the kids was sick in the night and she'd got up to see to him and stubbed her toe. When Paul turned up to see if Darren wanted a pint, he felt chilly in a jumper.

Darren and Mandy had a beach wedding. Paul still remembers how fit she looked in her sleeveless dress, the sea as warm as a cuppa and both of them so happy. Back in the day. They hardly even speak of it anymore; a hefty mortgage has dragged them out to sea and away from sunsets. On certain angles, he still sees the way the light kissed her hair.

Bloody Mandy. She'd kept Paul waiting long enough. He had always fancied her, but she went with Darren and half the time she was off her tits, so they were all proclaiming their undying love for each other and trying to piece the night back together in the morning.

She had made it worth the wait.

Friday night was Paul's.

Darren stayed home with the kids.

For a few hours, they were twenty-one again, hope and music running through their veins. Paul and Mandy, his best mate's wife. *I fucking love you* she mouthed but she never stayed the night.

# All Systems Nominal

## Angeline Schellenberg

I'm chopping carrots for a stir fry as he walks in from work; kisses my cheek; says the usual about his aching neck, the roads, and spreadsheets; then trudges to the bedroom to nap before dinner. The dog snores beneath the table, ears perked for the sound of falling cheese.

What I wanted in a marriage:
a listening ear
a dish dryer
a spider killer/mouse catcher
a motorcycle
sperm

I ring the "Christmas 1998" bell to call them all for dinner. We still eat together every evening: weekdays in the dining room on Grandma's china; weekends with pizza or grilled cheese in front of the TV.

What our kids believe in:
maternal servitude

the dangers of Teflon
total honesty
elves and vampires
Elon Musk's bright future
sleep

After I wipe the table and walk the dog, my son and I snuggle on the sofa to read *Frankenstein*. Between chapters he tells me about SpaceX's latest static fire.

"Sorry: what is that, again?"

"They test-fire all six rocket engines while Starship remains anchored to the launchpad."

His sister comes in to kiss the cat goodnight.

Before I fall asleep:
I lift the arthritic dog onto the bed
My breasts bound from their wire cage
I tell the back of my husband's Kindle what I will do tomorrow.

# For Life

## Kathy Miller

People say Onondaga Lake is the best place for viewing bald eagles, especially this winter when as many as fifty have been seen at one time. My husband and I bundled ourselves into our heaviest down parkas and ventured there on a recent blustery Sunday afternoon, binoculars in tow. As we trudged along the narrow lakeside trail, we stopped frequently to scrutinize the patch of lake not covered by a film of ice. Whenever a huge bird cruised overhead, I could feel my heart race. Finally, one bird with a wingspan wider than I am tall landed on some ice. Peering through my binoculars, I could confirm he was an eagle. Or was it a she; maybe so, since the females are up to a quarter larger, hence easier to spot. All I could see for sure was the snowy head, and the way ducks and shorebirds kept out of range of this apex predator.

As we walked, we passed several other people in ones or twos. "Did you see the eagles?" "Yes, we must have seen at least thirty. Go to the pedestrian bridge."

And so we plodded on, even though our toes and faces were growing stiff with cold and snow. The trail became more treacherous as we neared the bridge, the snow packed down into ice by many boots. Suddenly the shapes we'd been seeing in the trees of the wetlands revealed themselves as the accipitrids we were seeking. As we watched, several birds proudly soared into the air, revealing the dark wing feathers on top and the lighter ones beneath. The yellow, hooked beaks and deadly talons became visible, as these majestic birds of prey circled overhead or dived towards the water, sometimes joined by a brown-headed fledgling.

Suddenly one eagle headed straight for the bridge where we stood. Catching the thermal convection current, she spread her powerful wings wide and simply coasted to within a few yards of where we stood -- close enough so we could see her golden eyes. Those eyes can be used together or separately, providing even sharper vision for hunting and evading the attacks of other eagles vying for food.

Back home, my husband and I sat side by side under a fluffy throw as we looked at the eagle photos in the bird guide. I remembered the way two eagles sometimes flew together, one leading the way, one following, perhaps proof that they do indeed mate for life. Both of us had other lovers before marrying in our thirties. I wondered, *does forty years qualify as life?*

# The Honeymoon

## Caroline Jenner

It had been Megan who'd come up with the idea of surprising her parents, Vera and Michael Stokes, with a short break in Lyme Regis for their fiftieth wedding anniversary, a town they'd last visited on their honeymoon. The family had all chipped in and a taxi had come to take them to Waterloo and then another collected them from Axminster and drove them on to Lyme Regis. Their children had even booked them into the very hotel they'd last visited fifty years earlier, the Royal Lion. It had been a lovely three days. They'd walked along The Cobb, admired the ammonite street lamps, paddled in the chilly sea and, on the one rainy day, drunk lots of coffee in the plethora of artisan coffee shops that peppered the High Street. As they strolled along Marine Parade on their final morning, they'd spotted a minty-green beach hut. Almost simultaneously, they remembered a day fifty years previously, when walking along hand in hand they had seen a young couple, rather like themselves, sitting in deck chairs in front of a beach hut and pouring tea from a flask into two metal camping cups.

"Maybe one day we could have a beach hut on the front," Vera had said.

"Perhaps next year," Michael had nodded. But life had swept them along and they'd never been back – till now.

★

The following year Vera turned 70. Michael had co-opted his son into arranging another surprise mini break to Lyme Regis. He'd popped round and the whole trip was done and dusted in the hour and a half that Vera spent each week at her Pilates class. She'd been delighted by another trip to Dorset, even suggesting they might make it an annual event. In fact, she'd whispered quietly one night as they were lying in bed just dropping off to sleep, it would be lovely to live in Lyme Regis, although they both knew their children would be horrified if they moved so far away.

The receptionist at the Royal Lion had greeted them like old friends – mentioning their golden wedding and congratulating Vera on her birthday.

Vera was bemused. "How did she know?"

Opening the door to their room Vera spotted the balloon, a great, big, pearly orb that read 70 TODAY, attached to a silvery weight. The weight sat on a tray that held an ice bucket, with champagne and two glasses.

"We could take it down to the bar to drink," Michael suggested. "I didn't book a table in the restaurant. I thought we might prefer a bar snack tonight, maybe after a walk along the front?"

It was then Vera noticed the parcel, a small package neatly wrapped in pale green tissue paper. She picked it up, feeling the shape, moving it from hand to hand.

"Are you going to open it?" Michael tried not to sound impatient. Inside was a key, a small brass key in the shape of a seahorse. The most unusual key Vera had ever seen.

"What's it for?"

Michael could hear the anxiety in his wife's voice. Her eyes scoured the room for a clue, worried in case she spoiled a surprise by saying the wrong thing.

"Let's go for a walk," Michael said, holding out his hand. "We could do with stretching our legs, maybe you should bring the key." There was a definite twinkle in his eyes, a gleam of expectation.

And then the penny dropped. Scrabbling inside her handbag she found a packet of tissues, extracted one hurriedly, blew her nose, trying desperately to hide the drops that had leaked from the corners of her eye.

"Sorry, sorry, just me being a daft old thing," she muttered, pushing the tissue into the pocket of her cardigan and carefully rewrapping the seahorse key in the pale green tissue paper, before stowing it in the inside zipped pocket of her handbag.

"Yes, but you're my daft old thing," Michael said taking her hand as they headed off to explore the minty green beach hut on Marine Parade that would open at the turn of a seahorse-shaped key.

# Sunday Morning Coming Down

Gary Percesepe

Cal heard the old Kris Kristofferson song playing as he walked the streets of his Brooklyn neighborhood and it stopped him cold. Sundays belonged to the first year of his marriage, before he learned to get on without her. Young as they were, both twenty-three, they would laze in bed, nowhere to go, Jules with skin the color of a madrona tree when the bark peels away, and as smooth, softly kissing his chest as they made love on the rough Army blanket that had once been his father's. Cal listened to the song as it drifted down from the open window of a brownstone and calculated she'd been gone five years and he wasn't yet thirty.

Twice on their wedding day he'd stepped in to save Jules, the first during the ceremony when her veil almost caught fire lighting a candle on the altar, and then, as they exited the church on Fifth Avenue, she'd stepped off the curb and he'd had to grab hold of her dress, tearing it at the waist, as she nearly walked into the path of a speeding cab.

When the driver of the black sedan cried into his sleeve after the accident that had killed her, having ran a light and slammed into Jules in the bike lane, Cal remembered thinking how ironic, she'd been spared by the medallion cab but killed by an Uber driver.

He braced for the chorus, and Kristofferson didn't disappoint. Cal remembered then that there is something about a sad song, sung right, that can be a comfort.

Once in the heat of lovemaking she had deliberately slowed him. When she sensed that he was finally seeing her, she said, "Will we always make love on Sundays, baby? Promise me, OK? I'm serious, baby. I want you to make this one promise to me. It's all I ask. Just this one thing."

"I promise," Cal had said. Jules had kissed him then and said sweetly, "We will, won't we?"

The song was over. The station DJ came on air, describing how Kristofferson had come to write that song, and how it was famously covered by Johnny Cash. "The man in black," the DJ said.

Cal walked slowly through the park and heard the birds chattering. A squirrel ran down the limb of a tree and leaped across to another. Linden trees lined the path he walked and smelled faintly of honey. A phrase came to him then from some poet Jules adored, *the broken jaw of our lost kingdoms.* She waited tables and read between shifts. Cal was a line cook.

Cal tried to concentrate. He remembered how one story can connect to another and one song can trigger something in you but not in another person who hears the same song playing and who doesn't know the music. He thought there was something in that, but he hadn't the patience to think it through.

He saw couples walking in the park and thought, they are coupled now, but they were once alone. And they will be alone again, maybe not soon, maybe not for many years, but just the same we die alone, and no one can make our death for us.

He left the park and passed a restaurant. Servers in starched white shirts were setting up for Sunday brunch. On the brick front of the restaurant brass carriage lamps glistened in the sun and there were tea lights on the outdoor tables. Brooklyn was a circus of smells. Maple syrup mixed with the smell of bacon on the grill.

As he walked Cal tried to pick up the thread of what he had been thinking moments before. No memory is innocent. Every thought has its joy and its bruises.

He breathed a prayer, *protect me from throwing any part of me away.*

Cal recalled how when Jules cried, her whole face went to pieces. "Don't cry, baby," he would say to her, and sometimes she would be able to stop, but sometimes she cried and cried and there was no stopping her. But when she was done it was as if she had never cried at all. Wiping her eyes with the cuff of her shirt, she'd go into the bathroom. She'd take a shower and step from the shower to the sink and do her face and come back to him in bed, and it was always on a Sunday in his memory. She'd had her cry. It was still Sunday then, Cal thought, but she'd had her cry and she went on.

Cal climbed the three floors to his apartment and closed the door. Then he fastened the double lock. He walked to their bedroom and lay down on the bed with his face in the pillow. He dreamed they were in the Adirondacks in a tiny A frame cottage. A puff of wind blowing off the lake caused the lake water to lap the shore, and a strong wind blew through the hemlock trees and grew stronger and waves were running high up on the lakeside beach and Jules was doing a funny dance, slapping her bare feet in time with some song in her head, her long body just one step in front of the biggest wave as it chased her higher up the beach and then suddenly she stopped her dance and looked him dead in the eyes and he woke up and was awake a long time before he remembered that it was Sunday.

# Seventeenth Inning

## Michael Webb

I do not like how my wife drives.

She is very aggressive, zipping into small spots, only to have to stop short suddenly, then pressing forward again. She seems offended by the fact there are others on the road. She has never been happy being anywhere, always on the way to somewhere else. I say nothing, because I know better.

We are caught in airport traffic, which seems to grow worse regardless of how many lanes the planners add to the sprawling complex. She pushes the car into a slot behind an expensive sedan, slamming the brakes millimeters short. I try not to wince. The radio purrs in the background. I can hear Bruce Springsteen's "Hungry Heart". Wrapped up in the backseat, the baby mumbles something, and then sighs.

"We wish you didn't have to go," my wife says. I wonder about that, how much of the "we" is "I miss having someone to distract the kids" and "I need someone to keep me in $400 shoes and designer bags." Sometimes I feel like an ATM with feet.

"I know," I say. I am thinking about the kids' farewells that morning. My son tried to look impassive, but he held onto my neck a beat too long, the pressure of his hands communicating his anxiety. My daughter was histrionic, as usual, but calmed right down again after I showed her on my phone how many days it would be until I was home again. Then she trotted off, distracted by thoughts of ponies, or candy, or whatever it is little girls ponder. Children and relief pitchers have necessarily short memories

My wife said last night that I wasn't hard enough on them, that she gets tired of having to be the bitch all the time. I see her point, but I also don't want to have the time I get with them spoiled by tears and whining. I left that argument alone, preferring sleep over logic.

She pulls up to the terminal, jerking left and right and then snapping into a spot that opened up just a microsecond ago. She turns towards me, her visible knees and calves trim and appealing, and we kiss. I can already feel her restlessness, already ready for the next thing, the next item to be checked off the list before the kids return from camp and another summer Tuesday winds to a close.

I hop out, and retrieve my bags from the back. I set them on the curb, and turn to open the back door, hoping for a last kiss on the baby's sleeping forehead, but she has already pulled out, the electric engine humming. I watch the car recede and merge back onto the highway, and I take my bags from the hot sun into the cool of the terminal, another soul on the way to somewhere they aren't.

# The M Word

## Nod Ghosh

"No." Ronan glanced at the curtain. The light fabric danced in the breeze. "Things are fine as they are."

The low light brought dust motes to life and turned the down on his skin golden. He pulled his legs towards his chest and the quilt fell to the floor.

"We've waited so long," I said.

Ronan flicked an invisible speck from his knee, something he did when stressed.

"Why now?" he asked.

"They can't tell us what to do anymore."

"So you're telling me what to do instead." He rubbed his knee and flicked again, as if casting away a demon.

"It's what you want, too." I stroked his arm. His skin was cool and clammy, despite the heat. "It'll redefine us. Make us clean."

"How do you know what I want?"

"You might not be sure now." I hated the whine of my voice, but continued. "But one day you'll know I'm right." I felt like a sixteen-year-old, rather than a woman in her prime. I was coming across as a sycophant, rather than a lover. I sounded like a kid, rather than an adult, a mother – the mother of someone we both loved. I was a loser, not a respected schoolteacher – except I wasn't a schoolteacher anymore, not since events had caught up with me. Caught me out.

"Maybe one day." He rubbed my ankle with his foot. "Why the hurry?"

Naturally, an average eighteen-year-old wouldn't rush into marriage. But Ronan wasn't typical for his age. He wasn't like the teenagers I'd taught. He was different from my own son. Kyle would also turn eighteen in a few weeks. I wondered whether I'd see my child when he transitioned into adulthood, then flushed the thought away. It hurt too much.

My Ronan wasn't a child. He was a man. He worked hard, used his limbs to build the future. His school days were over. His shoulders were broadening, arms like the branches of a mature tree. He wasn't a sapling anymore.

I tried again. "You'll want a solid foundation. Security."

I was bargaining, negotiating. Not begging.

"And how would becoming your husband help that?"

I didn't have anything left to lose, nothing more I could give, beyond what I already had. I couldn't provide him with an answer, so I asked a question instead.

"Don't you want to make a statement after everything we've been through?" Surely he wanted to fight after years of everyone telling us we were wrong – years of people saying our love was unnatural. This was a way of showing those people they were the ones who were wrong, not us.

"Who would we be making a statement for, Madeleine?" Ronan twisted over, looked me in the eye.

"Us," I said. "You and me."

"But statements aren't for you or me. They're for other people. Do you think Mum would give a shit whether we were married or not? Would it make everything all right? Would your old school welcome you back into the classroom?"

"It's not about that. It's what I want. For us." My voice was hoarse, barely a whisper. "I thought you'd want it too after everything that's happened. We can be together forever now. No one can stop us."

He touched my shoulder, ran a finger down my body, but didn't say anything.

The early evening light turned the walls amber. We'd leave the bed again soon. Perhaps I'd open a bottle of wine. Maybe we'd have something to eat. Then my man-child would fall asleep and I'd watch him breathe. In. Out. In. Out.

Ronan's work exhausted him, but that wasn't why he rushed to the bedroom when he came home. He needed me – my hands on his back, my lips on his neck.

How long was it since we'd first spent the whole night together? Nearly two years? I'd booked us into a hotel and savoured the sour sweetness of his skin when I woke. We had a whole night together without fear of discovery.

Ronan had been sixteen.

No one could criticise me for taking advantage of him anymore.

We could be together every night for the rest of our lives.

No more sneaking around.

I'd sacrificed so much for this.

*

My life had imploded when people found out about us. Ronan had been painted as victim, and I was labelled a paedophile. We lost those closest to us. His mother Jacqui had been my friend. And Kyle. My son didn't understand. Ronan had been *his* friend.

*This is fucked up, Mum.*

*How could you?*

*There's a word for people like you.*

There was more. It ended with *I hate you.* I hadn't seen my son for over a year.

Ronan slid out of bed.

"So?" I asked.

"What?"

"Shall we do it?"

"Do what?"

"Will you marry me?"

"We've got this. We don't need anything else." He picked up his guitar, sat on the armchair and strummed some chords, the same ones he always played. He used to be an adept musician. Had I robbed him of that as well?

The late sun inched its way down, dipping towards the horizon. Sweat trickled down my back.

"Come back to bed."

Ronan cast the guitar aside, flicked his knee again as if shooing away a demon. I knew what the demon was. I knew what would happen if the demon pushed Ronan further. He'd squash it. I knew he'd discard the demon if it tried to ensnare him. Yet I knew the demon was persistent.

So I tried again.

"We don't have to get married here. We could go somewhere nobody knows us."

"A non-public public statement?" He sneered at me and walked out of the room.

He'd be back. He always came back.

A door banged. I heard the stomp of Ronan's boots on the path, a crunch of gravel, the gate closing.

If he was coming back, it wouldn't be any time soon.

# Traditions, Stories, and Old Truths

## AR Neal

Victoria watched as the sunlight bounced off the needle in Sister Browning's hand as it moved up, down, back, and forth. She was amazed at the pattern taking shape.

Mrs. McCray, seated on the other side of the room, cleared her throat and stood. 'Come on with me, Victoria. A watched pot don't boil and a watched deaconess won't sew any faster.' She pointed an arthritic finger toward the door.

Like an obedient child, Victoria stood, walked out the door and to the stairs. When she reached them, she waited for Mrs. McCray and held out her hand to help the elderly woman.

'What's that for? I been coming up and down these steps since your father was a child.' She smacked Victoria's palm and it sounded like a slap. 'Let me go on down and worry about yourself.'

Victoria watched as Mrs. McCray used both hands to hold the banisters as she stepped on each stair, one foot at a time and her heart skipped a beat. She wished she'd descended first, in case the elderly woman stumbled. Letting out a held breath, she thought about how spry all the senior church women were. They seemed to have been old since she was small, but like the others, Mrs. McCray took care of herself. She never drove but walked all over town, occasionally leaning on a roller cart on colder days to go to the market. She seemed to get down to her knees a bit more slowly these days when she picked fruits and vegetables from her garden, but other than that, she still kept after the smaller children in Sunday School and according to those teens who had been caught doing wrong was said to still have a vice-like grip as she held their biceps and marched them to the principal's office as part of her duties at the school.

Mrs. McCray put one foot, then the second, on the floor at the bottom of the stairs, then turned left and walked into the front room. 'Hey, Sister Smith. How you doing today?'

Beyond being John's mother and Victoria's future mother-in-law, Sister Smith was the senior deaconess at church and wore her authority like a sigil. She'd taken to spending more time with Victoria after John had proposed. She had already discussed living arrangements for the newlyweds with Reverend Claymore, who agreed that after the wedding, Sister Smith and John would move into his home. The Reverend Doctor claimed that he needed both John and Victoria close to ensure that he could properly oversee their leadership training. Sister Browning, who still acted as the pastor's house manager, knew he'd convinced Deaconess Smith to move because the three-story parsonage was much larger than the four-room shotgun shack her family had lived in for the past several generations.

'I am blessed, Sister McCray.' The deaconess didn't look up from her intricate crochet. She had announced to all that she would be making Victoria's wedding veil by hand. It was a pale blue, so pale the color was only visible in the brightest light. The gown she'd wear had allegedly been in Victoria's family for several generations. The reverend had said his grandmother, who had worked in the big house as an enslaved cook, had worn it when she'd jumped the broom on the plantation.

Victoria knew it wasn't true, since Deaconess Smith had told her the true story of the dress Victoria had found in the back of her mother's closet. Her mother's mother had started saving up when she was a young girl. She and her mother, Victoria's great-grandmother, had not been enslaved but lived in a poor little enclave of maids and sharecroppers. They took in washing from the wealthy people in town and according to Sister Smith, who'd heard the story from Victoria's mother, the young girl had dreamed of a fancy-dress wedding. She bought the dress, got married, and it was then passed down to each girl. Victoria's mother had also wanted to get married in it, but the good Reverend, who hadn't yet received his honorary doctorate from the correspondence bible school, wanted his betrothed to wear his mother's dress, which Sister Claymore had been buried in, meaning Victoria would need to make other arrangements for the day she would walk down the aisle of The First Apostolic Church of Christ, Inc. on the day she would be married.

'Why does Daddy tell the story about the dress?' Victoria had asked Sister Browning again that morning.

'Well, honey,' the elderly deaconess said, blinking her rheumy eyes and thinking for a moment. 'He does keep in the part about earning the dress from washing, so I guess it's nearly true, isn't it?' Sister Browning would never accuse Right Reverend Doctor Josephus Claymore of lying. Men his age, she figured, were entitled to their stories.

Other than the dress, which she and Sister Browning had carefully cleaned and repaired together, John's mother had taken control of things. She'd arranged for Victoria to carry Sister Browning's evening bag, so the old and borrowed items were taken care of. Since the veil was newly handmade in that lovely shade of light blue, Sister Smith's contribution took care of the remaining elements of tradition, and everyone had been satisfied. Especially Victoria. She would take with her everyone she cared about: her mother, Sister Browning, John because of his mother's beautiful contribution, and her dad through his story about her dress.

The older women watched Victoria, who walked to the window and looked out. As her eyes filled with tears, they whispered to each other and prayed over the day to come.

# Indestructible

## Edward O'Dwyer

She stepped suddenly on the brakes and caused the ring I'd been stowing away for just the right moment to come leaping from my pocket and, to my horror, land in her lap. We were in the middle of an argument so it probably wasn't the right moment. Then again, when is the right moment? Is there any such thing?

"Is that what I think it is?" she asked.

"That depends on what you think it is," I said. Sometimes a line sounds cool and smooth in your head and the reality of it being the opposite only hits you when you can't undo it, but then who wants to marry somebody cool and smooth? Those people have affairs. They are the people you possibly have affairs with. You don't marry them.

She let both of her hands fall away from the steering wheel to open up the little box. A brilliant smile showed she was pleased by the expense I'd gone to. That restored some confidence lost from the unfortunate timing.

"Well, go on then," she said.

"Go on, what?"

"I presume you're going to get down on one knee. I couldn't possibly say yes if you don't get down on one knee." She frowned to make it clear she was quite serious.

It isn't easy getting down onto one knee in a very small and cramped car, I can tell you, but of course, I gave it my best shot.

I had no choice after all. I had to undo my seatbelt, which I wasn't feeling good about, since she had only a minor interest in negotiating the car out of the way of oncoming traffic.

I finally managed it, the glove compartment pressing cruelly into my kidney, and she burst out laughing at the difficulty I had contorting myself into the position needed to perform the traditional proposal ritual. It was a laugh I cherished profoundly, and so I wasn't deterred by it sounding then at my expense.

"Will you marry me?" I asked quickly. I was naturally in a hurry to get out of the strenuous position before doing myself a serious injury.

She said yes, or at least I think she said yes. It was difficult to hear properly through her laughter and the crash of the truck slamming into us.

We should have died instantly but there are moments when you are almost indestructible because of sheer happiness, and it was one of those moments. We simply refused to accept death, and so we both lived

It was a miracle, an amazing story of love triumphing over tragedy.

Her full body cast was pristine white on the day, just like a wedding gown. She was perfection itself as her father wheeled her up the aisle of the church. I watched in awe. In normal circumstances I'm sure I'd have been rendered speechless. As it happened, I hadn't yet recovered the power of speech since the accident. Still, I was in no doubt I would do so when the moment came to say "I do". I would find a way. And so I did. There was a lot of drool involved but I got there. The words came out. The priest was satisfied they did. He was satisfied on God's behalf.

We were both pretty much entirely crippled and the experts were not optimistic. They were all telling us we'd be this way for the rest of our lives, but we had dreams of kissing, and of holding hands, of walking on a beach as the sun was setting, and a million other dreams, and so we just laughed at them all, holding their charts and clipboards and with their grave expressions. We didn't credit them one bit, because there are no experts who can tell us what love can and cannot do. Sure, it's twenty years later and nothing's changed, but that hasn't shaken our belief, not one bit. We'll show the experts. We'll show them all.

# Also from Pure Slush Books

pureslush.com/store

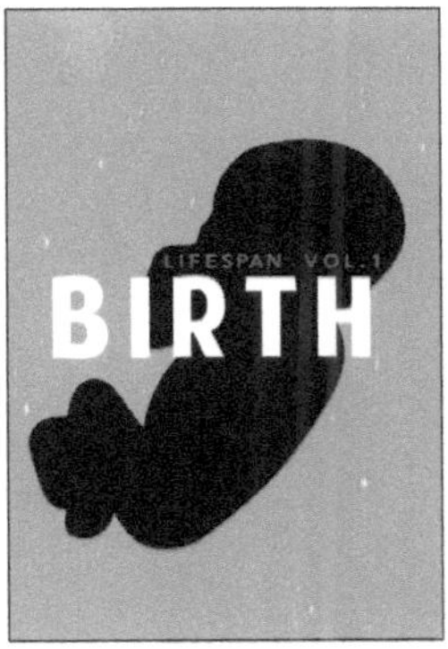

- Work Lifespan Vol. 5

ISBN: 978-1-922427-28-1 (paperback) / 978-1-922427-29-8 (ePub)

- Love Lifespan Vol. 4

ISBN: 978-1-922427-26-7 (paperback) / 978-1-922427-27-4 (ePub)

- Friendship Lifespan Vol. 3

ISBN: 978-1-922427-24-3 (paperback) / 978-1-922427-25-0 (ePub)

- Growing Up Lifespan Vol. 2

ISBN: 978-1-922427-22-9 (paperback) / 978-1-922427-23-6 (ePub)

- Birth Lifespan Vol. 1

ISBN: 978-1-922427-20-5 (paperback) / 978-1-922427-21-2 (ePub)

- Wrong Way Go Back Pure Slush Vol. 19

ISBN: 978-1-922427-06-9 (paperback) / 978-1-922427-07-6 (eBook)

# Also from Pure Slush Books

pureslush.com/store

- The Tyranny of Bacon Pure Slush Vol. 18

ISBN: 978-1-922427-02-1 (paperback) / 978-1-922427-03-8 (eBook)

- The Beautifullest Pure Slush Vol. 17

ISBN: 978-1-925536-23-2 (paperback) / 978-1-925536-24-9 (eBook)

- The Shitlist Pure Slush Vol. 16

ISBN: 978-1-925536-90-4 (paperback) / 978-1-925536-91-1 (eBook)

- Happy$^2$ Pure Slush Vol. 15

ISBN: 978-1-925536-39-3 (paperback) / 978-1-925536-40-9 (eBook)

- Inane Pure Slush Vol. 14

ISBN: 978-1-925536-17-1 (paperback) / 978-1-925536-18-8 (eBook)

- tall…ish Pure Slush Vol. 11

ISBN: 978-1-925101-80-5 (paperback) / 978-1-925101-98-0 (eBook)

# Also from Pure Slush Books

pureslush.com/store

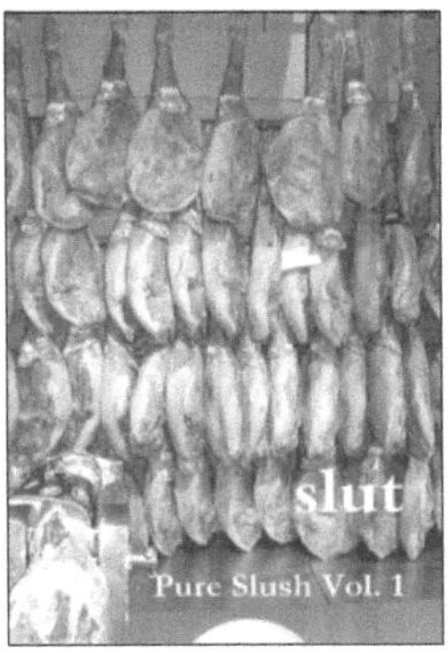

• Five Pure Slush Vol. 10

ISBN: 978-1-925101-71-3 (paperback) / 978-1-925101-72-0 (eBook)

• Feast! Pure Slush Vol. 9

ISBN: 978-1-925101-63-8 (paperback) / 978-1-925101-66-9 (eBook)

• Barcode Pure Slush Vol. 8

ISBN: 978-1-925101-00-3 (paperback) / 978-1-925101-01-0 (eBook)

• Catherine refracted Pure Slush Vol. 7

ISBN: 978-1-925101-78-2 (paperback) / 978-1-925101-79-9 (eBook)

• Slut Pure Slush Vol. 1

ISBN: 978-1-4716-0674-8 (paperback) / 978-1-925101-99-7 (eBook)

• Pride 7 Deadly Sins Vol. 7

ISBN: 978-1-925536-72-0 (paperback) / 978-1-925536-73-7 (eBook)

# Also from Pure Slush Books

pureslush.com/store

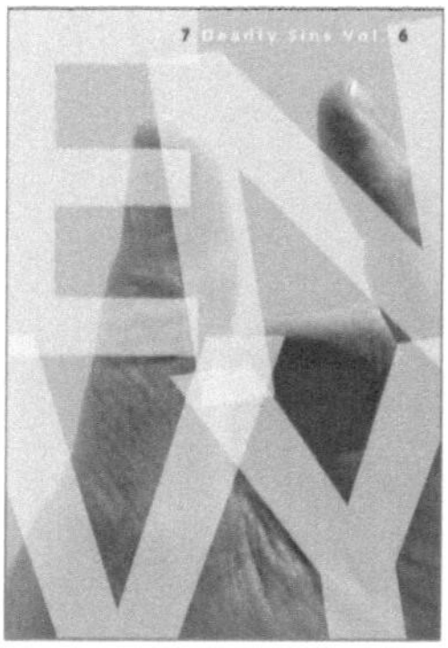

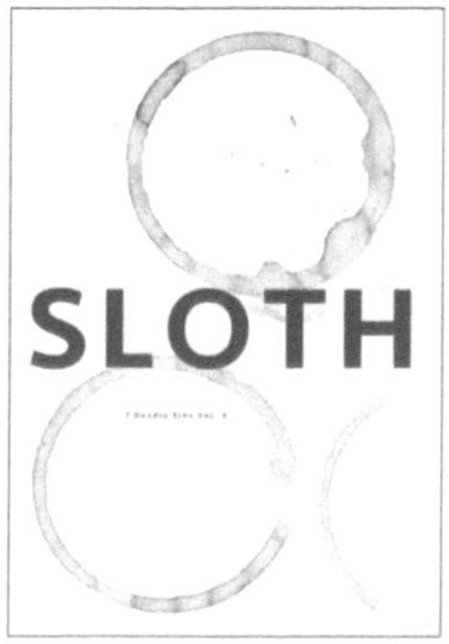

- Envy 7 Deadly Sins Vol. 6

ISBN: 978-1-925536-70-6 (paperback) / 978-1-925536-71-3 (eBook)

- Wrath 7 Deadly Sins Vol. 5

ISBN: 978-1-925536-68-3 (paperback) / 978-1-925536-69-0 (eBook)

- Sloth 7 Deadly Sins Vol. 4

ISBN: 978-1-925536-66-9 (paperback) / 978-1-925536-67-6 (eBook)

- Greed 7 Deadly Sins Vol. 3

ISBN: 978-1-925536-64-5 (paperback) / 978-1-925536-65-2 (eBook)

- Gluttony 7 Deadly Sins Vol. 2

ISBN: 978-1-925536-54-6 (paperback) / 978-1-925536-55-3 (eBook)

- Lust 7 Deadly Sins Vol. 1

ISBN: 978-1-925536-47-8 (paperback) / 978-1-925536-48-5 (eBook)